Joan was born in 1950 and now after many years of moving house for her work, lives in Malvern, Worcestershire. Joan is very happily married to Keith, having met him when she was sixteen. Several years later three offspring appeared in quick succession and after much trying; life has never been the same since.

Wonderful successful years in commerce and design, usually working seven days a week because she loves work, have left Joan with hundreds of stories about her observations of life in general. She decided to 'slow down' to forty hours a week, to spend time with her husband and all the grandchildren before it's too late, and then she was inspired by the Chris Evans Radio 2 show, to try writing a story.

This is the result of her labours, with much help on the commas and apostrophes.

To my fabulous husband Keith, our children, Laura, Andrew and Peter, and their wives Lucy and Teila. Grandchildren Felix, Summer, Callum, Ife and Joshua.

Joan Edwards

A MOST CARELESS DEATH

AUSTIN MACAULEY
PUBLISHERS LTD.

A CIP catalogue record for this title is available from the British Library.

ISBN 9781786129512 (Paperback)
ISBN 9781786129529 (Hardback)
ISBN 9781786129536 (E-Book)
www.austinmacauley.com

First Published (2016)
Austin Macauley Publishers Ltd.
25 Canada Square
Canary Wharf
London
E14 5LQ

This is a work of fiction. Names, characters, businesses, places, events and incidents are either the products of the author's imagination or used in a fictitious manner. Any resemblance to actual persons, living or dead, or actual events is purely coincidental.

Acknowledgments

Blame Chris Evans, he started me off on this journey. There I was driving along listening to his Radio 2 Breakfast Show, Chris was discussing with two authors some tips on how to structure and write a competition entry for his 500 words story competition for children. As I sat in the traffic, I was inspired to see what I could do, not of course to enter the competition, as I was many years too old, but just to see if I could write an imaginative 500 word story.

I scribbled down the beginnings of a story that night whilst watching television, and thought perhaps I would try and write some more the following evening. After several nights enjoying myself writing fiction, I started writing in the daytime in notebooks until I had an embryonic story. I had only just discovered that one of my loveliest neighbours, Jeanne, had taught English locally for years before her retirement. I plucked up courage to ask her if she would mind reading my fledgling story, and give me a professional view, asking her to try and ignore my terrible grammatical mistakes.

Jeanne Titley was my inspiration to continue, and without her encouragement I would not have written another word. I miss her terribly, as very sadly she died not too long after her initially helping me. She remains in my thoughts, especially when I am gardening in my front garden, and she no longer passes by and stops for a chat.

Cherry-Anne Osborne and my cousin Alison Stone responded to my cries for help with the grammar and have been so wonderful in spending hours correcting it and removing all my use of repetitive words and phrases. I am blessed to have such wonderful friends that have been so patient with me. Madeleine Gilles and Mary-Rose Hughes both also have spared time for me, when none of us knew if this book would ever be published.

My son Peter designed the initial book cover, which was sharpened up by Greg Carter at Austin Macauley and my friend Roy McAdam took my photograph for the inside of the cover. So you see how lucky I am to have such wonderful friends and family. It is lovely to be able to tell you about them in print.

Chapter 1

47 days to deadline
9th February, 2015
Princess Margaret Gardens

'Goodness Anne's nervous. Let's hope it's a yes and she doesn't have to wait too long today to hear.'

John bent down and removed the large dandelion plant from the front garden of number six. The supposed retirement bungalows were positioned on three sides of the large central grass area, which was divided by an old grey concrete path, that led from the 'reception' area of the entrance hall down to the Eastnor Road out of Malvern.

'If the PM has got his way, it will be amazing, amazing for the whole team. All these years and it could finally be going to be rolled out. Let's hope the final adjustments work or it's going to be a bloodbath. Gosh and if people find out the cause, then the lawyers will have a field day. The government will fall, that's for sure.'

John breathed in the cold, sterile air as he continued along the narrow concrete path that divided the tiny front gardens from the lawn. It was still dark and the gardens were lit by the streetlights.

They must continue the illusion of housing for retired gentlefolk, even if they were rushed off their feet at the moment. Weeding their front gardens was just one more detail to maintain this impression and was imperative. However, this could wait until after the deadline for Jean and Anne's project. He also noticed how some of the posts of the post and chain fencing by the pavement were listing; the excavations had loosened the soil. Best get them seen to at the same time, lest the Council come to reinstate them and notice the soil disturbance and start asking questions.

John swiftly walked around the end of the bungalows and along the veranda that joined the three blocks at the back. He reached the back door of his bungalow and inserted the keys into two security locks, opened the adjoining covered security pad, entered his code and when the door opened, stepped into the kitchen. After stooping down to remove his well-polished brown brogues, and slipping into indoor leather shoes, he crossed the kitchen and removed his thick, navy wool coat, and hung it on the coat hanger on the back of the kitchen door, together with his red fleece scarf. The bungalow was lovely and warm. John walked through the living room, into the hall. Removing the newspaper from the front door, scanning the headlines, he placed it on the small, round mahogany hall table.

'I will read it tonight, after work,' John thought. 'Better get on, loads to do.'

He opened the door to the hall cupboard. He pressed his hand over the security pad on the back wall, and waited the second for the airtight door to slide open, then walked through the doorway onto the stairwell landing. The automatic lighting slowly illuminated the bare concrete

14

walls. Descending to the first floor, he wondered where to start this morning. He would be the first one down today so he decided to go to the lower floor. His feet danced down the metal mesh stairs with knees flowing, he did a little skip down the last two – still got it even at seventy-five years of age, he thought smugly. Losing a bit of the excess weight from the Christmas over indulgences, would be a good idea though. It would not be too much of a hardship, after all, just apply some self-control John thought.

Pressing his hand over the security pad, he opened the Command Centre's heavy metal door and entered the dimly lit room. The command map glowed with the signal from Major Ross's Segway; he was over half way here. No surprise, he was always on time, leaving Credenhill at 05.30 precisely, and arriving at 06.30. Credenhill, Hereford, the home of the 22 Special Air Service regiment, known just as 'The Regiment', was only eighteen miles away, and the new transport had really improved the journey. To be honest it was still a bit slow, so he knew that Major Ross had been looking at the newest electric bikes; one of these would save his war damaged hip from any agro, and take about twenty-five minutes off the journey time.

John thought back to the previous SAS Major, Major Harris, when he came over during the period of the initial briefings, early on in the project. He ran the whole way, with just a headlamp to light the tunnel, sometimes wearing a fully packed Bergan, just for the fun of it and at the end of his day, he would set off again. 'Good example for the troops,' he used to say. Fit as a fiddle – wiry old bugger. John had never been fit; mentally agile yes, but he couldn't even run a mile. He had been asked once to cycle the route in an emergency when he was only sixty-seven, it scared him almost to death cycling into a dark void, with the small circle of light from the battery cycle lamp, illuminating at the most, only a couple of feet ahead – the pot holes in the muddy floor, jostling him the whole way. Never had he been so glad to see daylight as that day. That bike ride had been nearly eight years ago, when the connecting tunnel was in its infancy.

John had been seconded ten years ago to the Princess Margaret Gardens Communications Project from QinetiQ in Malvern. He had worked for the previous twenty years at the QinetiQ site, when it was known as the RRE, the Royal Radar Establishment, and had been government owned. They had been great days, he remembered. Government money poured into projects on the success of their previous developments. Amongst them was the work on the power of radar, especially Maurice Wilkes' working on the electronic radar, helping produce commercial computing in 1953, and also in the fifties with the development of thermal imaging machines.

The old boys loved to tell anyone who would listen, about the time the Queen visited in 1976. The old place had been completely spruced up, painted, with new chairs and tables and everything made shipshape. Even the folders and box files had been replaced and re-labelled. Donald was presented to her, and showed her how to press the computer controls to send the very first email from a Head of State. The tension in case it did not work was immense, as several trial runs had experienced problems. They had all gone to the pub as soon as she had left, and sunk a few by way of celebration,

There had been many pioneering developments in key scientific, research and technological areas during his time at QinetiQ. The two projects they were now working on were certainly just as pioneering and would cause huge ripples of excitement amongst academics. The impact would be worldwide, if these projects succeeded.

At last the latest excavations had finished at Princess Margaret Gardens. Everything could be moved back into place and most importantly, they could use the new communication tunnel to GCHQ. The cost had been incredible, especially considering the relatively small size of the bore. The need to physically move messages and documents in secret underground had been proved of late to be the new thinking, the most advanced technology and the most secure. 'Funny old world,' he thought.

There had been a significant security lapse at GCHQ, Britain's most secure facility this year when the private mobile phone number of the Director was given out to a member of the public. Even John's project would not stop this type of lapse. He was tasked with coming up with a new and innovative solution to the twenty-first century problem that computers and spies were shaping the future, and what once was the preserve of a few intelligence agencies such as GCHQ, now mattered to everyone. Computers were now transforming espionage from the Cold War years of spying to the data-driven pursuits of terrorists and the industrial-scale cyber espionage against corporations by hackers and governments.

The communication tunnel to GCHQ was so high tech that it was deemed foolproof – it was genius. However if John's new communication and tracking system using nanotechnology worked as predicted, it would become obsolete.

The boring of the tunnel had caused some disturbance to the gardens above which must now be made good by the weekend, lest someone discovered the excavation. The local Gazette had stopped running stories about the constant road works on the Eastnor Road outside the gardens. The Gas Board was forever digging up the roads nearby, and the works caused by the building of the Peak View retirement village next door a couple of years ago, meant that it was not thought out of the ordinary. The temporary traffic lights had caused massive queues and quite a stir as this was, after all, Malvern and traffic backlogs were not an everyday occurrence; that is, until work had started.

If anyone had looked hard at some of the workmen, they might have noticed how super fit they looked, but that's the SAS for you, what else would you expect?

The door opened. The smell of Rive Gauche filled the room. Anne was here. As usual, when they were alone, she came over to John and gave him his morning hug. Last night had been good, very good.

"Morning my little songbird," John said.

She smiled and blew him a kiss, before sashaying over to the control panel, kitten heels click clacking on the bare polished concrete floor.

"We have mail," she said, picking up three new canisters from the collecting tray.

"GCHQ seem to have been busy last night," she said more to herself than John. She unscrewed the caps and revealed the yellow pages. Looking at the codes, she laughed to herself; as usual, each one was headed with the words 'TOP SECRET'. Considering their mode of transport and their destination, it would seem rather obvious. In advance of Major Ross's arrival, she fed them into the decoder then put the decoded messages into his in-tray in his adjoining office. It was 06.25, five minutes until his arrival. He had been here every day recently because of the pressure placed on him by the politicians, in particular the Prime Minister. He could no longer manage the project from Hereford. Deadlines had been set for Jean's project that must be met.

"Morning all." The booming voice of Major Ross filled the room, reverberating around the walls. It was 6.30am.

Anne approached him, "Have we heard yet?"

"No, I understand we will be informed by about eleven o'clock," Major Ross replied.

"They definitely had the meeting yesterday?"

"Yes, I am sure that a decision has been made, it's just a case of waiting now, Anne."

She and Jean were on tenterhooks. Should the deadline for production to start be passed, it would be another whole year before the vaccine could be rolled out. Due to the extremely sensitive nature of how the drones were to be introduced, they were not at all sure if permission would be granted. It had been the politicians who had pressed for absolute secrecy.

"The waiting is killing me," Anne replied.

The next couple of hours passed in a hive of activity punctuated by coffee and biscuits.

The faltering steps of Jean could be heard as she descended the metal stairs. Anne made a mental note, to talk to Major Ross about getting a stair lift, after all their average age was now seventy years.

Jean paused outside the door, to catch her breath, and compose herself. First impressions of the day were important. She straightened her purple boucle jacket, brushed down her tweed skirt and pushed open the heavy door.

"T-t-t-t-today's th-th-th-the day," she stuttered as she entered the room, her brogues squeaking as she walked. "Good morning all."

They turned round and smiled,

"It sure is, Jean," Anne confirmed. John turned and smiled.

"Morning Jean," John replied. They had both noticed her stutter and knew this meant she was stressed.

Jean immediately concentrated on the techniques she had learnt to control her breathing enabling her to talk fluently.

"Have we heard yet?" Jean asked Anne.

"No, and I'm going crazy," Anne replied. "About eleven o'clock, apparently."

She rarely stuttered nowadays. It had been such a bugbear all her life, from when she was bullied all the way through her schooling, right from primary level through to when she was eighteen, even though she was by then at an all girls' school in Worcester. It was one of the reasons she had buckled down to her studies and had got into a top university to take her maths degree followed by her Masters. She had been a shining light, taking immense joy in solving complicated problems. MI6 took note and she was recruited to GCHQ. Jean had not looked back and had risen up the ranks to one of the top jobs, involving new forms of communication and code breaking.

Her new life fulfilled her mentally, and she had thrown herself into the project. There had been such a steep learning curve when Anne had joined the project. Anne's background was in medicine and she complemented Jean's problem-solving mindset. She and Anne became firm friends, living on site adjacent to each other. Her older years were now full of work and enduring friendship and companionship, things that had been lacking all her life. The immensely sensitive project filled most of her waking hours, which suited her, as she had no longer had any relatives save for a brother with whom she had very little contact. She had never been a sociable person.

Major Ross from the ORW [Operations Research Wing] of The Regiment had set up this covert research establishment back in 2005. Jean and Anne's research had for the past ten years been focused on nanomedicine. Its purpose was to research the uses of nanotechnology within the fields of interest to them, particularly national security, using the high tech laboratories on site and their small team of highly skilled researchers. Worldwide research was discussed and dissected to see how it would impact on their top secret plans.

They were isolated from the main researchers in nanomedicine, with all communication 'air-gapped' so that research remained only on the internal computers, not linked elsewhere. Jean's team were researching how to use the new nanotechnology to diagnose life-threatening illnesses. The main diseases being researched were the curse of the NHS budget; dementia and Alzheimer's disease, and how early diagnosis could be used to decide on future action. It was this further action, how and when it was dealt with, that was the most sensitive part of their research. High-level security even within their very controlled facility was at maximum. All electronic Internet devices were prohibited from being brought into the facility and computers used for research were signed for and locked away each day in the safe in Majors Ross's office, signed in and out by Jean or John.

The researchers had exceeded expectations and after a couple of false starts, had almost completed the work on the vaccination project. Final trials were almost complete.

GCHQ and QinetiQ staff were in constant contact with the main researchers in Cambridge and Boston USA about their work on nanomedicines. This ensured there was no chance of them getting any hint of the location of the top secret Princess Margaret Gardens research centre and the ground breaking work going on. They were not to know how the plan was to use the new technology for a totally different outcome.

Anne wondered out loud if anyone had heard from the others.

Major Ross replied that he had heard Bill and Isobel upstairs when he had parked his Segway. The old ground level laboratories were at full strength today, all staff being in.

"Bill still seems to be a bit gloomy. I think he is finding the stress is getting to him," Anne observed. "We will have to get Isobel to cheer him up. Reassure him. She is good at that, especially after having been married to Jonathon all those years. He was such a prick."

"Anne don't say such things."

"Well he was, we all knew it."

"Yes but don't speak ill of the dead," Jean replied disapprovingly.

A canister dropped into the basket. Major Ross retrieved it immediately, removed the lid and quickly took the paper over to the decoder; Jean and Anne looked over to him and waited for what seemed an eternity.

He smiled and gave the thumbs up sign "Well girls, we have lift off."

"My goodness," exclaimed Jean.

Anne did a little jig and her smile could have lit up the room "Wow. It's full steam ahead. Is the deadline still 26th March?"

"Yep sure is," replied Major Ross after double-checking the paper.

"Right, we had better get our skates on." Jean strode over to the door. "Let's get upstairs and congratulate the team. Celebrations of tea and biscuits now, but just wait until the 26th, then we can really push the boat out."

Anne skipped over to Jean and they both disappeared upstairs.

Chapter 2

48 days to deadline
8th February 2015
Apartment No 11, Downing
Street

"Hi kids," The PM shouted as he strode into his living room, slung his briefcase on the sofa, and waited the fraction of a second for the tribe to bound into the room.

"Hi luv, how did it go?" Lucinda asked.

Before he could answer, three pyjama-clad children flew into the room with a chorus of "Daddeeeeee" and squeals of delight as they surrounded Alan. Two-year-old Joshua raised his hands to be picked up, whilst the twins rushed around his legs, still shouting. The PM bent down and lifted Joshua into his arms. He looked adoringly at his little boy, such a sweetheart. Chloe and Jack ran out of the room, continuing their game of chase with whoops of delight.

"Well it went exactly as planned," he replied. "Such a relief, the majority said yes to both projects. It's all systems go Lucinda. We are up and running. Look, I'll get the children off to bed shall I, and then we can sit down and have a drink and talk about it."

"Ok, I'll just finish getting the dinner ready."

"Kids come on, its bedtime, no ifs and buts, let's go." He carried Joshua out of the drawing room, and down the corridor, whilst Joshua played with his father's hair and giggled.

Living above the shop had lots of advantages They, like all the recent previous PM's, had chosen to live in the four bedroomed, number eleven apartment, as number tens' apartment only had one bedroom. The accommodation had not been to Lucinda's taste when they moved in, but over the last five years, they had stamped their style, chic and contemporary look, on the apartment. Access to the garden was another advantage, as the children needed somewhere to shout and play in the fresh air.

Currently all three children shared the same large bedroom, but hopefully when they returned after this years' May election, they would each have a separate bedroom. Certainly it looked as though they should win the election by a landslide, so they felt secure thinking this far ahead.

"Chloe where are you?" he called. Giggling could be heard from her favourite hiding place underneath her bed. The same game was played most nights. He pretended to search the room everywhere, all the time saying "Chloe, where are you?" and "Are you behind the curtains? Are you inside the wardrobe?" and all the time Jack would be shouting,

"No, she's under the bed Daddy, she's under the bed."

After a few minutes, he would look under the bed, "Oh there you are," and they would all laugh whilst she crawled out, always being told to mind her back, after the time she had scrapped the skin off her backbone whilst not keeping low enough.

"Right children, pick your books. Joshua shall we have The Farmyard book tonight or The Zoo? "

Joshua pointed to the Zoo. He loved the noises his Daddy made, when asking him the names of the animals. "Chloe? Which book? Go and choose it then." She ran over to the bookcase, and chose Little Red Riding Hood. It was her favourite and read most nights, so it was no surprise. "Jack, which book tonight? Come on make a choice, Daddy has got work to do." Jack walked up and down, and picked out three books. "Sorry Jack, only one tonight. Jack chose The Emperors' New Clothes.

They all positioned themselves on Jack's bed and Alan started with Joshua's book, with Chloe and Jack joining in the identification of each animal, and making the correct noise for them. Joshua loved this time of night and looked adoringly at his Daddy as he decided what to call each animal, and Alan smiled and confirmed his choice. As he sat on Daddy's lap, Alan could smell his post bath time smell, all clean and lovely. It was a scent that you could not bottle, but was the most wonderful in the world.

Chloe and Jack both tried reading their books, with help from Daddy. Now that they were at pre-school, their reading was coming on really well. Joshua of course wanted to take the books from them, but they managed to concentrate enough to read them.

"Right, everyone it's bedtime now. Joshua that means staying in your new bed, no walking around. OK?"

Joshua had not got over the freedom of not being in a cot, since he was sleeping in a bed. He kept strolling around the bedroom disturbing the other two. Things were improving slowly.

The PM closed the bedroom door, and walked back down to the kitchen for supper.

One hour later, with the sound of the dishwasher swish swashing in the kitchen, they were cuddled on the orange sofa. The PM started to contemplate this momentous day, with a large glass of red wine in his hand.

"The majority of them with only one abstention, approved both the trials. It got rather heated in the morning but I got my way in the end. You know how much this means to me Lucinda. It is such a very sensitive idea, and I am so aware that it must go the way we plan. It's the huge step we must take. You must know how much I have worried about the idea, but now I am certain it's right for all of us."

They both sipped at their drinks. Lucinda looked admiringly at him.

"This will be your legacy won't it?" she asked.

"I hope so. The end results should be an absolute election winner in five years' time, as long as we get the go-ahead now. It is imperative that the researchers complete the trials by the 26th March, in time for the dissolution of Parliament.

"You haven't changed your mind about stepping down then have you?" Lucinda looked at him directly.

"No don't worry, I will not renege on my promise to you and the children. I know you want to go back up North. The children will love living on a farm, the fresh air and romping around the fields. I will step down don't worry."

Lucinda sat back and took another sip of her wine and thought how in five years, Joshua would be seven and the twins nine. The perfect time to live on her parent's farm, and go to the local village school. Her parents could start converting the barn for them now; they had been discussing it only last weekend when they visited.

"Do you think our parents will have the special flu vaccine Adam?" Lucinda asked.

"Well I know that I want it and I presume you do. There is no way on earth I want any of them to suffer. We can't tell them of course, so I would say yes, they should have the benefits the same as everyone else."

"There's no danger that the activation point could be wrong?"

"Well that is why we are still waiting for the go-ahead from the researchers. The deadline given to us by the pharmaceutical company is thought to be in time for them to confirm that everything is ready. I am told the deadline is very tight though especially from my point of view, as it is only four days before I dissolve Parliament prior to the election. I hope to goodness we don't have to leave it a year. We need two full years after the initial three year roll out for the results to be visible, so that we can maximise the position for the next election in five years' time."

They resumed drinking their wine, and sat back and contemplated the situation.

Chapter 3

The Park Lane Hotel
London 2005

Jean patted her mid-calf length navy and white pleated skirt
to smooth the pleats. She checked her boxy navy jacket,
and then looking in the mirror ensured that there were no
stray hairs from her bun. She had not known what to wear
today; she was not even sure why she had come – curiosity
probably. She felt very nervous and quite out of place.
Satisfied that she looked as good as possible, she left the
ladies rest room, and walked quietly across the marble and
carpet floor, her polished brown brogues silently disguising
her arrival at the reception desk. She waited to be noticed.
A very beautiful, polished Japanese receptionist
approached.

"How can I help?"

"Could you please let Mr Gormley, of International
Hemp, know that Mrs Harris is here for her ten o'clock
appointment." Jean spoke softly.

"Of course Mrs Harris. Would you like to take a seat
and his personal assistant will be down soon."

Jean turned and looked around to select where to sit.
She chose a seat to the side of the reception area and sat

down, putting her brown-framed handbag squarely on her lap. She looked around at the comings and goings of the business classes. One of the lifts opened and two ladies exited. One came straight over to the reception desk, whilst the other lady, with short, stylish blonde hair, swished away, click clacking on animal print kitten heels towards the hotels' exit to Green Lane.

She heard the receptionist point her out to the lady at the desk, who was smartly clad in a navy business suit. She suddenly felt very out of place, in her plain clothes. The bowler-hatted doorman, the uniformed staff, the suited men, all seemed to overpower her. She was unused to such smart places, never having needed to come to London hotels in the past. 'Keep your breathing pattern calm, otherwise you will start stuttering,' she reminded herself. The lessons Jean had had years ago to lose her irritating stutter, had been very successful, but when stressed she tended to forget the managing techniques.

"Mrs Harris?" the refined voice enquired.

"Yes," she replied to the smiling, warm friendly face.

"Do come with me, Mr Gormley is expecting you."

"Good morning Mrs Harris, so very pleased to see you." A gentleman of distinguished appearance stood up and greeted her. "Thank you so much for coming all this way to see me. Do come and join me over here." Mr Gormley indicated a chair adjacent to his. Jean noticed his silver grey hair, receding at the temples and how elegantly he was dressed. His demeanour was really friendly with a lovely open face and a smile that spread to his blue eyes.

"You must be wondering why I asked you to come and meet me here." Jean nodded.

"Well let me explain. I know all about the very impressive work you have been responsible for at GCHQ. I understand that you are due to retire next year. What do you think about that Jean? Are you looking forward to relaxing and perhaps travelling?"

"Absolutely not. I have spent all my working life fully engrossed in solving very complex problems, but I am quite unsure about my retirement. I have built up all these years of experience and feel at the peak of my performance, yet I must retire because of my age. It just doesn't make sense."

"I could not have put the argument better myself Jean'" replied Mr Gormley smiling.

"Well to be truthful, I have been concerned about my future, knowing that I have to retire. I have no family apart from my parents whom are both suffering from the onset of Alzheimer's," Jean continued.

Mr Gormley nodded his head and leaned forward in his chair. 'That confirms my personal file on her,' he thought.

"They have both just reached the stage where I am going to have to make the most terrible decision, and put them into a nursing home. Poor Dad has been trying to keep Mum at home, but she's become more violent and forgetful. Now I realise that my father is also getting to the stage where he will no longer be capable of making decisions for himself either, let alone for both of them. You may already know, but it is the most terrible disease."

Mr Gormley nodded sympathetically. "I know it completely robs you of them and their souls, and you lose the person you knew, it's a terrible disease."

"Yes, it does," Jean appreciated his insight. "My parents were both lawyers, very successful and highly intelligent, but all that is changing daily. It is breaking my heart if I am truthful." Jean paused "Gosh I am so sorry to have burdened you with my problems, I do apologise." Jean looked down into her lap, undid the clasp of her handbag, and pulled out the folded triangle of her daisy embroidered cotton handkerchief, and dried the tears that had welled up in her eyes. She kept her face lowered.

"No, not at all. Are you all right?" Mr Gormley enquired.

Jean nodded.

"You are one of the country's most accomplished scientists in your field, as you know, and I simply cannot afford to lose you, when I have a project of the utmost sensitivity and of national importance, that I think you can head up."

"Well that sounds very interesting. I am confused though as I was asked to meet you as a representative of International Hemp Associates. Are you suggesting a job within your company, only it does not sound like that to me?"

"Well of course, you are right. The job is for the state, exactly as GCHQ.

The Official Secrecy Act still applies, but the establishment we are in the process of completing is unknown to all except those with a need to know. Security levels will be, as you are used to, at the very highest level Jean. We want all the researchers to relocate to the new facility. Although GCHQ is not that far away, we will have other experts from different parts of the country working alongside you Jean, and want you all to live in our newly converted secure accommodation."

"By the sounds of it, the facility is still in England," Jean asked.

"Yes, that is all I can confirm today. We will, of course, pay all costs for relocation plus the usual percentage of your salary for new fittings etc. I will ensure that you will not be out of pocket. As I said, we want all research personnel to live on site, each person having their own separate accommodation."

"What is the size of the establishment?"

"In its initial stages, we shall have a team of just six researchers."

"Only six, that's a very small staffing level," Jean replied.

"Yes, each member is the top specialist in their field, and everyone that we hope to recruit is in your age range. I need the most experienced researchers for this trial. You will head up the initial team Jean. Age is of no concern to me at all. This research, if successful, will have a global impact. The technology is a new and emerging one and you will be expected to be up to speed very quickly. We will provide all the training necessary. We want your capacity for solving problems Jean, which you have proved time and time again."

"How much time do I have to decide?" Jean asked.

"Well I would like you to go away and consider your options, not least how are you going to cope with your parents' situation, if you decide to accept the position. I will need you fully committed from the start, so your parents must be settled by the time we are ready for you. Come back with your questions, contacting the telephone number on your letter. Do not give any information; just confirm that you wish to speak to me. I will then meet you again. Jean, I do hope that you are not only interested but excited. I cannot divulge any of the details of the research until you commence, but suffice to say, I have full details of your expertise, and know you are the most qualified person for this project. The salary offered is the next scale up to your present level, which will confirm to you just how seriously we need you." Mr Gormley stood up, Jean rose, they shook hands, and she turned and left the room. His personal assistant Juliet came to meet her, and escorted her to the lift.

"Are you alright for getting home?" she enquired with a condescending voice.

"Of course I am. Thank you." Jean always rankled when addressed as though she was eighty, and losing her marbles.

As she travelled home by train, she wondered where the location would be in England. Wow, that was quite a thought. She fancied a challenge, she was not ready to retire, and to be honest the income would help her fund her parents care after she had sold their home.

Jean decided she would sit down and work through the list of pros and cons as soon as she got home.

Mr Gormley, or Major Ross to give him his correct name, sat back, running his hands through his hair and stretching out his legs.

'Today's recruitment seems to have gone well,' he thought. There was a knock on the internal door.

"Come in." Juliet entered the room.

"That's everyone then sir. Was it a successful day?" she asked.

"I think so Juliet, I think we have both Jean and Anne on board, a few more to see tomorrow."

"Yes sir. I will be here at nine o'clock. Goodnight Major Ross." Juliet left the room as Major Ross collected up his briefcase and coat, checking the room before he left.

Chapter 4

Pershore Horticulture College
July 2005

Sarah paid for her coffee and cake and took the tray over to her normal window seat in the students' canteen. She was going to miss studying at Pershore Horticultural College. The past three years had been brilliant. Her parents had been so impressed with her results, when she told them she had got a first. They had taken her shopping for the new road bike she had been saving for. To get a first had not been that much of a surprise, as all along she had shown a particular aptitude for the degree course. Her parents were particularly delighted to hear that she was the top student of her year.

Her father had even managed to get his boss Ken Burrows at QinetiQ to put her forward for a prestigious research job at the Royal Botanic Gardens, Kew. Ken had known Sarah for years and had followed her progress with a special interest. Her father had told her previously that QinetiQ sometimes used research from Kew, especially from the department that dealt with Toxicology and the medical use of exotic plants. The research job Ken had helped her to obtain, was working under the Professor who was a world-renowned expert in toxicology. Sarah's understanding was that she would be refining previous studies on the toxicity of plants. Pershore College had singled her out, as having an unusual ability to think outside of the box in her studies. This had helped her to discover new properties for the genus of plants in her dissertation.

She had been down to Kew with her mother to search for accommodation, and had found a flat share with four others, two girls of about twenty and two men of a similar age. The flat in Kew was going to be a far cry from her parents' home; it was a typical student digs. The bedroom was small; it only had room for a desk and chair, a single bed and a small freestanding wardrobe. She did wonder how on earth she was going to manage sharing a kitchen and the bathroom with four others, especially as she had lived with her parents in Malvern whilst studying at Pershore. She was a very relaxed laid back person she thought, but her friends had been telling her horror stories about the problems of flat sharing. They had taken great delight when they were in the pub the other day, telling her about the annoying things such as disappearing food, no one buying toilet rolls or washing the kitchen towels. Hopefully if this happened, she would just have to laugh and cajole her flatmates to share and all have fun together.

The flat had a basement where she could store her bike. This was brilliant as she was going to cycle to Kew every day, rain or shine, as it was only fifteen minutes away, and mainly down the small side roads, with very little time sharing road space with huge honking monster lorries, belching out fumes in her face that she had experienced during her flat hunting trips.

"Hi Sarah, any room for a little one?" Jenny plonked her tray down next to Sarah and sat opposite her. "What have you done with your hair today?"

"Hey cheeky, what do you mean?"

"Well it looks even more unruly than usual today," Jenny observed laughing.

Sarah pushed back her long naturally curly hair from her face and drank her coffee. She had become accustomed over the years in Pershore, to being compared to Charlie Dimmock the TV gardener from Ground Force.

Jenny had been her soul mate throughout the three years of studying. She was everything Sarah was not. Jenny had immaculate chin length black bobbed hair, cut every five weeks. Her clothes also always seemed clean and pressed, whilst Sarah looked as though she had fallen out of bed and had just picked her clothes off the floor, which most of the time she had.

"I was sat here thinking about Kew Gardens. My God, I'm so looking forward to the night life around London." Sarah took another sip of her coffee.

"You mean you are so looking forward to the men. I know you so well.

Sarah Jones, you are so transparent. I think I'm going to put up a sign in Kew saying 'Beware lady prowler on the lookout for gullible young man.' Jenny laughed again.

The trouble is she was right; Sarah could not wait to get out of sleepy Malvern into the metropolis. She planned to taste all the fruit on the trees, and see which variety of which species she fancied most.

Chapter 5

Riverside View Nursing Home
June 2006

"Well it looks lovely in the sunshine today, Jean. The gardens are well tended. You said they were settling in well?" Anne asked, as she took the keys from the ignition.

"They are fine now, but I still have the most terrible guilty feelings. Mum was so upset when she first got here. She couldn't understand why she didn't recognise her bedroom, and who all the other people were. Dad did his best to comfort her, and on good days she seems very content. As you know, it was by far the best home that was in my price range. Do you remember some of those awful ones? The smells, the untrained, uncaring staff, and the poor residents who just seemed to have been neglected. Some residents didn't even seem to have their own clothes on. How on earth would I have coped leaving them there?"

Jean and Anne got out of the car and walked over the gravel to the steps leading to the porch. The sun was very hot today.

"What a beautiful day, Anne." Jean said climbing the stone stairs. She rang the lovely old-fashioned doorbell. Alison the care worker let her in.

"Good afternoon, Jean. Your mother and father are in the lounge." She knew Jean would sign in as she had been coming for months.

"How are they today?" Jean asked.

"Up and down. Your mother is having a very bad day today. She was shouting and hitting your father this morning, so we took her back to her room. Joanne did bear the full brunt of her anger, but she managed to calm her down. Your father was, of course, upset, but he has not been with us much today, so he soon forgot. Go on through and see for yourself how they are today Jean."

Anne and Jean walked through into the large, airy room. Around the edge of the room were placed the typical nursing home chairs; high backed with arms and covered in a waterproof fabric, with high seats to make it easier to stand up.

Some of the residents were sat engrossed in their own private worlds. One or two looked up to see who was visiting. Reginald nodded a welcome, and Jean waved and went and kissed him on the cheek.

"All right, Reginald? Good day today? It's beautiful and sunny outside. It makes you feel happy to be alive." He smiled and watched as Jean went over to her mother and father.

"Hello ducks, do you want the toilet?" The care worker loudly asked Reginald.

Jean lent into Anne.

"He used to be a County Court judge." Jean whispered. Anne looked surprised.

Sounds of lungs being cleared and the odd burp, and dropped cutlery from the adjoining kitchen filled the air, almost drowned out by the unwatched television blaring out a daytime quiz show in the corner of the room. The smell of urine and stale food filled the air. This was a very well run care home, but this seemed common to all the homes Jean and Anne had visited. She had been so glad that she had met Anne before she had to choose which home to put her parents in. Anne had helped her select this home, after visiting so many.

Doris continued as usual calling out for help every five minutes. The staff knew she was fine, and ignored her calling but continued to check on her occasionally, just to make sure. She would be moved soon, to give the others a break from the continuous pleading, which unsettled them after a while. Joyce, another of the care workers came through with Gladys, who was moving her walking frame slowly, concentrating on each step.

"Other foot Gladys, next foot." Joyce instructed. Joyce eventually settled Gladys in her chair and brought her a blanket for her legs despite the warmth of the day.

Anne knew that this care home would not take long to swallow up all the value of Jean's parents' rather lovely home, and then Jean would either struggle to continue paying for their care out of her earnings, or let them go into funded care. This would really unsettle Jean, as the funded care had to be run on such a reduced budget, that the care was unlikely to be as good. She just knew that Anne would continue to pay as long as was humanly possible.

They approached Jean's parents, who were sat adjacent to each other, but both mentally in their own worlds, they could have been in different rooms for all the notice they took of each other. They turned to look at the persons approaching them. They both recognised Jean as a regular visitor but not who she was. Some days one of them would know it was Jean, and Jean's day would be made. She could chat to them and remind them of what they had done years ago, however today did not look like being one of those days.

"Hello Mum, Hello Dad." She bent down and kissed them both.

"Hello luv, I know you don't I?" her mother asked.

"It's Jean, Mum, your daughter."

"Oh. Joyce, Joyce is this my daughter?" her mother shouted out to the care worker.

"Sure is ducky, she comes every day." Joyce responded and continued to settle Gladys. "It's not been her best day today, Jean." Joyce spoke so loudly that everyone was reminded of her mother's lack of memory. Jean winced.

"I've brought Anne from work to meet you Mum."

"Hello Mrs Harris, hello Mr Harris." Anne gave them her warmest smile.

No response from either of them. Her Mother looked past Anne to the window and then reached down to scratch her ankle. Mr Harris just sat with his mouth open, dribbling onto his bib, which looked very wet. Jean reached down and took a tissue from the box on his table and wiped his chin.

"Pull up a chair, Anne, whilst I go and get him another bib from the office," Jean suggested.

They sat and talked to them both for the next fifteen minutes. Nothing was said in response, but Jean was not put out, she just kept talking to them, reminding them of past events and happier days. She even sang quietly a couple of songs from The Pirates of Penzance, which both parents sang along to, looking quite content.

"I always think that they know someone who cares and loves them, is talking to them, even if they have no clue who I am."

Anne was very taken by that thought. Thankfully her parents had both died suddenly, and she never had to suffer the pain of seeing them in a care home, and then thinking of Jean, she suddenly felt very guilty thinking that. She sat there feeling very out of her comfort zone, very aware that everyone was listening to their conversation.

The mantle clock struck four o'clock. It was time for afternoon tea.

Those that could stood up when Joyce and Alison told them to go through to the dining room. They shuffled along, mostly using Zimmer frames to go through to the dining room. Anne noted that the tables and chairs were designed for easy cleaning and not comfort.

Jean and Anne helped her mother and father through and sat them down at their places. Jean's mother ate her sandwich in total silence. Jean helped her father, feeding him each mouthful. She liked to take over this task from the staff, as she had the time to make sure his food was not removed from the table before he had had time to eat it. Feeding him, reminded Anne of feeding a toddler, slow, laborious and messy.

"Was that nice Dad? Ready for your cup of tea?" Jean waited for his response.

They left the home shortly afterwards; Jean making sure her parents were seated back in the lounge area comfortably.

Driving home, Jean asked Anne what she had thought of the afternoon.

"Jean, it is so sad to see their minds slipping gradually away. It really spurs me on to find a cure or a solution for their plight. We must solve this riddle. It is unthinkable that we are on the brink of curing cancer, AIDS and all the other major diseases, but we are no nearer to understanding how we can help with dementia. People like your educated, professional parents are surviving in another world to ours. Jean, I know you find it so upsetting. Do you think we can solve this problem?"

"Yes I do. Mum and Dad were so well respected, on so many local committees, very sociable people, always out at some fundraising event or other. Mum loved to dress up; she used to look so elegant, pearl necklace and earrings, always smelling beautifully of expensive perfume that Dad would buy her and she wore the most beautiful shoes, my goodness she loved her shoes, she had dozens of pairs, all neatly laid out in rows. So unlike me!

Do you know Anne, no one visits them now, who can blame them? Mum and Dad just don't recognise them, let alone each other many days. Usually they are sat next to each other. Mum has been getting quite angry and violent recently. The disease is of course progressing. She was such a softly spoken person, kind and thoughtful, especially to Dad. Dementia is so very cruel. At least I don't have to worry about the care of my parents, from the point of view of abuse from care staff. There were more cases only last week in the papers, did you see? I expect you noticed how Joyce spoke to the residents, like they are children? It is so common, if only they had known them before they were ill, and they would have known what intelligent people they had been. My mother would be so offended to be called 'luv' or 'ducky.'

44

We must find the method of identifying the point at which the brain is affected so badly that people lose the ability to be independent. We cannot let so many people suffer, it's just not right."

They drove home, both deep in thought. Anne was thinking that there was no way she would ever allow herself to get to that state and suffer the indignity of being cared for. It would Dignitas or similar, if their vaccine was not ready.

Chapter 6

Princess Margaret Gardens April 2007

Jean put the phone down slowly. She sat back in her chair and took a long deep breath. 'Better call a team meeting'

Jean's team had now been working for almost two years on the ideas that had originated from Jonathon whilst at Cambridge. Major Ross had formed a very tight team to develop the idea. Jonathon's expertise in nanotechnology and visionary thoughts had combined with work gleaned from The Royal Botanical Gardens in Kew's toxicology unit. MI6 had been using Kew to develop subversive methods of elimination, and also for the investigation of unusual deaths by Communist countries' defectors. Initial testing of the new inoculation using nanotechnology was in its infancy, and Jean had just received feedback from the initial trial subjects in Hereford.

Anne, her second in command, as Major Ross called her, Isobel and her husband Jonathon, with Bill, sat in a semi circle around Jean's desk at the far end of the brand spanking new laboratory. Desks and equipment lined each side of the long, narrow room.

Bill was sat back in his chair, legs splayed out in front of him, looking impassively at Jean; Bill had never been one to show his emotions. His balding fair head, large ears and his thickset nose, belied a very clever intellect. He was single and the oldest of all the researchers. Anne on the other hand was sat upright, alert like a coiled spring, eyes fixed on Jean, attentive just waiting to hear and react to whatever was going on. As usual she was smiling at everyone as they arrived. She flicked her slender skirt to smooth away imaginary flecks of dust and held her pen poised above her notebook ready for action.

"Well the first results are in, they're sending them through by courier this morning, so we can work on them immediately," Jean reported, "the overview is that the nanodrones are in place, so now we must see if they are going to activate at the right time. The retirement home has reported that Test subject A103, has already started to show that his dementia is progressing, but not yet at the level to warrant intervention from the drones. The other test subjects are still in the early stages, with two progressing from the earliest signs of dementia."

Bill looked at his notes. He had been back and forth to Hereford over the last few months, selecting from amongst the residents that had agreed to be on the medical test team, those who seemed the most likely to benefit from the trials. The men were all ex-servicemen, with wide-ranging experiences and conditions, but all had agreed that they preferred to give back to society and hopefully find a cure to the problem of care for dementia patients once they became incapable of caring for themselves independently. From the many conversations he had had, both with the test subjects and the staff, it was obvious that the men all feared having to leave their homes in the independent living housing if they developed dementia.

The work that the team had developed so far was still in its infancy and the first hurdle to overcome was getting the nanodrones in place. Hopefully these results today would enable them to analyse if their latest adjustment had worked sufficiently to develop the trial further. Jonathon's ideas were so ground breaking and had entailed tremendous input from the team's various areas of expertise, together with research from Boston and Cambridge.

Jean's code-breaking mindset was able to look for patterns and thinking outside of previous solutions. Anne's medical research was needed for the methodology of the drones activation point, calculating when was the brains' decline was at the stage when intervention was most effective. Bill was the expert on not only the face to face interaction, determining the pace of decline of the brain cells, but also the analysis of the CT scans, and collating both elements. Jonathon was the main innovator, the instigator of the research with years of study on nanotechnology and its potential use in industry and medicine. He had worked on various uses, in particular on coatings for use in the space industry.

"Well team, as soon as these results arrive I'll distribute them accordingly. Isobel, can you concentrate on A103's scans, as he appears to be the volunteer who will activate first?"

"Of course, Jean." Isobel was pleased that she was chosen to work on these CT scans, as if A103's drones activated at the correct timing, then she would be able to confirm that Jonathon's research was working.

Isobel and Jonathon walked back to their desks together.

"What are we having for dinner tonight my lovely?" Jonathon asked.

"Well I thought I would make a lasagne with a salad, and I've bought some strawberries for afters."

"I'll get us out a lovely bottle of red then to go with that, eh?"

She loved working with Jonathon, at the old place in Cambridge they had been in different departments. Jonathon even then tended to work late into the evening, and then come home flaked out, too tired to talk. Here they worked together on his idea and could have intense discussions anytime of the day.

"Are we going to Chepstow then on Saturday?" she asked.

"Of course. I've got a couple of sure winners lined up."

Isobel was more than used to Jonathon's 'sure winners' that very often did not perform. They both loved the atmosphere at the races and Jonathon was the most generous of hosts to the connections. He held court at the bar, able to chat in detail about bloodlines as easily as the cost of living or any other current topic. Isobel was the perfect filly on his arm. She was slender with immaculate hair and with her fine, expensive dress sense, making the most of her womanly figure. She was more than content to stand adjacent to him, drink, smile and laugh at his jokes and asides to his cronies at the bar.

"Shall we stay over at The Lion for a change?" she asked.

"If you don't mind darling, I want to get back and work here on Sunday. I'm developing those ideas we looked at yesterday and am really keen to expand them. Do you mind?"

Isobel laughed, he would never change. He would work twenty-four hours a day when really fired up, a little bit like John next door in the other laboratory.

It was planned that the initial trial activation would not have any effects on the trial subject; it would just release the minute nanoparticles of dye that would indicate that the drones had opened. These would be picked up on the scans. They would later release the agent, currently being developed by Kew toxicology department, once it was known to be the correct strength and purity. The entire group of test volunteers were aware that the research was to develop a method of shortening the life of sufferers from dementia who wished to avoid the later stages of the disease affecting their independence. That was about the total of their knowledge, but they understood that they would be given the choice of using the 'live' product, if it was developed to the production stage of clinical trials. All of the test subjects were still bound by the Official Secrets Act, having worked at the highest level of security within the forces.

Jean's team had been informed by Kew that the Professor of Toxicology had real hopes that the new researcher could solve the problems they were currently experiencing. Once they had increased the toxicity, they hoped to be able to combine the nanodrones with the toxin, and start live trials. They understood that if not toxic enough, then the side effects could span diarrhoea and sickness even possibly paralysis. The work at Kew would be as important to the trial as their work, ensuring the correct activation point.

As the security forces might use their research in addition to the NHS, it was incredibly sensitive, as Major Ross reminded them from time to time, usually when they asked if they could correspond with Boston or Cambridge.

There were of course major doubts about IF they could get their pilot to work, and if so, would the general public, and the unions and interested parties, allow it to be used. As this point was obviously quite some way off, the researchers gave little thought to the future problems of implementation.

In the other smaller laboratory, converted from a single bungalow, John was working tirelessly trying to develop a replacement system for the Internet as well as a new communications system also using nanotechnology. It was as a direct result of Britain's National Infrastructure Security Co-ordination Centre, who had warned in June 2005 that a cyber attack called initially 'Titan Rain' was causing real alarm within the military by 2003, with hundreds of US Defence Department systems being penetrated, and its allies being aware that something significant was going on with the other members of the 'Five Eyes' club of Western powers. The warning said that nearly 300 critical businesses and government departments in the UK had been targeted. Titan Rain began by going for the most sensitive industries, those in defence, telecoms and related to national security, as well as government systems.

John had been involved as the radar design and engine schematics of the Joint Strike Fighter plane had been a leading target, with terabytes of data stolen. They reckoned that the cost of the theft of defence secrets was estimated in total at a staggering trillion US dollars. Britain's BAE was also reporting as being hit this year, with a suspected steal of the secrets of the F-35 technology.

During this time John had been developing ideas at GCHQ with input from QinetiQ about trying to create a replacement system for storing information. Cyber hacking was now so out of hand with China, in particular, stealing so much R & D from around the world, saving it trillions of dollars in terms of the cost of research investment, and at the same time, giving them the opportunity to develop other countries previous research. It had been agreed, that as his research was so sensitive, a secure core tunnel would be built sometime in the future, at enormous cost, to enable coded messages to be sent direct from GCHQ. Although the facility in Malvern was air-locked, preventing any transference across the Internet, and computers were kept on site, locked in a safe when not in use, this research was so ground breaking that it was a matter of National security that it must not be penetrated by cyber hackers.

John had not asked for any extra input on site, as his ideas were so new, that he needed to be able to concentrate all his energies on them in solitude. Sometimes he would sit for hours just staring into space, formulating the complex structures and strategies. Major Ross knew not to disturb him during these intense periods of concentration. When necessary, John would talk to Jonathon and Jean about their trial using the same nanotechnology, as there were areas of crossover in concept. Major Ross obtained all the up to date research from around the world gleaned from establishments above board, as well as by the usual subversive methods deployed by states.

John's ideas had started when he had heard about Robert Morris, a world-renowned computer expert, who had given a talk, in 1997 advising students not to even think about using email for financial transactions, as it was not encrypted. When asked about the most secure way, he replied 'Probably the US mail.' It set John's mind thinking that rather than making the existing Internet secure, why not find an alternative, perhaps using the nanotechnology that he had been reading about? He had been working for years and years on compromising radiation, and knew many of the secrets remained classified at GCHQ, under the code name 'Tempest.' The tiny amounts of radio frequency emitted by electrical devices, although only carried a few hundred feet, could be picked up by antenna.

However, he set about considering alternatives to electrical devices, and began experimentation on the power of the brain. Terrorism also was altering warfare, with the unknown location of the enemy far more worrying than just cyber-security and spies. Major Ross suggested he also look at combining in his research, if it was possible, a way of identifying using GPS tracking, where the communication was coming from. This idea was now taking on a life of its own, as this was easier to achieve, and John was working flat out trying to develop the idea of GPS tracking using nanotechnology to so that trials could begin.

Major Ross was now considering reducing his workload in Hereford, to concentrate solely on these projects, thereby increasing his visits to four or even five days a week as his input was needed more, and even more intelligence being sought through him.

Chapter 7

Joe's Bar, Kew
2009

"Tomorrow at mine?" Andrew suggested to Sarah, who was perched on the very high bar stool, legs crossed flirtatiously, quaffing her cider.

"Sorry, couldn't hear you," Sarah put her cupped hand to her ear and bent towards Andrew.

"Let's get out of here," Andrew indicated the exit with a nod of his head, and started to walk off. Sarah drained her glass, and plonked it on the bar, following him outside to the smokers area.

"Whew, it was noisy in there tonight," Andrew breathed out a sigh of relief.

"I think Daniel was in charge tonight, he always turns the volume up to the max."

"I was saying, do you fancy coming round to mine tomorrow night? I'm just off the High Street, about five minutes from here."

"Yeah why not, what time?" Sarah asked.

"Say nine."

"Yeah, great, I'll bring some drink. Yeah?"

"Great. You on WhatsApp?" Sarah nodded, and Andrew typed his address and sent it. Sarah's phone pinged receipt. "Basement flat. Ok?" Andrew confirmed.

"OK, I'm off, see you tomorrow." With that Sarah sauntered away, off down the street past the takeaways, shops and bars. Fabulous, another conquest, she thought, it's like a sweet shop here, loads of choice. It was such a massive difference to Malvern, which was the original back of beyond. She had been having a ball since she came down to Kew; all varieties, all nicely packaged, different backgrounds and colours. Such a choice!

She had been talking to Andrew for a few days in Joe's. He was a little straight-laced, but quite acceptable.

Sarah had no difficulty finding the large Victorian house, but finding the flat's entrance was quite another challenge. The steps up to the front door, only gave numbers one to five, where on earth was the basement flat? She retraced her steps to the muddy patch where cars were parked in the front garden. As it was a semi, she thought perhaps the entrance was around the side. She walked away from the light emitting from the streetlight, and down the side of the building, the ground sloped down and there was only long damp grass to walk on. Her heels were digging into the soft wet ground. It hardly looked as though it had been walked on much. Perhaps she was in the wrong place. She carried on in the semi-dark, worried what she might tread on. She still could not find the doorway. She rounded the building to the back. There was a wall of wheelie bins, and then she saw it, a small flight of brick steps, down to a dingy, litter strewn, recessed doorway. The ceiling light bulb was not lit, so she walked carefully down the steps holding onto the wall to steady herself. The doorbell push emitted a glow and she pushed it and waited. She could hear his footsteps echo, as Andrew walked to the door. Two seconds later the door was partially opened, and Andrew peered around the edge, and then smiled at her and opened the door fully.

"I've brought the drink." She proffered the carrier bag with the cider in. "God you were difficult to find."

Sarah stepped inside, giving Andrew a cheeky grin.

To say the long hallway was barren was an understatement even for rented. The bright blue walls had a missing strip where once a wallpaper border had been stuck at dado height. The light bulb must have been 40 watts at the most and squeezed just enough light out for her to see.

Andrew led the way through the battered door at the far end of the hallway. The room was also lit by a dim, bare light bulb, and the unlined pink curtains which hung precariously from a thin wire draped across the wide high window, were shut.

Two camping chairs were arranged in the centre of the room either side of a camping table. Sarah looked around. She was just about to speak, when the only other door opened and a very smart man in his fifties walked in. Sarah looked quizzically at Andrew, fear beginning to rise. Who on earth was he?

"Please don't be alarmed, take a seat." The gentleman spoke calmly and gestured to the two chairs. Andrew smiled at her to reassure her.

"OK what's going on?" Sarah asked bullishly. "Andrew?"

"Do sit down, I can reassure you everything is fine, you are safe with us," the gentleman continued. Sarah sat down cautiously, choosing the chair which was facing the two doors, so she could see if anyone else came into the room. The silver-haired, bespoke suited gentleman sat down in the only other chair, whilst Andrew stood adjacent to him, facing Sarah.

Andrew placed a slim, black folder down in front of the gentleman on the table and stood smartly upright, with his arms behind his back and legs slightly apart. The gentleman opened the folder cover, and read the first page. He looked up at Sarah, and repositioned his glasses high on his forehead.

"Do call me William, Sarah. Now, obviously, you are wondering what on earth is going on, and quite rightly so. Andrew has asked you here for a purpose, perhaps not the one you were thinking of." He smiled knowingly. Sarah continued to stare at them both. "He works for me," he continued. "We have been monitoring you for months, since your arrival at Kew. Your Professor had already marked you out as suitable. We think you could be very useful to us.

You are, of course, fully aware by now of the significance of the Gelsemium elegans project, which you have shown great aptitude for. We need someone with your knowledge, and your sassy personality for a very important long-term project. You will need to sign The Official Secrets Act, and commence training, which will take place here in London, so that you can continue your research.

We need you initially to be a 'sleeper', helping us develop a major project.

Sarah leaned back, and tossed her mane of hair back off her shoulders. She defiantly kicked off her muddy high-heeled shoes, which had been killing her.

"Can I have a drink? I've brought some cider," she asked Andrew.

"Andrew, go and have a look. Give them a clean if there are any cups."

Andrew disappeared though the door into the kitchen. Cupboard doors could be heard being opened and closed. The tap was turned on, and water spluttered in spurts from the spout.

"Oh bloody hell." Andrew could be heard to exclaim. William raised his eyebrow and continued to read through the file on the table. Andrew returned holding two builders' type mugs, chipped and only one having a handle. Sarah noticed Andrew's trousers were splashed with water.

"All there was." Andrew confirmed as he put the wet mugs on the table. If it were not for the fact that the cider was in a two-litre bottle, Sarah would not have bothered with a mug at all. Andrew poured cider into the better of the two mugs and handed it to Sarah, who quickly drank a couple of good gulps.

"Now let's get this straight," she began, "Is this all kosher, you know, all above board? My father works for QinetiQ on government projects, and he will kill me if this impacts on his career."

"No way. Do you mean Ken? Ken Burrows? I only thought he gave me a reference." Sarah took a minute for this information to sink in. She knew the competition was fierce, and had been surprised to be offered the job, but was disappointed to think she didn't win it fair and square. She had another couple of mouthfuls of cider. William and Andrew waited, in no rush.

"You cannot mention either this meeting to your father or the project, just as he does not discuss his work at home," William continued.

"I just thought he had a bloody boring job,'" she responded.

"No, not quite. Andrew will be your contact, once you have been security checked. He will organise your training. You can expect to continue with your research at Kew, but sometime in the future after you have had training, you will be advising on a project, before moving at a later date, to live on the site of the project.

So you will need to be willing to move at anytime, anywhere, once you become active. Now, I cannot give you any more information. We need to establish, just between the three of us, if you are interested.

"Are we talking about the HQ being along the Embankment?" Sarah asked.

"Yes, Sarah we are," William confirmed. At this stage he did not need to tell her if he worked for MI5 or MI6, most people were unsure of the difference – plenty of time later on.

"Oh wow! How exciting. Why me?"

"We have already established your aptitude for research in toxicology, and despite, shall we call it, your free lifestyle...." William paused and looked at Andrew and smiled, looked back at Sarah, and then looked skyward and raised his eyebrows, "You have applied yourself well, exceeding expectations, in fact it could be said, and well it has been said, excelling. Your perception is just what is needed, plus the organisational skills you have used in your research. All these talents will be needed, plus of course our specialist training, which will be implemented, as required."

"Wow!" Sarah sat back, crossed her long bare legs, finished her cider and, putting the mug down on the table, looked at them both and said "Right, let's do it. Fancy, me a spy."

William looked at Andrew and sighed. Not exactly the response he had hoped for, but at the same time, he had heard it countless times before, and his judgement had rarely been wrong.

"Just remember, Sarah, it is vital," he paused, and looked directly into her eyes for a couple of seconds before continuing. "Vital, that you only speak to Andrew about tonight. Is that very clear?"

Sarah smiled, threw her head back, laughed loudly, uncrossed her legs, leaned forward and said in a conspiratorial voice, whispering. "So when do I sign the Official Secrets Act?"

As Andrew and Sarah walked around the corner of the house, through the grass, he took her arm by the elbow and spoke clearly and directly. "Sarah, no one must know, not even your dear Professor. You do understand?"

"Ok, ok, I'm not stupid, I got that. Trust me."

"We will be."

"So, I presume you have a company car? Home James and don't spare the horses, save my poor feet from these blasted shoes."

William aka Major Ross locked up the safe house and left for his club in town. It had been a long time since he had stayed over. 'I wonder who is in tonight?' he thought as he negotiated the steps and then the long grass. His leg was playing up tonight. The wound was still painful even after his latest op. 'We had better be right about Sarah,' he thought as he drove away.

Chapter 8
Jean's bungalow
Saturday afternoon
2009

Anne knocked on Jean's back door rapidly.

"I'm coming, I'm coming," Jean shouted, as she walked to the door.

"Hello Anne, come on in. What on earth is wrong with you, you look distraught?"

Anne walked slowly in and took a seat at the kitchen table. She continued to dab her eyes with a tissue. Before she had time to speak, Jean picked up her kettle filled it and switched it on.

"You look like you need a cup of tea." Jean continued. "Have you had some bad news?"

"Jean, the most terrible thing has happened. Major Ross has just phoned to let us know. He tried you first, but you did not answer. Jonathon has been found by Isobel at their Cambridge home. She has just let Major Ross know."

"Is he alright? The way he sped off yesterday worried me. He looked very troubled and Isobel looked terribly upset," Jean asked.

"No, she found him hanging from their landing bannister. It looks as though he had been there for hours, according to Isobel."

Jean took a sharp intake of breath, held onto the back of the other chair, and sat down with a thump.

"Oh no!" Jean raised her hand to her mouth and looked wide-eyed at Anne. "What a terrible thing to do. Poor Isobel, poor, poor Isobel. Where is she, did Major Ross say?"

Anne got up and filled the teapot, put the knitted cosy on and placed it on the table between them.

"Thank you Anne."

"Major Ross said she would be needed by the police and would need to stay there for a few days. Unexplained death I think they classify it as to begin with. The coroner will ask for a report," Anne replied.

"Oh my goodness, I really can't believe it. Jonathon. What on earth caused him to do that, to commit suicide? Isobel must be beside herself. Does she have anyone to look after her?" Jean asked, getting up to get the cups, saucers and milk jug.

"Well I have never heard her talk of anyone, have you? Her Dad died years ago and I'm not sure about her Mum. She would have to be in her eighties if she is still around. They never had children, so I don't know if there are any other relatives. She never got over not having children did she? I bet she is aware of that now as there is no one there to care for her. We must go across to her Jean, if you think she would appreciate it. It's quite a journey, but if we can get the time off this week, I think we should go." Anne suggested. "I'll phone her and see what she wants us to do." Jean poured the tea.

"Biscuit Anne?"

"No thanks." Anne stirred her tea and looked distantly into the cup.

"I just can't believe it. Jonathon was always a bit eccentric, but that's not unusual for such a mathematical genius. I've worked with many at GCHQ, and most of them are a bit on another planet at times. Jonathon was in a league of his own wasn't he? He has developed so much of our programme. Did you know how they came to own two such lovely houses?" Jean leant forward over the table.

"No."

"He won nearly all the money playing poker," Jean answered.

"Well I knew he played, but I never knew he had been successful. Wow!"

"He won the money for the house in Cambridge and the one in the South of France, at the same time, years before they came to work here. He won it during a marathon poker weekend, and walked away with enough money to buy them almost outright. Isobel told me about it a couple of years ago." Jean explained.

"You never said."

"Well I don't think she had wanted it to be common knowledge. She and Jonathon were very close, weren't they? Although he could be very difficult, I always thought she knew how to handle him. You know, calm him down and make him listen."

"That's the understatement of the year, I found him very difficult at times," Anne replied. "Do you think he had a bit of a drink problem?"

"Well I wasn't going to mention it, but I think he kept bottles of booze in his locker in the rest room, and he always went home at lunchtime for a drink or two."

"Umm. I think you are right."

They sat and finished their tea, tidied up and then Anne went home, leaving Jean to talk to Major Ross about taking some time off to help Isobel, and then tell the other researchers.

Six months later

Cambridge.

Isobel placed the vacuum and the dustpan and brush by the front door and turned to look one last time at her home of the past twelve years. The rooms echoed, the house felt so sterile, devoid of all their belongings -the paintings, the furniture, their love. It was just an empty shell now. She avoided looking up at the landing bannister, as she had done ever since that awful afternoon six months ago. The image of Jonathon hanging there haunted her every night. Every night she relived the drama, the realisation of what had happened. The 'what if's' that would have changed everything. She knew the 'what if' list was pointless, but she still replayed it, when she was driving, when she was sat relaxing, and every night, all night. The doctor said it was Post Traumatic Stress and she had no reason to disagree, but it was so difficult to live with.

She had walked around each room this afternoon and remembered the good times, the happy days filled with laughter. She remembered the absolute joy of being able to afford to buy such a wonderful home so close to town. Despite neither of them being gardeners, it was the garden that had sealed the deal and they had paid the full asking price to ensure they got the house.

Jonathon had proved to be a genius at poker, and the winnings from that weekend, had enabled them to buy outright a gorgeous home in a small village in the South of France, and put down a substantial deposit on the Cambridge house.

They would decamp in the summer, Christmas and every other moment possible to the warmth of France and immerse themselves in the local village culture.

Matthew had been employed as their gardener to keep Oak House in pristine condition. Lawns were trimmed, mowed and nurtured by him twice a week in the summer. The stripes on the lawn were much admired.

Isobel had stood at the kitchen window moments ago and looked at the garden paths strewn with debris, the flower beds were now covered in weeds, and the lawn was unkempt with the grass at least a foot high. Matthew had had to be let go, straight after Isobel saw her financial situation after Jonathon had died.

She had no idea that Jonathon had run up massive gambling debts that were in both their names. She had found it most upsetting that small local business had not been paid their money. Everything had had to go to try and pay off the debts. The house in France sold quite easily to another English couple, and that had helped to pay off some of the extended mortgage that Jonathon had taken out on their Cambridge house. Despite every effort she made, she could not settle the debts or pay the mortgage. She put the house on the market, but the market was really sluggish, two buyers fell through, both because they could not sell their own houses. She had come to terms now with the fact that the building society was repossessing it today. She would walk away with nothing at all. The furniture that would not fit in her bungalow in Malvern had been sold off for a song, with the remnants going to the local house clearance shop round the corner.

If only Jonathon had stopped gambling when he was winning, but he was like his father, he became addicted, even before his alcohol problem became an issue. He had so cleverly hidden all the problems from her. It was only when she went to pay for a lovely sofa and her credit card and debit card were declined, that she found out from Jonathon what dire financial circumstances they were in. That had been the terrible Friday. They were working in Malvern and he said he would sort it out and that he would see her later and had driven off in their Range Rover in a rage. She never saw him alive again. Jonathon had chosen to evade the problem; with what he thought was the only solution.

Isobel had continued with the research project for three months, through all her problems before taking three months compassionate leave. She had needed that time to sort out the sale of both houses, and her financial situation.

In a way she was looking forward to going back to Malvern. Her research work would hopefully totally absorb her, and the flashbacks and 'what's if's' would have less space to occupy in her mind. Also whilst she had been living in Oak House, she had expected Jonathon to come into the room or come home constantly, she was so used to his presence. It had been hard doing the chores that he had always done, putting out the rubbish, mending fuses, reaching into the loft. Each in themselves was a small task, but each time she needed him, she missed him more. She had let herself go, she knew it; she had been so consumed by the grief of losing her lifetime's partner her appearance just did not matter. Who would notice anyway? 'I really must lose some weight' she thought as her shapeless trousers strained around her waist, sitting below her roll of spare flesh. She had packed up all her pretty dresses and jackets the other week and realised that none would fit her at the moment. She had thought then that she would start her diet, just as soon as she finished off the doughnuts downstairs. Here she was dressed in her current uniform; taupe stretch waist polyester trews with a sewn-in front pleat, beige round necked long sleeved jumper over a simple white blouse, with beige flat lace up shoes for comfort. Everything looked as though she was trying to blend in with the background, to be ignored.

She had filled her old vanity case that morning with all the lotions and potions she used to use daily. Hair products to give shine and bounce, various brushes, blushers, eyebrow pencils and mascara, as well as seemingly dozens of lipsticks, all in lovely coral or red shades. All had been sitting undisturbed in her dressing table since finding Jonathon. 'I'll get round to using them again, when I have lost the weight, once I get back to Malvern.'

She would miss Cambridge. It was where they had both studied, and where Major Ross had recruited them for the Malvern project, her knowledge being medical research and Jonathon's nanotechnology. They had lived for the past four years, weekdays in Malvern, and weekends in Cambridge, apart from their visits to France. It was quite a drive to Cambridge from Malvern, but they shared the driving and it had become mundane after a while, and meant they could have a good, long uninterrupted chat during the journey.

'Oh well, it's no use standing here any longer.' Isobel picked up the cleaning materials and left the house for the last time. The sound of the door closing rebounded around the empty property.

Chapter 9

Kew Royal Botanic Gardens. The Professors office. February 2010

"Sarah, your latest results are improving but as you are aware, the potency is still nowhere near the required strength. It just will not have the outcome we need for the project at this strength. The Operations Research Wing requires a ninety per cent success rate to commence the initial trial roll out, with a final ninety-eight per cent efficiency. At the moment, we have a drug with only a guaranteed thirty-eight per cent mortality. We must look outside the box, and I also think we must establish that we have the strongest raw materials from which we are working. I travelled to Fujian in China to collect the plants we have been using a few years ago, but I think now what we really need to do, is harvest material from all the other sites where it grows, which are all to be found in Southern China. I understand from my contacts that the nine areas in China, although remote and relatively far apart, all still grow the Gelsemium elegans in the wild. It's quite a trip, I can tell you. I am loath to use our contacts to collect plant samples as the Mussaenda Pubescens is so similar, but does not have the toxicity. We just cannot afford to lose any time, Sarah, by having the wrong plants sent."

It was agreed that Sarah would take Thomas, a fellow researcher with her, as much as anything for company and to help haul all the bags, as it could be quite a challenge dealing with the Chinese in the remote areas. Thomas was only a couple of years older than Sarah, very studious and set in his ways. He always wore smart trousers, long-sleeved tailored shirts and very shiny black lace up shoes. He could be good fun though, and he liked a beer or two, so he and Sarah had always got on well. Thomas was to be her companion as he spoke a little of the local language. He had pulled her leg that she was going to frighten the local people with her height and blonde curly hair. He advised her to tuck it up, into a traditional douli hat, to avoid too much attention. She was also told to exchange her usual garb of combat shorts and tee shirts, for long trousers and shirts, similar to the local women. Better safe than sorry.

Sarah did rather fancy Thomas, but thought she had better behave as they worked together. Perhaps a little flirting would be fine. It could be a rather boring trip otherwise.

Sarah was so excited about going on an expedition. She had not been to China before, and thought the mad food they ate would be interesting. She loved eating in the Chinese quarter in Birmingham, but knew that the food she would be offered would be very different. Still she was always up for anything new and frankly, if she did not eat much it would not hurt her figure. Andrew had approved her visit, and had ensured she knew enough diplomacy not to end up in prison there; she was still a bit of a loose cannon at times, despite all the training.

They did not want to lose her before she began her alternative work.

The eleven and a half hour journey from Heathrow was quite fun, she thought. Thomas slept most of the way, until breakfast was served. She had spent the night, whilst most travellers were sleeping, walking up the aisle and standing at the back chatting to the crew. Mind you, when she got off and it was late afternoon, she wished she had had at least some sleep.

The southern airport of Guangzhou Baiyun arrivals terminal was no different from any other destination she had travelled to; modern, large and impersonal. If it wasn't for the impenetrable Chinese signs, she could have been anywhere in the world.

They walked out of the arrivals hall to see Sarah's name on a card being held by a dark-haired young handsome Chinese male. This, she thought, must be Cheng. She had been told about his studies at Kew and also warned by Andrew, that he was known to be working for the Chinese state.

Their driver packed all the many bags and luggage into the car and they were off. Sarah and Thomas sat back and knew they were in for a very exhausting time. The areas were all in the south of China, but that still meant an area covering seven thousand square kilometres. Luckily they had been given all the locations within each province, but there was going to be a lot of air travel, and hauling masses of baggage and samples.

The cover story was that Kew Royal Botanic Gardens were researching the use of the plant in the treatment of cancer, and that different strains of the same plant might react differently, this being the reason to collect all the varieties.

"Did you know, we call it – I think you would say – Heartbroken Glass?" Cheng mentioned on the first day of travel.

Sarah replied, "Yes, Heartbreak Grass." Thomas bent towards the front seat where the interpreter sat.

"Yes, I understand the hill tribes use it to commit suicide," he said.

"Yes and in South East Asia. Of course no one would do that unless they were very ill." The interpreter suddenly thought he would not want them to think any Chinese person would want to commit suicide. He knew, of course, that China was the very best place in the world to live.

"Of course, they would have to have a mental problem to resort to that," Thomas replied, saving the honour of the interpreter.

The first hotel was modern and clean. The evening meal had been fine, as they were still in modern China and even Thomas had found something to eat. They had both locked their laptops and phones in the safe during dinner, for security. The area of China that they were in, Guangzhou, was known to be the centre of cyber espionage. The instructions had been clear from Andrew. The first place anyone from the state would look for their information would be in the hotel safes. Nothing about the project must be transmitted or stored on the devices that would give their research away. If it proved absolutely essential to send information, then Sarah was to use the old one-time pad she had been given. This would encrypt her information and it would be impossible for anyone other than the recipient to decode.

Cheng recalled to Thomas and Sarah that evening how his parents had moved back to Guangzhou after the Cultural Revolution had collapsed, as they had been school teachers and classed as 'intellectuals' and had been sent out to the countryside to live. He hoped that Thomas and Sarah would like to visit them on their return to Guangzhou. His parents had heard so much about The Royal Botanical Gardens from their son that they would love to return the kindnesses that Cheng had received when he had visited and hear more about their work.

The next day was the beginning of the hard trek around the scrubby forests, to harvest the plants. Rural China was both a shock and at the same time fascinating. The amazing mountains that seemed to leap out of flat paddy fields reminiscent of St Lucia's Pitons, very old rundown houses which were just so picturesque, not that Sarah would want to live in them. The seeming poverty of the rural workers was just a world away from the urban areas they had left behind. Everyone they met seemed so happy, so content. Many of the young men were working away when Sarah and Thomas were there, as they had gone to the cities to work in low paid jobs, as migrant workers, but they would be back come the harvest season. Life certainly seemed a struggle, but Cheng said that everyone was happy, as this was all the life they knew.

The weeks flew by and all too soon they were on their way home. As promised, Cheng's parents insisted they go and have a meal with them. Cheng has told them that Sarah was very keen to eat with them at home, rather than the usual custom of eating out in a restaurant. The five of them sat around the circular table in their small apartment in the high-rise block of flats. The table groaned with a selection of dishes on the central Lazy Susan turntable. Sara was in her element by now. Her chopsticks were flying from dish to dish, as Thomas picked a little here and a little there. He did manage to keep his dislike of the food to himself, thank goodness.

In the morning they loaded up the van with their suitcases, just finding space amongst the packed boxes of plant saplings. At the airport, Cheng organised the four trolleys needed for their luggage, and after they had paid the excess baggage fees, Sarah and Thomas turned to Cheng and shook his hand.

He had got used to this in England before, so knew the appropriate response.

"Cheng, it has been a tremendous honour to have known you these last few weeks. Your parents were so kind last night; please pass on our gratitude again to them. Thomas and I cannot thank you enough for all the help you have given us. It would have been impossible to collect the specimens without you and your knowledge. We did have some fun didn't we?" Sarah opened her huge handbag and dug out a box. "I brought this over from Kew for you, to thank you. It's not much, but I hope you enjoy it. Open it when we've gone." Sarah handed over the box of sweets that she knew Cheng had had a passion for when he was working in Kew. Cheng took the box, and turned it over to inspect it from every side, looking for clues. "Enjoy. You never know we might see you again, here or at Kew." She reached over and gave him a hug, whilst Thomas shook his hand again, and thanked him. They left Cheng at the Passport controls, with him smiling and waving his box in the air.

Thankfully the plane left on time. Sarah sat by the window and looked for the last time at the most stunning scenery.

"Glad that's over," Thomas said.

"You have no sense of adventure young Thomas," Sarah smiled.

"Hated the food, hated the travel and, apart from Cheng and the plants, I will never come back again."

"You are an old fogey. The food was great, if you had tried it. It was good honest food, different yes, but that's what travel is all about."

"No thanks, those muesli bars I brought with me were lifesavers. I should have starved otherwise," Thomas moaned.

Sarah chuckled. The hours they had put in, plus the hundreds of miles in that car over difficult terrain, had taken its' toll. She put her seat back and rested her head. Still, the hold was full of their samples, all labelled and wrapped securely to withstand the flight.

She closed her eyes, and thought about the lovely Cheng and the firmness of his body.

Chapter 10

MI6 Headquarters.
The Embankment, London.
March 2011

"Good morning, Sarah," Andrew had phoned Sarah nice and early before she got stuck into her research.

"The time has come for your briefing. We need you to start work on your project – additional training ok? Monday next week nine am, same place. Come to reception as before and ask for me. I'll see you there." Andrew put down his phone. He looked out of his window at the view. The Houses of Parliament to his right were looking spectacular, broody and grey with huge rain clouds dominating the skyline. The Thames was bustling with the usual river traffic and tourist boats getting ready for a busy day. The sun was due later if it could struggle out from behind the clouds, hopefully to provide some welcome warmth after the biting winds of the past few weeks.

'I'm so glad I chose this office, facing the river,' he thought, as he drank his fourth coffee of the morning.

He did not expect any problems with Sarah's training. She had already proved herself to be very quick at picking up new ideas and developing them. Very bright girl, they had chosen well.

Sarah would now have to liaise with the security planning department here, who were advising their architect on the plans for the new medical trial village in Malvern, now that it had been finally been given planning approval after much interference from Whitehall. It had been essential that it be built next to Princess Margaret Gardens. The only land suitable was in front of the town's recycling facility. Not ideal, especially as a small stream ran between the two sites, which could affect the underground connection between Sarah's laboratory and next door. The architects being used were the same firm that had designed the 'Doughnut' for GCHQ in Cheltenham. The Doughnut was probably the most secure site in Britain; every possible defence against attack had been installed. Peak View Village, as this site was to be called, required extra security measures to be installed just as covertly and thoroughly.

Now Sarah needed to design the research facility for her needs, as the plant production was going to be moved from Kew, so that she could combine it with her new role in the village. Her specialist research rooms were going to be installed behind the village's plant room, where all the mains services such as electricity, gas and water supply for the needs of the village, were to be controlled. The outer door was to be labelled "Plant room" which amused the architects who had labelled a ground floor room used by the Cyber Defence Operations (CDO) at GCHQ 'Defending the UK one bit at a time.' Humour was alive and well even in high security areas!

The location of the Plant Room was to be the lower ground floor, where the only other rooms were to be Sarah's apartment. All access to this floor was restricted, by having the Access Control System extended from next door. Lifts and stairs would have security built in to avoid residents and their visitors having access. The Plant Room's specialist growing room would contain all the latest technology, as the plants were to be grown in artificial conditions and harvested by Sarah. Access to the rooms was to be through secure concealed doors inside the Plant Room.

The building's security was being worked on by GCHQ, as most areas were to be monitored, and almost all areas would also be under camera surveillance.

Sarah booked time off from her project to visit Head Quarters. Dressed in her usual quirky style of short khaki combat shorts, with her trademark multi-coloured scarf as a belt, dangling down nearly to her tan bovver boots, as she called them, with her thick socks pushed down to her ankles, she showed off her long, lean legs to full effect. She had chosen her favourite bright orange long sleeved tee shirt to wear today and despite the possibility of showers, chose not to wear her leather bomber jacket. Her shoulder bag was slung over her shoulder and was as usual, crammed with everything she might need; phone, lip salve, purse, receipts plus all the usual detritus she never bothered to remove. She hopped onto the underground at Kew to head to Victoria station.

Having left plenty of time, she decided to walk today rather than take the tube connection to the Secret Intelligence Services [SIS] building, at Vauxhall Cross, the fairly new headquarters of MI6. Its stunning architecture, she thought, must have won several awards; it was such an iconic building. She loved crossing the river at Vauxhall, usually standing for quite a few moments to look at the river traffic. She was rather pleased that she was working for MI6, rather than MI5, as she loved the modern aesthetics of the building. She had only visited a couple of times now, but was starting to know her way around.

Andrew met her as before in the reception area and accompanied her to meet the architects in the planning department.

Later, as she walked back to Victoria station, through the evening rush hour, she paused again at the bridge and leaned over the parapet to observe the comings and goings on the river. It was really amazing how her life was turning out. Who would have thought she would have been getting involved in such monumental research, especially having studied horticulture at Pershore, rather than Oxford or Cambridge. Sarah, as instructed, had not told anyone, not even her Mum and Dad about working for MI6. She still found it unbelievable.

She had really enjoyed today. She was to provide a comprehensive list of all the requirements she needed for her laboratory. It was a good job that Kew was going to help the planning department with this. Her facility was going to be state of the art. She thought her fellow researchers would be quite jealous if they knew what equipment she was going to order. Money was not an issue, so she planned on using the very latest technology.

Sarah was now partially briefed about the village's purpose and was amazed to find it was being built in her home town of Malvern. She had really hoped for some amazing new location to move to. Whilst she loved Malvern, she had hoped for a much livelier town or city, rather than a rural retreat. She understood now, why it was Malvern. Who knew about Princess Margaret Gardens? She had lived in Malvern most of her life, and had driven past them day in, day out, hardly ever looking at them. She had presumed they were full of old folks, living in God's waiting room. Still living in Malvern meant she would be able to have dinner at Mum's occasionally. She must catch up with her old university friends, and see who had stayed around the area. It might not be so bad after all.

As she sat on the underground, she wondered about Cheng. Should she contact him with this news? Perhaps leave it a little while, until she had more information.

Chapter 11

Princess Margaret Gardens
Major Ross's office
June 2012.

"So you think that the timing is right now, do you John?"
Major Ross leant back against his office wall.

"Yes, you know those couple of researchers we have
been keeping track of at GCHQ, Mark and Paul. Well I
think that we need additional input now. I have come to the
point, where I am certain we can do the nano GPS tracking,
and need far more input and research, and then shortly we
can start a full trial. Did you say you had approval to use
the troops?"

"Yes, after initial trials have been completed, the MoD
has agreed to a limited trial, probably using my guys. They
want to see how it acts in a conflict situation, and consider
its full potential. They are chasing me for dates, as they see
another potential use, as we did in the tracking of suspected
terrorists. Do you know what? I reckon we could use it as
an inoculation, as we are with the dementia flu jab, but on
anyone travelling in or out of the country. I have even
thought further outside the box, John. Is there a way we

could develop where the nanodrones can be transferred through either a drink, or even some method that it could be absorbed through the skin? Think of that potential John, how easy it would be to track people. MI5 and MI6 would be well up to using that wouldn't they?"

"Right, shall we say you can get me two researchers pronto, and then very soon after we have as least got the system working with an intravenous method, we get more researchers on board to develop and trial the system?" John asked. "There is no point getting too many on board now, as I need to concentrate on the basic method first. They will only distract me at the moment. Do you agree?"

"John, it's your research, you know what you need. The resources are there when you need them, so just ask. I will get onto the department today to organise things, and then we can go over to GCHQ to chat to Mark and Paul. I'll let you know how things are going, ok?" Major Ross walked to the office door. "I'm getting really excited about this, John. If we can crack this, we will be so far ahead of the game, it will give us such an important advantage when tracking people if we can get the GPS nanos covertly in place."

John rose and was about to walk out of the office when Major Ross stopped him.

"Have you been exchanging your latest developments with Jean's team? The crossover of ideas working so closely has been very successful, and you both might have some outside the box ideas. Sarah's knowledge of plant absorption could well have some bearing on trying to administer the Drones through the skin. I'm thinking something like on a fingerprint pad, or paper coffee cups. Have a chat, and give her the problem to look into. "

John left with his mind buzzing with ideas. Ross was perhaps really onto something there.

"Jean, how is it going? John will probably tell you, I am doing a catch up day with our resources, checking if you have enough personnel for the trial and development." Major Ross had called Jean down to his office straight after seeing John.

Jean straightened her skirt, and played with her pencil on the fresh pad of paper she had come downstairs with. Her computer was open at the latest results analysis.

"Well I must say the completion of next door can't come soon enough for me, sir. Sarah's work down in Kew has come on leaps and bounds. Her input has been thought provoking. Whilst we still do not have the toxicity we demand, she has improved the strength dramatically. Once she is up here, we can have our discussions face to face, which is always a good way of bouncing new ideas around. We have been training her on the trial subjects we are going to need. Anne has been training her on the symptoms of dementia and Alzheimer's, and we placed her as you know, for three weeks in that care home for retired personnel, to give her first-hand knowledge. Anne thought that she picked up really well the early symptoms and mannerisms for identifying visually the residents who should be tested by Bill, to see if they were at the right stage to have the nano flu vaccine. With next door opening in October, it's perfect timing to give the new 'flu' vaccine to at least seventy residents. Feedback will be instant with Sarah on site. We are all very excited. This village will speed up and intensify our trial results, so that hopefully we can go into production in the near future.

"Since Jonathon's death you have been understrength. Is it time to get in some additional personnel to deal with all the new results now? I am thinking it's going to take at least two months to recruit and then we need to train them, before the results start coming in from next door."

"Yes, I have been thinking of asking you about extra help. I reckon we need three additional researchers. Do we have accommodation for them next door?"

"No problem, we have reserved ten apartments for our use, but of course as other apartments come up, we can always put the extra security in them if we need to." Jean nodded.

"Then could I ask for three new personnel? I have some contacts already that might be able to suggest suitable candidates. We could also try Cambridge and what about one of the pharmaceutical companies? Someone more medically rather than scientifically trained."

"Definitely not the pharmaceutical companies, Jean. They must not get wind of our research, as if they do not get awarded the contract for production they stand to lose so much of their other business if the trial works. No, leave it to me, I don't think I did badly with my initial selection do you?" Jean smiled.

"Right sir, I await your selection."

"Now, we must start work on the exact course we want the trials next door to take. Come back to me soon Jean with your plans."

Chapter 12

Peak View Village
October 2012

Sarah met up with her site manager, Amanda, who had been seconded from GCHQ, in the new manager's office. Rows of filing cabinets were lined up against the long wall, ready for action, waiting for more medical notes and CT scans of the new residents, to add to their initial results. The building work was now nearing completion, and today was to be the first of several 'Meet and greet' meetings for batches of new residents.

Sarah and Jean had worked so hard choosing the right residents from the hordes of applicants. Bill had arranged all the medicals, and written up all the initial records and filed them with the CT scans. It was only a few weeks to go before the first residents moved in, and the new trials could begin.

Although Sarah had moved all her belongings into her apartment, she still had to work in Kew on average three days a week. She could not risk moving her precious plants here until the electricity on site was on one hundred per cent of the time. The new state of the art controlled environment was essential to their survival.

The new plants from her visit to China had been a huge success with a vastly improved toxicity. The success rate was averaging eighty-five per cent. The aim for the project to enable it to be rolled out was ninety-eight per cent. It was essential that not only was the timing of the nanodrones activation accurate, but that the toxin from her plants caused an immediate heart attack, and not a debilitating illness or paralysis. The great thing was that no autopsy carried out outside of Hereford, had picked up the Gelsemium elegans in the blood or urine. However the thirteen per cent improvement in toxicity was proving difficult to achieve. Her knowledge and expertise were being fully tested. No one else could help her, as she was way ahead of even her Professor on this one. She had become quite the expert on nanomedicine, an area she had known nothing about six years ago.

Sarah was also excited to learn yesterday that two new younger researchers were coming to join them and they would be living in the specially adapted accommodation here. It would be great to have others nearer to her age. 'I think Ross said they were about forty years old, still about ten years older than me, but at least not in their seventies,' she pondered. They were both males, never a bad thing, if only to have a laugh and a beer with. She smiled at the thought of company.

Inaugural 'Meet and Greet.' Session

Peak View Village

"Well hello Mr & Mrs Partridge, come on through and meet some of the other residents." Sarah showed them the way to the bar and lounge area. "Have you met the Smiths before?"

"No, hello I'm Steve Partridge and this is my wife Margaret," Steve shook Mr and Mrs Smiths' hands. Margaret nodded and smiled at them. "Excuse me a minute I just want to ask Sarah a question." Steve quickly darted off after Sarah, "Sarah, how long will this meeting take?"

"I expect a couple of hours, with the tour of the facilities," Sarah replied.

"Excellent, as we have to go to the doctors later on. Will we be able to have a look at our apartment today?"

"I am waiting for a list from the site manager for today's meeting, to let me know whose apartments can be viewed. Yesterday your floor looked as though it might be ready for you to access today. So how is your house sale going?"

"Well we have signed the contracts, and it's just a case of tying up the moving dates to when the apartments are ready for us."

"Excellent, that's good news. How is Margaret?"

"Not too bad, some days she is worried about her memory, but then she is still driving, so not too bad."

"Oh that's good. If you will excuse me, I have just seen the Evans family coming into reception. I'll be back soon." Sarah strode off in the direction of reception. Her low heels and knee length skirt, felt very alien, but her image was important as the 'face' of the new village.

"Are you alright, Margaret?" Steve sat down next to his wife at the coffee table with the Smiths.

"Yes, we have just been discussing how wonderful it all looks. I cannot wait to see the facilities. Barbara was saying how brilliant the deal seems to be, with the discount and the monitoring of our health included." Barbara nodded.

"It's quite something isn't it? It looks even better than the brochure. What did your family think of you coming here?" Barbara asked.

"It took then quite a while to accept we were selling up the family home. Frankly, we gave them the £60k discount that we had made on the purchase price for being on the health trial. It's meant they can put deposits down on their first homes. So now they are really pleased," Steve replied. Barbara and Bob looked at each other.

"So have we," they both laughed. "It's the only way they can afford to buy a home I don't know about you, but we were able to buy our first house when we were in our early twenties, but now, they cannot seem to get the deposit until their mid-thirties. Our two are nearly forty, and still haven't managed it." Barbara confirmed. "It's an amazing discount just so that they can monitor us, don't you think?"

"Did you tell your family about the medical research?" Margaret asked them.

"We did have to convince the boys that it was in our best interests. I think they worry that we are going to be experimented on. I have explained, exactly as Sarah said, that the trial is to see how our lifestyle affects our development, and that it can only benefit us, especially with all the facilities here on our doorstep." Barbara replied. "We should be fitter than ever, I think I will have a daily swim, might even try the gym," Barbara continued. Bob laughed.

"Pigs might fly," he chuckled.

"You never know," Barbara laughed and patted his knee.

"Yes I might also do some exercise, as you say, you never know. The pool appeals to me," Steve said. "What about the food? We don't even have to cook unless we want to, and then it's all free anyway. The sample menus looked lovely, as long as they taste as good as they look. My Margaret is such a good cook," he looked at Margaret lovingly, and she glowed in response. "I am sure I will still be spoilt by the occasional apple pie or two," Steve finished. Margaret gave him a lovely motherly look. They had been married almost fifty years now, and she really had had enough of cooking, especially since the children left home. If she was honest, she also worried about her weak wrists as she found it difficult to lift saucepans when they were full. She worried about losing her grip and scalding herself, especially when she drained the potatoes. Recipes were also harder to follow; her concentration was so poor lately, she would forget where she had got to in the recipe, and add ingredients twice or miss them out altogether.

Sarah called the meeting to order. The room was almost full. Sarah had counted fifty-four attending. The average age was sixty-two years, exactly as required for the trials.

"Hello everyone. It is lovely to see you all here today. I hope to spend some time explaining how the system will work, what you can expect and then take you all on a walk around. The swimming pool is not filled yet, but you can see the size of it and the other facilities. Do be careful of the barriers. Carl, our site manager, will be there to ensure we don't lose anyone." A ripple of laughter flowed around the room.

This was her first 'Meet and greet' meeting and she hoped that the future residents were also going to be impressed with the village. It was a shame not all the apartments could be shown to the residents, but the site manager Carl had strict instructions to keep everyone safe by complying with the site's Health and Safety policy, as the building contractors were still on site, and were working all over the village. The central gardens had been landscaped and were beautiful. Sarah had been allowed to commission the landscape gardener and had chosen Jenny, her friend of many years, who had graduated with her. They had had such a laugh working together.

Jenny had decided to have plenty of old fashioned sweet smelling roses and pinks, with lavender hedges along many of the paths. Social seating areas had been located to provide shade for hot days and others were positioned in full sun. There was even a large greenhouse for any green-fingered residents, who would miss growing a few vegetables or flowers for picking. The whole atmosphere was one of tranquillity and homeliness. Sarah had suggested a few cannabis plants but thought the residents might recognise them. They did laugh at that idea.

Sarah had selected every resident herself, using the criteria from Princess Margaret Gardens. Health issues had to match the requirement for their research needs. Pre dementia symptoms and / or family history of Alzheimer's were the very basic requirements. Of course this was completely unknown to the applicants for the apartments. As expected the demand, due to the discount, was enormous, despite the recession. They could have filled the two hundred private apartments several times over. It had been a relief to realise how many people with the carrot of a heavy discount on the purchase price, free food and facilities, were willing to be monitored, supposedly to take part in a trial on how the effects of lifestyle affected quality of life. Everyone had had to take a full, thorough medical and a brain scan before being selected. This had been essential to sort out those who were already showing signs of dementia. The future residents had been told it was so their health could be checked thoroughly and they had to give a full medical history for themselves and their parents where possible. In return for being accepted, they would have a full medical each year, complete with brain scans when necessary.

Besides the private residents, there were sixty apartments for Housing Association residents. Some had lived in houses that were on the site before the development. They had been rehoused during the building work but had been promised a new apartment in the new village if they wanted it. These residents only had to be over fifty-five to qualify. All Sarah had to do was to have them have their health checks, so that she could use them if they proved suitable.

Jean and her team were so looking forward to starting the research on the residents next door; it was going to be far better for immediate reliable feedback.

Chapter 13

Peak View Village lounge
December 2012

Christmas decorations hung everywhere like Santa's Grotto. Lights trailed from decoration to decoration, causing lovely reflections around the walls and ceiling. There was an enormous Christmas tree to the right hand side of the small performance stage in the entertainment lounge. Its colour scheme of black and white had caused much conversation amongst the residents, rather like Marmite, they either loved it or hated it. To satisfy them, Amanda had decorated the reception areas' tree in red and gold, to everyone's satisfaction and delight. Sarah was a bit peeved, as she thought they might all like her taste, but Amanda could see it was better to keep with tradition on this one.

Mark and Paul drank their coffee. There were a few others in the lounge, sat in ones and twos around the small tables that were dotted about. They were mainly in their sixties and seventies, which made the two of them easily the youngest in the room.

"They really have decorated the place up well, haven't they?" Paul commented. Mark looked around and nodded.

"Did you hear some of them discussing the tree? Quite controversial it seems. I suppose we will get used to some people seeming to be set in their ways," Paul continued.

Mark and Paul had been briefed on the special security adaptions of the village before they had agreed to move in. John had warned them that when the other new researchers moved in, they must not congregate as a group, so they would not bring attention to themselves in the village. Mark and Paul had no idea when the others were due to start, although they had heard the other research trial was going to have about four more scientists.

"John seems very likable don't you think?" Mark spoke quietly.

"Sure, he seems pretty straight. He liked the work we brought with us. I was a little surprised that it will only be the three of us initially working on the tracking. Still, he obviously is years ahead on the nanotechnology side of it. I think Jean's team will bring their expertise to the table as well," Paul replied, a little bit too loudly for Mark's comfort.

"Paul, let's not talk about it here, eh?"

"Oops, of course." He looked around the large coffee lounge and thought. 'Bet most of them can't hear us anyway, I expect most of them wear hearing aids.'

Mark and Paul knew each other from working together at GCHQ in Cheltenham. They had always got on very well, during work hours. It should be quite fun living in the same building, although Mark was not sure what his London based girlfriend, Helen would make of it. There were two bedrooms in his apartment, so plenty of room when she visited at weekends for her stuff to be stored.

Mark was quite fussy about tidiness and could not bear it when Helen left things hanging around. At least her overnight bag and other rubbish could be put in the other bedroom when she came. Helen was used to Mark being engrossed in his research, and being second fiddle to his work. Mind you, her job was equally demanding, and there were weekends when she could not make the journey.

"Well, what a day!" Paul said looking at Mark, whom was now people watching. "Isn't it odd when you start another job; I felt like a fish out of water today. Not knowing where anything was and having to ask all the time. Jean was surprised our security passes worked; they are always having problems with them. Do you remember all the problems at Cheltenham initially? It sent me potty. Anyway they seem a really nice bunch."

"Yep, certainly can't wait to start working with them on this research. It's amazing, if it can be made to work, it will be world changing. No wonder the security is so tight," Mark replied. "It's an immensely complicated project, I've certainly not heard anyone else working on this line of research. I also reckon that Major Ross is one smart cookie – he used to be operational apparently for The Regiment. I think he had a bad Gulf War, which accounts for his limp. Hey, what a great idea using the Segway to get home. I fancy a go on that sometime." Paul nodded, and drank his beer.

"Never asked you Mark, do you cycle? We could try the Thursday night ride that Simon goes on. They do a ride, and end up at a local real ale pub," Paul suggested.

"I used to ride a while ago, I was quite fit at one time. Simon who?" asked Mark.

"Simon Hughes, you know, who worked for QinetiQ before they made the redundancies. Do you remember he was at Cheltenham for a while? He helped us with the compromising radiation research."

"I remember him. He wears glasses and has sandy coloured hair?" Paul nodded. "Well why don't we go out a couple of times first and see if we are up to it? How far do they go?"

"I'll phone and ask him, but I seem to remember him saying it was about thirty miles. Just thought we could get some fresh air, and keep fit at the same time."

"Anyway Paul, how's it going with Julie? Is she going to stay in your old home and pay you off?"

"Well you know that Callum and Gemma have both left home, and that Gemma is expecting her first baby, this February?" Paul asked.

"Yes, you told me last week."

"Well, Julie doesn't need such a large house, but I think she wants to stay there, after all we've been there for 24 years, since we married. She's looking into getting a mortgage at the moment. "

"How is she coping?" Mark asked, drinking his beer.

"Well we both feel it's very sad, but to be honest, we haven't really been a couple for years. I think we stayed together for the children, but now they have gone, we both feel that life is passing us by, and that perhaps for both of us, there is something better out there. Just at the moment, I cannot see me looking for anyone else after all these years, but who knows?"

"I hope it works out well for you both. You haven't met Helen yet have you? I must say she has perked up my life. I just wish we could spend more time together. It would have been great if the research facility had been down south. Never mind, she is coming up this weekend, as long as there is no last minute panic at work. She's going to help me with the unpacking and putting up my pictures and curtains. How are you getting on with your apartment?"

Just at that moment, a guy walked slowly into the lounge, said hello to both of them and found a seat over by the window.

"Hi Bill," a lady raised her glass to him.

"Hi Cilla, didn't see you there," said Bill.

Bill got up and went over to the bar. "Coffee please, I'm over with Cilla. Thanks." Bill signed the slips and went over to Cilla's table. He sat down in the very comfy chair and was soon engaged in conversation.

"Must get to know Bill, he is working on Jeans' project, seems to be the oldest researcher. I think he is the person who carries out the yearly medicals on the residents. His apartment is at the back, on the ground floor I think." Paul said. "Anyway I'm off, got some work to look at. See you tomorrow, Mark."

"Fine, see you. Actually I think I'll also go up." They both got up and went to the lifts. The reception area was empty. The lift opened.

"Second floor?" Paul asked.

"Yes please. Hey, has Sarah pointed out all the security features they have put in for us? She was telling me why the internal corridor windows were put into our kitchens. I must say I thought it was odd, having a window looking inward onto the communal corridors, but apparently that is so we can check who is coming to our doors or passing our apartments. That's neat isn't it?"

"Why, what do they expect, a rush of spies knocking on our doors?" Paul laughed.

"Well to be honest, this is very sensitive research, who knows?" Mark responded.

"I hear they insisted on it, and planning agreed. However the bugging etc. has been put in by GCHQ I think. Of course it might be by The Regiment, but our apartments are as tight as possible," Paul replied.

"Goodnight Paul," Mark replied as he left the lift at his floor.

Paul carried on up to the third floor, and then walked down to the end of the corridor, turned left and walked to his front door. He undid the two security locks, passed his pass over the reader and entered his apartment and made straight for the fridge for a beer. He wondered if they would be able to start work on the project tomorrow.

Bill saw the two recruits leave the lounge. 'They seemed pleasant enough, young though. They can't even be fifty yet. They both look pretty healthy and athletic; I expect they will use all the facilities, when they have time.'

Cilla was talking about how her mother had phoned her to tell her off for coming in late last night. There was no doubt now, she obviously had dementia, her mother had been dead for years. If Sarah knew she would have already added her to the list for residents coming up for trial use, but Bill had hidden the CT scans of her brain from this year's medical reports, and Sarah had not yet missed them. He had only known Cilla a couple of months but already they seemed to have bonded.

He got up and went over to the bar, and ordered two more drinks. Cilla, on his return, was asking him about gardening, and if he thought she should buy some seeds, and plant them in the communal greenhouse. He knew the moment had passed and she was his again.

Mark made himself comfortable on his sofa, feet up on the coffee table and turned on his laptop, read his emails and messages and thought about sending a reply to Helen.

It wasn't so bad here after all. His furniture had fitted well, and soon he would unpack and hang his paintings. Perhaps Helen would help him choose the right positions for them? She was bringing the curtains she had ordered for him off the Internet.

When she came up for the first time last weekend, she had found it very odd, Mark living in a retirement village. Even though it had a gym and all the other facilities, it was for old people. His old rented house was so much more private than here. Being 13 years younger than Mark, she felt out of place. Mark hoped she would still come regularly up to Malvern as he wasn't sure how easy it would be at the moment to get Friday afternoons off, to drive down to see her in London. It might be a few months before he could ask, especially as he and Paul were seconded in due to the pressure of work on the project. Security forces were getting desperate for the new systems, he had been told in John's briefing today.

Helen, working for MI6, had no problem getting Friday afternoon off, as it seemed quite the norm when in the office. Last summer the traffic had been terrible, but she so enjoyed the hills and the countryside, that it was still worthwhile for her to come to Malvern, especially as she really enjoyed Mark's company. She and Mark were not committed to each other, but the relationship was developing.

They had met two summers ago on a course at GCHQ about counter terrorism, and had fallen into a lovely relationship. Their mutual interest in communication technology had overcome the age difference. Julie was always intrigued about his progress at GCHQ, and loved discussing his projects and making suggestions.

She hadn't met Paul yet, but Mark had told her, that he thought they would get on well together. He must tell her about the cycling idea; she might like to cycle around the area, next time she was up. She had said in her email last night how busy she was on her project. Her project was as sensitive as his, and they had not discussed it at all.

He had been emailing her, to make sure that their conversations were not overheard by GCHQ. Of course, they could read them if they really wanted to know what he was up to.

He had checked when he moved in, and had only seen the bugging devices. He felt confident that they did not have cameras. He and Helen did sometimes talk about issues that were confidential to their separate trials so they needed to think more carefully in future about it.

He sent a quick message, and decided to call it a night.

Chapter 14

Peak View Village footpath
December 2012

Mark and Paul scurried along the slippery pavement with their chins buried in the collars of their coats. The rain whipped around them, and they squinted their eyes against it as they half ran up the concrete path to the reception doors. Rushing through the doors, stomping their feet to remove the excess water, they stood and laughed.

"Whew, what terrible weather. Where did that come from?"

"God knows. It was so lovely yesterday," Mark replied.

"It was a great weekend wasn't it?" Paul asked.

"Brilliant. My apartment finally looks homely. Helen is a brick helping me with the positioning and hanging of all my pictures yesterday afternoon. She also put up two full-length pairs of curtains in the living room and the bedroom. Mind you, it took me several goes at putting up the curtain poles. Not my forte using a drill. I've polyfilled all the unnecessary holes, and I've just got to give them a touch up with some paint, which I'm hoping Sarah can get me. Did you enjoy yesterday's ride?" Mark asked.

"Loved it, beautiful views. That pub lunch was great. It was the first proper Sunday roast I have had since I left Julie. One of her good points was her Sunday lunch, always with roast potatoes, parsnips and Yorkshire puds, all the trimmings. Oh well, those days are over," Paul commented.

"Sarah sure tucked in," noted Mark.

"Didn't she just. Likes her food does our Sarah. She is a bit of all right isn't she?" Paul said.

"Well I think she thinks you are."

"Do you?" Paul asked.

"Helen loved her, thought she was as mad as a hatter, and was great fun especially when we were in the swimming pool Saturday night. She also thought she was pretty hot on you. Yes, I think if you played your cards right, she might be interested."

"Little bit too soon for me. Julie and I have been married such a long time, I'm not sure about dating just yet."

"Well, there's no rush is there?"

"What did you say Helen did?" Paul enquired.

"She works for M16, on the Embankment. She is mainly office based, but does go to conferences all over the world. In fact she is off to Brussels this morning, just for the day."

"So how did you meet her?"

"Do you remember I went to a counter terrorism meeting at GCHQ about two years ago?"

"Sort of."

"Well, there, we hit it off straight away, even though she is so much younger than me. She still is not sure about me living here though, even though she knows the reason."

"What's her problem?" Paul asked.

"Well the age of everyone, don't forget she is thirteen years younger than me, she's two years younger than Sarah."

"No wonder she flew up those hills on her bike." Paul laughed.

"Come on, let's get started." They disappeared down to their lab.

Chapter 15

November 2013
Heathrow Terminal 5
Coffee Lounge

He sat facing the concourse, his coffee getting cold on the table in front of him, sat on the very edge of his seat, checking everybody as soon as they came into view.

His stomach churned again, he still felt sick with nerves. Would she be late? Would the traffic hold her up? Was an airport the best place to meet her? He had been told that the terminal was the most transient of places and that no one would look twice at them together. Business people scuttled past on the way to Passport control, looking anxiously at their mobile phones and checking their watches, having left it to the last minute to leave home. Families shepherded their children, keeping a careful hold on their passports and boarding passes, their carry-on bags full to the brim. Mothers calling to their excited children, who were either dashing around or clinging to their legs, staring out at the strange environment. Around him sat travellers having a last coffee and snack with relatives or friends that were being left behind. The chatter of the barista, and the whoosh of steam as they prepared with theatrical flourishes the mundane cups of coffee. Names being called out when finished, as the paper cups were distributed correctly to the waiting queue.

All the noise and bustle was disturbing him, as he waited. What if she missed him? Should he stand on the concourse?

Suddenly the crowd separated, as a lively, tousled haired lady brushed through.

"Excuse me excuse me, in a rush. Thank you." Sarah stopped and looked around, and the man stood up and waved.

"Cheng!" Sarah rushed over, gave him a hug and plonked herself down adjacent to him. "It's been so long. I could not believe it when you phoned." She grasped his hands and looked into his eyes. He looked relieved.

"How long have you been waiting?" she asked.

"Half an hour, I wanted to get here beforehand to make sure I did not miss you."

"When is your plane?"

"I'm not flying home until the morning."

"Why are we here then?" Sarah looked puzzled. "It's one hell of place to get to. We could have met in Kew."

"Sorry, they thought here was safer."

"Now I am really confused. Safer? They? You've lost me now."

Cheng looked away from Sarah, and changed the subject.

"I have missed you so much. My parents have asked constantly about you. I thought at one time that I would never see you again. It broke my heart. Your letters have always been so loving, that I had hoped we might get together again.

My boss sent me to Washington, to do three days' translation for them, and now I am here in London at the embassy for four days."

"Cheng that's wonderful. Can we go out tonight?"

"Sarah I have to speak to you urgently, and we are being watched, so please act naturally."

"Gosh this sounds ominous, I couldn't understand why you said not to tell anyone about our meeting."

"You know that I, like you, work for the state." Sarah nodded. "I have been under tremendous pressure from them recently. They know all about our liaison when you came over. They have read all your letters to me. They know how much we loved each other. I have been taken to Shenzhen and interrogated several times Sarah. They want information, they want information from you." Sarah looked quizzically at him.

"Why?" she paused, "What sort of information, for goodness sake?" Sarah looked around her, to see if she could see who was watching them.

"I wouldn't be asking you, if it weren't for them bringing tremendous pressure on me and my parents. They have been threatening me for about a year now, they will send my parents back to the countryside if I didn't get you to co-operate. They know now all about your research using the Gelsemium elegans; I have had a terrible time, being interrogated about what I know." Cheng lowered his chin, and stared at the table. He thought back to his weakness that had made him give information to them. Sarah sat back and thought.

"Another coffee?" she asked as she pushed back her chair and stood up. As she walked through the maze of chairs and luggage to the counter, her mind was in turmoil. She queued up behind three others, and began to wonder what on earth Cheng was thinking about.

"Next please. Excuse me, do you want to order?"

"Sorry, I was deep in thought. Two large lattes please."

"Name?"

"Jones." The man scribbled her name on two paper cups.

"Next please."

Sarah took the couple of steps to the end of the counter. She watched as the performance of producing two cups of coffee was staged. 'Why can't they just make an instant coffee, it's a bloody site quicker.'

"Jones?" Sarah held up her receipt and grabbed the two cups. Winding her way back, she saw Cheng looking over towards the concourse. Was that where they were being watched? Was she in any danger? She put down the coffees and sat this time with her back to the concourse.

"What did you mean 'the state want some information?' Why on earth would I give them any research?"

"Sarah, they hope that by them threatening me and my parents, you will help them. I am so sorry, so really very sorry to put you in this dilemma. It has taken a year for them to break me, so that I will ask you. I have resisted all their pressure, but now they have found my Achilles Heel. They have told me, that unless I ask you to co-operate, they will send my parents back to the countryside, they will lose their apartment and live again in the very poorest area, in a hovel. Do you remember how I told you that they had been sent to the countryside during the Cultural Revolution? The labour camps, the complete lack of food, how they ate grass to survive. I could not do that to them again."

"Surely there are no labour camps now?"

"No, but you saw the living conditions in the most rural areas we visited. No sanitation, shelters rather than proper homes, how tough the life is and how the farming only pays enough to survive on. They are too old for physical labour now. My parents are now so urbanised, they are professional people, teaching in local schools. They have a lovely apartment in metropolitan Guangdong, with full sanitation, washing machine, heating and near to a huge selection of shops and entertainment, a large circle of friends to socialise with, in fact a lovely life. How could they leave all this for the basic living conditions and hard physical labour of the countryside? It would bring back all the deprivations of their past, and it would kill them. I will cope whatever, but I could not dishonour my parents like that. It is my fault all this has happened."

"Of course it isn't. I fell for you, the second day of our trip, and it was my fault. I never ever thought it would cause any problems for either of us. I wondered why your letters seemed more distant recently. You were such a breath of fresh air, a truly genuine, lovely person. I worried about our different backgrounds, our cultures. Truly I have thought about you and your parents constantly since we met, you know that from my letters. Then when your letters seemed more distant, I took that as a sign that your love for me had cooled. Perhaps even that you had met someone else. When you phoned for us to meet today, I half expected you to tell me you were getting married. To hear that you still love me, rekindles all my passion for you."

Cheng looked up at her beautiful natural face, framed with her long, blonde, madly curly hair. His heart sang, and he forgot just for a moment, how he was asking her for the ultimate betrayal of her country, just to save his parents. It was too much to ask.

His face crumpled as his emotions overtook him. He looked down into his lap as the tears flowed down his cheeks and dripped onto his trousers, leaving small dark patches on the beige fabric. They were shed for putting Sarah in such a terrible dilemma; they were shed for his parents and were shed in frustration at the situation he had caused. Cheng picked up the menu, and tried to hide his emotion by studying it. Control yourself Cheng, breath slowly, control yourself.' Sarah reached over and put her hand on his arm. Nothing was said, nothing could be said. Her thoughts raced, darting from the vision of his lovely parents, the rough rural housing, her parents and what they would think, her research and how it was developing so well – all this in jeopardy because she loved Cheng.

They sat silently for ages, whilst all around them people came and went, and queued and bustled around, lugging bags and suitcases, mobile phones being scanned and last minute dashes being made to Passport Control. Were they still being observed? What did they want to see?

Sarah touched his knee underneath the table whilst she took in the full impact of what was unfolding. Cheng put his hand on top of hers and looked up.

Helen was due in Zurich today for another counter terrorism meeting. She should be back tonight, if it all goes to plan. Heathrow was as usual at this time of day, full of commuters like her, all in a rush, and married to both their phone screens and their laptops. Everyone seemed to live in a parallel universe. On line rather than life in front of them, she often thought. She preferred to sit down, have a coffee and observe everyone around her. She had half an hour;

perhaps she would have time to go to the coffee lounge she preferred. She would have a look at the queue, and see if it was too long, otherwise she would wait until she had been through security and use the other one. It would probably be safer anyway, in case security had long queues today. As she breezed along the concourse, she thought she saw Sarah. She stopped and looked over. It was; she really was unmistakable with her amazing, naturally curly mop of hair. She seemed to have company, she wouldn't interrupt, might be someone she wanted a really good chat with. She tried to catch her eye to wave. No, she was deep in conversation. As she continued on, she thought it was a surprise to see her here, she hadn't mentioned going anywhere abroad on Saturday or Sunday.

She really couldn't understand why Mark wasn't as fed up as Paul, living with all those older people. It really would send her potty. Individually they were all lovely, but they had nothing in common with her or Mark. I suppose the gym and the pool were the only areas where they really chatted to them. They had managed a swim with Sarah and Paul last Saturday night when a lot of the residents had been in the lounge for the fortnightly entertainment. The pool was empty. They had had such fun. Sarah was like a dolphin, and an absolute nutcase. She had them doing timed laps, and she and Sarah had wiped the board with the boys. They complained that we were younger, which of course was true.

She had been surprised to see Sarah here at the airport. She was deep in conversation with the person who seemed to be upset. She didn't want to interrupt them, but at the same time, what was Sarah doing here? Was she flying out somewhere? Perhaps she was going on her hols, although she surely would have mentioned it. No doubt Sarah would tell her all about it when she saw her next. The chap had looked Chinese she thought, but she wasn't certain as his face was hidden by the large menu card. Perhaps he was an old friend from Kew.

Sarah gave Cheng a warm hug and left him at the coffee table, she was extremely uncertain about the whole situation. She had promised to let Cheng know as soon as she had made her decision. She had asked him to see if he could get his stay in London extended, so they could meet up again. Now as far as what Cheng had asked her to do, she thought she could start working on Paul straight away. It would be fun after all. 'Nothing ventured nothing gained' as the saying goes. Sarah had never been asked to seduce someone before and as long as Cheng approved, it was ok. She must go home and think about the serious implications to her and the project. Could she betray her country for love? Was she sure after all this time, that she was still in love and wanting to live in China? Certainly her heart had not stopped beating so fast yet from the excitement of hearing that he still loved her.

Sarah checked her watch, she had better get her skates on; she was meant to be at Kew in half an hour.

Chapter 16

December 2013
The Nags Head

"Inside or out?" Paul shouted over the throng.

"Bloody inside," Mark yelled back. Sarah followed them through the crowd. The Nags was always full on a Saturday night but this near to Christmas, it was heaving.

"See if we can find a table?" Sarah yelled as she led the way. The first two tiny snugs were full, but just then a couple got up to leave. She pounced on the table. "Mark, Mark, grab that chair." She sat down smartish. "Hey that was good timing!"

"Fantastic, didn't think we would sit down tonight." Paul agreed.

"Right you two, what shall we start off with? Sarah? The usual?" Mark asked.

"Ooh yes please, just a half to start off with, thanks."

"Paul, Hobson's?"

"Yes please." He raised his voice over the sudden outburst of laughing from the table next to them; Works Christmas party night out, by the looks of it.

Mark fought his way to the bar, and waited three rows back for his turn.

"My God, it's busy tonight. I knew it would be full, but it's rammed." Sarah said, people watching. She had also noted which groups were 'Firms do's' The mismatch of ages and people was so obvious; you could tell those that did not fit in, and those who had organised the venue. Mark and Paul came down with her most weeks; they were good company, always a laugh and some good educated conversation at times. She didn't think tonight would lend itself to the latter, due to the noise levels.

Mark emerged from the people standing near their table, and carefully put the glasses he had nurtured from the bar through the throng, down onto the sticky table. They sat and chatted and drank, and refilled their glasses for the next couple of hours.

Sarah turned around and unhooked her shoulder bag from the back of her chair and began searching amongst the detritus for her phone. A biro fell out and rolled under the table. Paul bent down and tried to retrieve it. Paul admired her long toned legs, from her baseball boots to her short shorts. Sarah was a strong gutsy bird, with such a raucous laugh and game for anything, he thought as he crawled under the table to reach the pen.

"What are you doing down there, Paul?" she laughed.

What would you like me to be doing?" Paul raised his head level with the tabletop and raised one of his dark, thick eyebrows with a daft quizzical look.

"Oh! Well the options are unlimited," she replied smiling encouragingly.

Paul firmly ran his broad hand from her ankle to her shorts hem and paused. He stood up and then sat back down on the wooden bench.

"Oh thank you kind sir," she doffed an imaginary cloth cap at him.

"No problem, my wench."

Sarah laughed; tossing her long mane of unruly hair back off her shoulders, she knew men liked it when she did that, and it was her trademark for attracting any passing man. She gave him her best 'come-on' smile, raising her eyebrows.

Mark stood up, picked up his glass. "Another?" he asked them both.

"Why not Mark, in no rush," Paul raised his glass.

"Sarah?"

"Yes please, just a half again."

Mark pushed his way to the steps, fighting his way down to the bar and disappeared into the throng.

"Well Paul, your place or mine?" Sarah suggested.

"What?"

"You heard me. Eleven o'clock tonight at mine? Promise you a good time eh? A few nibbles and a drink or two."

Paul was a little stunned, but not uncomfortable with the idea.

"Go on then, let's do it. Shall I bring a bottle?"

"Of course you idiot, we'll have some fun?"

Mark returned with the tray of drinks in his hands.

"You two look happy, have I missed something?" he asked.

"Not yet." Sarah threw her head back and laughed. Paul looked a little smug and gave Mark a wink as he took his glass off the tray.

"OK, I see, well enjoy," Mark replied. He secretly wished Helen were as flighty as Sarah appeared. Both he and Helen could be a little staid and demure at times. No great passion like Sarah, which made her such great company.

The rest of the early evening passed slowly, drinking and talking about all the news and about the funny personalities in the village, always a good topic of conversation.

"Well I'm off boys, leave you to it, some of us have work to do." Sarah rose, straightened her shorts, pulling them over the cheeks of her bum, threw back her hair, putting her bag over her shoulder and strode off down the steps.

"She's a girl isn't she?" Paul commented.

"Sure is Paul, fancy her?"

"Might do," Paul said thoughtfully.

Sarah's apartment

'Get the kettle on girl.' Sarah threw her bag onto the worktop and filled the kettle. Looking at her watch she saw she had just two hours before Paul came round. Really would have to make the effort tonight she thought. Not too much of a strain though; she had missed having a man with Cheng being back in China. My goodness one month, she had never abstained for such a long time since coming back from Kew. Malvern could be awfully quiet. Most of her friends, who had lived near, were either married, had children or worked away now.

She settled down in the living room with her tea and biscuits. She would need some energy. 'Damn the diet,' she thought. She kept threatening herself with one every morning. The news was on the television, so she flicked through the channels and decided it was all rubbish, and turned to her iPad for entertainment.

Tonight she would just get to know Paul intimately, and let things develop. Cheng's contact had said as soon as possible, but she did not think she could rush Paul, even though she had known him for three years now.

Paul rang her intercom and when she buzzed him in, he dashed down the staircase to her apartment.

"So this is where you hide yourself, eh?"

"Mmmmm sure is. Come on in." Her living room was all dark reds and purple with throws, cushions, and rugs, all mixed up together. Really homely but wild at the same time. The large lamp illuminated the room in a soft glow.

Sarah had changed and looked great in a tight short skirt, with a blousy girly top.

"You would never guess our apartments were the same. Yours is so wild and cosy. Mine still looks like a hotel room."

"You know why, you need a good woman. Come and sit down on the sofa. What would you like to drink?" Sarah asked.

Paul proffered Sarah the bottle of red wine he had brought on his way home from the Nag's.

"Thank goodness, I thought you were never going to hand it over," she laughed.

"What about a glass of this, you like red wine don't you. Seem to remember you quaffing it down before now," Paul asked.

"Certainly do." Sarah whisked the bottle from him, gave him a brief peck on the lips and half skipped to the kitchen. Paul could hear the sound of glasses clinking as she freed them from her cupboard. He had brought a screw cap bottle, so knew she would not need a hand opening it. Two minutes later Sarah appeared in the doorway, with two large, very full wine glasses.

"Where do you want to drink this, somewhere more relaxing?" She raised her eyebrow and tossed her hair back. Paul looked at her.

"I thought you promised nibbles."

"Oh I have got plenty of nibbles." Sarah lifted her right knee just far enough not to spill the wine, but giving Paul a view of what was nakedly on offer underneath her skirt.

"Will that do?" and with that she flounced into her bedroom. She had obviously lit the scented candles earlier, as the room was heady with musky perfume. Paul followed her, taking both the wine glasses from her and putting them down where he could find a space on her dressing table.

"Sarah Jones, you don't hold back girl do you, eh?"

"Life is for living, enjoy! Taste all that is there to be eaten, all that is offered, don't waste your time dieting." Paul was now getting very excited; his passion was rising at an alarming rate.

"Come here my wench." He grabbed her arms forcibly and crushed her mouth with his. She opened her mouth receptively, and played with his tongue.

Sarah manoeuvred towards her bed, and fell backwards with Paul still grasping her, onto the bed. Paul began madly trying to undo his trousers; Sarah was readily exposed, and removed her blouse and then her bra. Paul began by kissing her all over.

"Nibbles first?"

"Oh my goodness, yes please," she replied. Paul although out of practice, was masterful; in control, passionate and considerate but desperate at the same time. Sarah heaved with satisfaction, and purred and groaned. His tongue was afire, darting and surging, licking and tickling. My goodness this was brilliant. He suddenly thought of how Julie responded. He sat back.

"Problem?"

"No way, just wondering how to get your skirt off." He laughed and then continued to seduce Sarah.

Half an hour later, Sarah was sat upright whilst Paul staggered to the wine glasses.

"My God Sarah, I'm exhausted. You were insatiable."

"Yep, well you were so bloody brilliant. You certainly like your nibbles."

"Yes, Julie was very keen." Sarah took a long sip of wine.

"You miss her?"

"Yes and no. I thought I would never form another relationship after we broke up. I was out of practice. Tonight Sarah you have changed my mind. You really have." He leaned over the bed, naked as the day he was born, and kissed her first on the lips and then her breasts. Sarah ran her hands over the dark hairs on his arms and chest, following them down to his flaccid manhood. Worn out poor thing. He flinched.

"Good God Sarah. I am worn out."

"You must come round for nibbles more often. I'll help you build up your stamina." Sarah laughed.

"Mark and I have been cycling again but I must say I think your offer is far better." He slipped onto the bed, and stroked her bare legs with his hairy legs.

"Gosh it's hot tonight," Paul said.

"Sure is in here!" Sarah rose and blew out the candles, and opened the window. "I'll go and shower, you have a rest."

"Sure you don't want company, Sarah?"

"Not now, want to keep my hair dry tonight." With that Sarah sauntered off to the bathroom, and began singing out loud as she showered. Paul lay there remembering her lovely scent, natural and sweet. She was certainly some girl was Sarah Jones.

'Wow, if this is work bring it on.' Sarah thought as she tidied up the glasses after he had left. She still had been unable to decide about Cheng's proposition. It was such a momentous decision to take. She really needed to go to Cheng in China and stay with him and his parents, before making any rash decisions.

Chapter 17

Six months later
July 2014
Sarah's bedroom

It was only eleven o'clock in the evening. They were laid back in sleepy post-coital bliss. They had tried yet another of Sarah's new positions tonight, which they both really thought was brilliant; deep and satisfying. Paul was getting more adventurous on each visit. Sarah had quite a few more preferences to get Paul to try, but was keeping some of the best till last.

"Sarah, are you awake?"

"Just," she replied very sleepily.

"Do you love me?"

"Mmmmmm. Let me think about that?" she teased him. "Of course I do. How many times do I tell you that? Do you know it's been six months now?" she kept her eyes closed, half asleep.

"Six months and three days actually."

"I have hardly ever been with someone so long," Sarah replied, turning over to face him, with eyes now wide open. She smiled mischievously.

"I am so desperate to move out of here. I just can't stand the old folks any longer. They walk so slowly; they almost have a competition about whose ailments are the worst, who is suffering more. I need my own place Sarah. Julie has just told me she cannot get a mortgage to buy me out so either I have to sell the house and she has to move, or I have to stay living here. If I save up a deposit, would you share it with me?"

"Share it?"

"A house; the two of us living together in our own home." Paul looked away afraid of what Sarah would say. She cuddled up to him.

"The two of us together?" He turned and faced her.

"Yes. I love you more than all the stars in the sky!"

"Awwwww. That's lovely. I love you more…" Sarah had to think.

"More than all the money in the world." Paul rolled on top of her and kissed her softly and passionately. They stared into each other's eyes deeply. Sarah felt very mean, but Cheng was her one and only true love. She would leave asking about the project until Paul's next 'nibbles' night.

Chapter 18

The Malvern Hills
July 2014

"Paul?"

"Mmmmm?"

"I've been thinking."

"My goodness Sarah, don't strain yourself girl," he chuckled. They had set out on their bikes up to The Beacon. It was quite a hike, but Sarah said she wanted to see the view from the top of the Malvern Hills. Tourists and dog walkers did not usually come up here during the week day afternoons. Even if they did, she would easily be able to see them coming. Paul was studying the panorama, pointing out places he recognised.

"You know you were talking of moving out, and trying to buy a house for us?"

"Yeeeees. Why, have you discovered a long lost relative who has just bequeathed you a small fortune?"

"Well something like that."

"What?" Paul's attention was suddenly all on Sarah.

"I have an idea that could buy us a house."

"Tell me more." Sarah told him how the plan could work, and how Cheng could help them.

"Oh Sarah, I don't know about that. We could lose everything."

"Yes, but we could win everything. I thought you wanted us to live together? I thought you loved me? You've always said that it will take years to save a deposit for a house; we shan't be able to move from Peak View for ages. I want us to be together every night, all night. Don't you?" Sarah looked lovingly into his eyes, and held his hand.

"I must say my research is so different to yours. I think the Government will sell the technology in ten years after they have had the best years use from it. Your project is quite different."

"That's exactly what I thought. Rather than the Government make all the money from your work, what about us having our share, after all it's nearly all your work that has developed the system?"

Paul stared at the horizon, and then lay back on the grass looking skyward, as the larks soared overhead.

A young couple with a Golden Labrador could be seen walking towards them, taking in the views, and throwing sticks for their dog to retrieve. Obviously tourists Sarah thought. Eventually they walked past, their dog scampering up to them, smiling and wagging his tail, sniffing them and then retreating to continue his walk. They disappeared from view.

Ten minutes passed, before Paul rolled over onto his side, and stared at Sarah.

"You know that if we do this, there's no going back don't you. Are you sure you have thought this through? You want to risk everything in the hope we can live together and get out of the village?"

"I've been thinking about it for ages. I love you Paul, and want to live with you, and if this is the way we can do it, then let's do it. Life is too short to wait."

Paul grabbed her, and kissed her passionately, with urgency.

"Not up here Paul. Soon we can be together every hour of the day." Paul lay back thinking.

"How do we do it?" he asked eventually. By the time they got back to the village, they had decided in essence to do it. Of course it depended on the detail of the plan.

Cheng was going to be so relieved. He would sort out the financial side, and the parameters of the deal. Sarah thought that exchanging a little USB stick couldn't be that difficult could it?

Chapter 19

August 2014
The Growing Room

"I am going to need additional plants if the trial is going into production. When should I go back to China, Major Ross?" Sarah was showing him how the plants were thriving in the growing room.

"Where are you going to put them, Sarah?"

"There will be room, I am going to put in another level of lights, and I am sure they can be grown closer, without spoiling the volume."

"Well if you need more room, we can look at extending into the adjoining tunnel system."

"Well it's great to know that extra room is there if needed."

"Do you need to go, or could someone from Kew go for you?"

"It is so vital that we get the correct genus that I must go. This time I will only visit one area of forest, as I know where the most toxic plants are growing. I would like to use the same interpreter, as he was brilliant in gaining access. I should only need a week, two at the most. I can produce enough of the extract for the whole years' requirement I reckon by April if I go now."

Chapter 20

Guangdong
August 2014

Sarah glanced out of the window; they were flying over that dramatic landscape again. It was just so easy and fantastic to see it from the air, in the comfort of the air-conditioned plane. It would not be long before she was fighting her way through the forest scrub yet again to collect more plants and looking up at those incredible mountains, rather than down from a great height. Major Ross had authorised her visit without any qualms, now that it looked likely that production would be authorised for next year. They could not wait until the last moment to produce the volume needed. Sarah had heard that GCHQ had shown interest in using the poison for additional purposes; apparently the Russians were already suspected of using it to eliminate enemies of the state. If they didn't get the dose right, then all they would suffer would possibly be muscle spasm and tetanic convulsions. She knew of course that unless it was specifically tested for, it would be undetected in an autopsy. There would be no reason to test for the plant in an autopsy at present, as it was virtually unknown, also the test was a urine and gastric lavage, by liquid chromatography, which was not cheap to do. The way they had developed nanotechnology to administer it, was why it was going to be so successful in her trial. She preferred not to know about the espionage side of her work, and concentrate on the doctored flu vaccination, which she thought was going to benefit people in so many ways.

Cheng was to meet her as arranged at the airport. He had been allowed to let her stay at his parent's house, now that his side knew openly about their relationship. Sarah had booked a hotel room, to avoid any suspicion from London. They might go and spend a couple of days there anyway, as the facilities were beautiful, and it would give them some time away from his parents. MI6 knew he was an agent and working for the state, as was normal for interpreters. They must continue to believe that theirs was only a professional working relationship.

The 'Toblerone' she had brought with her, had been packed inside her case, with the extra secure packing she had been told to use. Apparently it would not show up on the security checks. She sure hoped they knew what they were doing. It had taken her ages to cover the USB stick with the chocolate. She had eaten all the trimmings from the two bars. 'Every cloud has a silver lining.'

She planned to be away for two weeks, which would allow her sufficient time for Paul's work to be scrutinised and the money obtained for her to ship back with her plants. On the face of it, it seemed so easy. Let's hope she was right, for her and Cheng's safety.

Two weeks later.

It had been a very tense couple of weeks for all of them. The terrain, although familiar, had been difficult.

Cheng yet again smoothed all the formalities, and had helped pack the money in the special cartons supplied for the plants. Hidden areas in the packaging had been created and checked to make sure detection was impossible. The plants unusual smell would prevent any of the special tracker dogs picking up the scent of the money.

Sarah was going to be incredibly tense going through security when she arrived home.

She and Cheng had had long discussions about their future, and his parents had been so welcoming. It was just a case of getting the timing right.

Baggage claim hall

Heathrow airport

The carousel number came up, and Sarah moved her luggage trolley closer to the revolving belts. The first suitcases started to slowly trundle around the snaking pathway. She kept her eyes firmly on the emerging cases. She was eager to be out of here as quickly as possible. Her black case emerged after a good fifteen minutes. Battered, it made it easier to identify. Dragging it off the carousel, she loaded it onto her trolley. Now she must make her way down to the large baggage reclaim area. She had decided, as before, not to risk commercial transport, but pay for her precious baggage to go in the hold with her. Except this time there was some even more precious cargo inside them.

The large, sturdy boxes were waiting for her, in perfect condition. Thank goodness. Where was the fourth box, there were only three. She started sweating. 'Oh goodness, had she been rumbled?' She stood there helplessly. 'What should I do?' She stood still, composing herself. 'Just stay calm, and act calm' Sarah looked around the area. It looked as though an orchestra was arriving, as large musical instrument cases suddenly came along the belt, and were being removed by a member of airport staff.

"Is there a problem miss?" he called, once he saw her looking around.

"I'm one box missing."

"Hold on a tick, I'll go round the back. Give me a couple of minutes." He continued to unload the huge volume of oddly shaped containers, and form them into a neat line. Just then, a large group of people came over to identify them.

"George, is this yours?"

"Sure is fella, thanks." The American accents were strong and loud.

"You look as though you could do with some help. Ma'am." The tall, muscular one looked over to Sarah, who was obviously waiting for something.

"No, I'm fine, thanks." She turned away, so as to not draw attention to herself.

Gradually the last item for the orchestra came off the belt.

"I'll go and have a look for you." Just as the man disappeared through the "Staff only" door, her last box juddered though the flaps on the carousel. The man popped through the door.

"Is that the one?"

"Thank you so much. You couldn't find me someone to help with the trolleys for me?"

"Just leave them there, and go over to the desk, they'll get you someone." It seemed hours before a porter came, but in reality it was probably only five minutes. Sarah kept turning over her keys in her pocket to distract herself.

'Oh please, please, let this go smoothly.'

"What you got here then?" he asked.

"Plants, loads of plants."

"You got your permits?"

"Of course."

The man loaded up the trolleys and they pushed them over to the Customs area.

"Anything to declare?" he asked.

"Nothing to declare," Sarah confirmed. She was so glad they were going in together; she could focus on the porter and not the boxes. As she exited the area into arrivals, she could see Paul waving at her.

"Hi my lovely. Gosh, I missed you. It's baking outside. It's been over thirty degrees today. I hired a van to get the plants back. You OK? Tired? Soon be home," and he gave her a huge hug that took her breath away. Sarah turned to the porter and paid him, leaving Paul to help move the trolleys.

Paul had parked in the short-term car park, so they pushed the trolleys over to the van. They weren't very heavy, just awkward.

"Fully loaded?" Paul asked covertly.

"Fully loaded, as arranged," Sarah smiled and Paul hugged her shoulder, and then patted her bum.

"Gosh, I have been hungry, missed my nibbles this last two weeks. Fancy some tonight?"

"It's a bit late tonight, I'm exhausted," Sarah made her excuses. She wouldn't have to keep this pretence up much longer. She must cool his ardour, now that Cheng was safe, and his parent's lifestyle not threatened. They had assured her, that they had what they needed, and Cheng was now fine.

Paul could be occupied with house hunting, and making the story about Julie getting a mortgage ring true, so he could buy a house next year. He deserved that at least.

Although it was the early hours of the morning when they got home, Paul was keen to unpack the boxes and check out the money.

"No Paul, I saw the boxes packed, it's there. Wait until tomorrow, when I can unpack them at a sensible time, in the seclusion of the plant room. OK?"

Paul looked deflated

"Never seen so much money, Sarah, can't wait to see what it looks like."

"The hiding place is ready?"

"Yes, it's ready."

"Remember don't tell me where it is, I don't want to know. If ever they interrogate me about all this, I want to be able to say truthfully that I had no idea where it went. OK?"

"Sarah, you worry too much. Everything is sweet, no problem."

The following day.

The Plant room.

The intercom rang about twelve o'clock, midday.

"Hello?"

"Hi, it's your favourite researcher."

"Mark, what are you wanting?"

"Hey you, it's me, Paul. Can I come down?" he asked, all excited.

"I was pulling your leg. I knew who it was silly."

"You are just like a little kid!" Sarah said when he came down the stairs. She stood back so Paul could squeeze past into The Plant Room.

"Lead on," he said. Sarah squeezed past the cylinders and meters, touched the entry panel, and waited for the concealed door to slide open.

"I've only been down here twice before." Paul went into the plant growing room. "Wow, it's quite full in here now. I thought you said you would have room?"

"I will have by the time I've potted them on and taken cuttings." She squeezed past him, putting her hands on his hips to slide past.

"Oh that was nice." Paul giggled.

'He giggled,' Sarah thought. 'He is so excited'.

"Look here," Sarah pulled up the matting on one of the plant trays; she had concealed the sealed plastic bags there for the moment. Paul looked at her and then again at the plastic bags.

"Is that all the room it takes?"

"Well that and about eight others under the other matting!"

"Wow, think what we can do with this!"

"Careful, I'm never sure if this room is bugged or not." Paul stood still and looked around the ceiling.

"I think it's a load of baloney all this saying that the village is bugged. It's like next door, no-one is sure. Nothing ever seems to have happened to make me think it is."

GCHQ.

Cheltenham.

Johnny smiled. He brought over his colleague.

"They still don't know do they?"

"Absolutely not. What were they referring to?"

"Not sure, but I'm going to pass it on."

"Are they the nibbles couple?" he laughed.

"Sure are." Johnny laughed out loud. "Glad she's back, missed my sport for the last couple of weeks.

Chapter 21

Guangdong
2nd December 2014

"Contact me. Then a 'Pay as you go,' telephone number. That's what it said at the end of the research. Cheng what do you make of this?"

"I don't know. Have you phoned the number?"

"Not until we had spoken to you. What do you think the person wants? Is it Sarah? Paul?"

"I'm not sure. Shall I contact Sarah?"

"Of course not, you bloody fool. Leave it us."

Cheng walked down the steps of the rather bland, modern building in the centre of Guangdong. He knew he was foolish to think the USB stick would be all he had to do, to save his parents. It looked like he was going to be involved quite a lot longer. The worry was almost unbearable. His parents had no idea, and could not understand his demeanour at home. He expected to have to do more very soon; no doubt he would be summoned in the next few days.

Peak View Village.

Paul's apartment.

"Hello." Paul had been in the kitchen fixing a snack when the 'Pay as you go' rang.

"Hello? Can you talk?"

"Phone me back in half an hour. Did you hear, half an hour?" The phone line went dead, and he immediately left the apartment and walked towards reception.

"Hi Paul, fancy a drink?" Mark asked as he passed him in the corridor.

"Hi Mark, no time, sorry. Have an appointment to go to." Paul walked into the Christmas decked reception and speedily through the revolving doors out into the car park. He pulled his fur-lined hood up around his face to protect him against the cold. He checked his watch again, plenty of time to get there, he thought. Driving out to the Quarry car park, he composed his thoughts. Now what was it he needed? He checked that his list was next to him in the centre ashtray. Stay calm, and be bullish.

Pulling into the car park, he parked away from the road and waited with the pay phone in his hand. Minutes passed, he checked his watch. Ten minutes still to go. He looked out over the view; the hoar frost had stayed all day, and looked beautiful in his headlights. He switched them off and shivered. His stomach churned with the drama of what was going to happen next. The shrill sound and the vibration made him jump.

"Hello?"

"Hi, whom are we speaking to?

"Paul, do you know who I am?"

"Yes, Sarah's contact. Yes?"

"That's right. Was the info to your liking?"

"Yes. Do you have more?"

"Depends what you are willing to do for me?" Paul spoke for ten minutes and then arranged to meet up with an agent in a week's time.

Chapter 22

MI6 Office

"Helen thanks for coming up so quickly. Had a worrying communication from the research teams' leader, Major Ross, where your boyfriend Mark works in Malvern." Helen looked surprised at the mention of Mark.

"Really sir?"

"Well apparently, GCHQ have been onto Ross, the Major from ORW who's in charge of all the research there, to say they listened into Sarah, as you suggested and something has come up. It may be nothing but needs checking out. She was in the Plant room of Peak View village, this is the transcript. He passed the paper across to Helen.

'Look here,' woman's voice, presumed to be Sarah, muffled sound heard.

'Is that all the room it takes?' male voice, identified as Paul.

'Well that and about eight others under the other matting"

'Wow Sarah, think what we can do with this.'

'Careful, I'm not sure if this room is bugged or not.' male voice.

'I think it's a load of baloney all this saying that the village is bugged, it's like next door, no-one there is sure. Nothing ever seems to have happened to make me think it is.'

Helen re-read the paper and handed it back.

"What do you think they are talking about? I don't think Paul is authorised to access the Plant room, my understanding is that only those on the vaccine trial have authorisation and then only when accompanied by Sarah."

"Well it could be vaccine, money, drugs, something Sarah brought back from China? Do the dates correspond with her return from her last trip there?'

'The day afterwards."

"Well it could be anything, even something for their home. I don't know. I would never have thought Paul would be up to anything underhand. He is so involved, as Sarah is with his R & D. He is a real professional. We have to get Mark and Paul to stop talking about it when we socialise. I did suggest some surveillance on Sarah only because of her meeting at Heathrow with a known Chinese state employee, when she had made no reference to it."

"What do you know about Paul and Sarah?"

"Well they are a couple, not living together yet, but hope to move to their own house when they can afford the deposit. Paul left his wife when he moved to Peak View village when he started the research. He has a grandchild, a little girl by his daughter. No money worries to my knowledge. Sarah you know about, Andrew is her controller. Never had any problems that I know about. Visited China twice where her translator and guide was

Cheng on both visits. He had studied for six months in The Royal Botanical Gardens at Kew before Sarah studied there. I see Sarah regularly as Mark and Paul work together and live in the village. She is quite mad, a free spirit, amorous in the extreme, but very intelligent and knowledgeable. She seems very committed to the 'flu vaccine' project, defends it if we doubt its legality, and I would not have thought anything was amiss if she had not covered her tracks when she met Cheng at Heathrow. There probably is a very simple explanation to the Plant room conversation."

"OK, you have confirmed all that we have observed as well as Andrew's information. I would like you to visit Mark this weekend and meet up with Major Ross, he will allow you access to the plant room, whilst he sends Sarah over to Hereford for additional research. I want you to do a full sweep and search of the room, as well as her apartment. Report back immediately. The sensitivity of the twin research projects cannot be compromised. It's essential we check to ensure that there have been no lapses in security.

Helen was soon back at her desk, sending a text to Mark, saying how she would after all be able to visit this weekend, her girly weekend having been cancelled.

MI6 office, one week later.

"Thank you for your report. Ross also came in this morning. The sweep and search showed no problems then? Apparently Ross said the Plant Room was in a fantastic shape. Nothing out of order. He told me over the phone about her apartment, which I understand was quite chaotic." Helen laughed.

"Yes we had quite a job searching it. Mind you, I think if we had thrown everything up in the air, she would not have noticed!"

"Just be aware of the two of them, just to make sure. It seems that nothing untoward is going on."

Quarry bank car park.

"Well what on earth did you want to come out here for in the wet and cold?" Paul dismounted from his road bike.

"Whew, I'm out of condition. I needed to speak to you." Sarah checked they were alone. "Now I hope I'm not being dramatic, but you know I was told to go over to Hereford on Saturday, and couldn't see you. When I got there, quite honestly I could not see the need, as the results were only as they send to me every month. When I got back my apartment had been searched, I am fairly sure."

"What?"

"Well it might look in a mess, but I know where everything is. Some ornaments go exactly in a certain place, facing a certain way. Well I noticed straight away that my dressing table had been searched, as well as the kitchen. What do you make of that?"

"Would they have found anything?"

"Nothing, I have nothing there to be found. You are the only one who has. I told you the rooms were bugged, didn't I? Have we said anything that incriminates us? Think hard."

Paul stood thinking for a minute. "Well, I came into the Plant room which I don't have authority to visit. You showed me the money; did we say it was money? Did we? Oh my goodness, what if they know?"

"Well as they won't have found anything, I think we should just be vigilant, and not discuss anything at all about the money. OK? My trip went well, there is no way they can tell about the USB stick, so we should be ok. Gosh this is so nerve racking."

"Hey, at least we will be able to get out of that flipping village in the spring eh?"

"Yes you're right." They mounted their bikes and free wheeled most of the way into Malvern.

Heathrow. Coffee Lounge

December 2014

Sarah shimmied around another of the massive Christmas trees on the concourse, huge Christmas baubles were also hung beautifully around the building, and Christmas music was playing. A sense of goodwill pervaded the extremely busy passenger terminal. Travellers on their way to visit relatives, to go home to loved ones. Sarah had booked three days off to go away. It had cost her a fortune to get her cover story to work in with Cheng passing through. She had booked a three-day visit to Munich's Christmas Fair. At least she would enjoy the festival. The boys had pulled her leg about the beer, and that being the only reason she was going.

"Hi Sarah?" Cheng waved as she went towards the coffee counter.

"Well fancy seeing you here, that's amazing. What are you doing here?" She walked over to him, and sat down after giving him a hug. Acting surprised was not as easy as she thought. She had practiced at home this morning, still not sure is had sounded natural.

"Well it's amazing to see you here," Cheng replied.

"Isn't it a small world? Another coffee?" Sarah asked.

When she returned with the coffees, she placed them to one side and took the newspaper out of her bag, and then placing her phone on top, put them on the table.

"I'm just passing through from America, I've been there working for the Embassy, and today I've been here in London, doing the same. I'm on my way home now. Cannot wait to see my parents and reassure them that everything is sorted." Sarah nodded.

"No problems at home, then?"

"Not now Sarah, not now." Cheng's body straightened and his shoulders went back. A confident smile beamed across his face. "I almost forgot, how are the plants? Did they all survive?"

"Two didn't but all the others are thriving under my tender care."

"Tender care – I should like some of your tender care." Cheng spoke softly.

Helen was listening from the other side of the concourse, out of view. She had hacked into Sarah's mobile phones' microphone. She had asked Mark if he knew about Sarah's work, and he had not been able to explain her previous meeting at Heathrow, as he thought she only went down to London, to visit Kew.

The sound quality was not bad, and their conversation seemed genuine. Nothing to report back by the looks of it.

Perhaps her mind was finding problems where there were none, could be the nature of her job.

Sarah picked up her voluminous bag, dropped her phone into it, and gave Cheng a hug and a wave and left him seated. Cheng sat a little while longer, and then with an anxious look around, picked up his flight bag, and tucked the newspaper under his arm.

"Helen how are you?" It was Ben who was travelling with her today to Cologne. He patted her on the back, and Helen removed the earpieces, and then whispered into his ear. They looked at the coffee lounge. Cheng had gone.

"Sorry bad timing?"

"Not sure, might be nothing."

Chapter 23

Christmas Eve 2014
Paul's apartment

Sarah was in jubilant mood, she had finalised her arrangements with her parents, and was going to have a lovely Christmas Day with them. This morning she had met up with Laura, Emily and Claire, who were all up in Malvern for Christmas at their parents' homes. They had met up in town in the newly re-opened Wren's Nest pub. They were all still single, just like her. Partners, fiancés and friends had all been discussed over several drinks throughout the day.

She rang the bell, and peered through the window. The door opened quickly.

"Hi lovely, you're looking brill," Sarah breezed in to Paul's apartment. The Christmas tree dominated the end of the living room. The decorations they had done were looking good. Paul had remembered to switch on the fairy lights, and had left the room lights off, giving a really lovely seasonal look to the room. Underneath the tree, were stacked loads of wrapped presents.

"My goodness what a lot of presents, Paul!"

"I have excelled myself this year. I have bought little Rosy so many lovely presents, dresses and toys. Her Mum and Dad wanted some electrical items for the house, you know Aidan has been wanting a Bosch drill for ages, and my daughter, Gemma wanted one of those posh steam irons. I haven't bought anything for Julie, but I am giving her money. You don't mind do you?'

"Of course I don't mind, but are you normally this generous?"

"No, but I thought I could splash out this year."

"How are you going to explain your sudden generosity? Won't they think it odd? Remember that money is for our house, not splashing around. You must make sure that it doesn't become common knowledge, otherwise questions will be asked. Don't be a fool and put us in danger Paul." Sarah was cross and worried. Paul went and sat next to her, deflated. He had so enjoyed the new experience of being generous to his family, something he would have liked to have done for years, and now Sarah was cross. Perhaps he wouldn't give her her own present just for the moment.

"I'm sorry Paul to be upset and spoil it, but you must be careful. You can't jeopardise our safety."

"I know, sorry. Look no-one knows I have bought all this stuff, so it shouldn't be a problem," Sarah sighed. How was he going to explain the large boxes and drums being delivered to Julie, God only knows? Julie had asked questions, why so many boxes were coming in from China, but he had said it was for a project he was setting up. Which of course was true! He had told her it was easier for him to have them sent to his old house, because he couldn't be sure the Village would take kindly to taking in the heavy boxes, and they might get lost.

"Would you like your present?" Paul couldn't wait, he was so pleased with what he had bought her.

"Oh go on then, you mad impetuous fool," she laughed and sat upright hand outstretched with her eyes closed. Paul went to the very top of the tree, and reached into the branches, and pulled out a most exquisitely packed present the size of a pen box. The box was almost hidden by the huge silk bow on top, and the gift card, which read;

'To my most precious treasure.'

"Oh, it's the most beautifully wrapped present I have ever received." She undid the bow, removed the expensive thick paper and opened the box. Inside, lying in the purpose made indent in the silk lined box, from the most expensive of jewellers, was a beautiful pendant necklace. The Christmas lights bounced of the pendant facets, and it twinkled brilliantly. Sarah was speechless.

"Oh my goodness Paul." She carefully removed it from the box, and examined it closely. "Are these real? Fuck they are! Paul this must have cost you a fortune?" She looked at him aghast.

"I wanted to give you a very special present this year. Do you like it? It took me ages to choose it. I just didn't know which one to choose. They have said you can change it if you don't like it."

"Like it, gosh I love it, it's amazing," she undid the beautiful clasp, and got up and went to the bathroom mirror. It did up so easily, not like the cheap crap she usually wore. Paul came in and stood behind her, looking into the mirror.

"What do you think?"

"What do I think? I think it is amazing."

"You can change it?"

"Change it, why on earth would I do that? When I wear it, I will have to pretend the stones aren't diamonds, otherwise people will think I have met a Saudi prince!" She turned round and hugged him, kissed him and then wrapped her legs around him.

"Hold on, I shan't be capable of visiting anyone tonight if you do your worst to me." He laughed and Sarah uncoupled her legs, and faced the mirror again, she kept moving the heart shaped pendant to catch the light.

"My present is going to be so small in comparison," Sarah said thoughtfully.

"If you chose it, then I shall love it."

"I'm not sure now." She walked back to the sofa, bent down and picked up his present. "I saw this and thought of you." She handed over her present, wrapped in inexpensive paper, with no flourishes.

"Can I open it tomorrow?"

"No, you must open it now." Paul removed the wrapping. Inside was a biscuit type tin, with the words 'Granddad's nibbles tin.' emblazoned on it. He shook it up and down, heard the rustle and opened it. Packets of peanuts and sweets were jammed inside.

"Delve a little more," Sarah urged him.

Paul emptied the contents onto the floor. He then saw the packet, which was carefully wrapped, looked over to Sarah and opened it. The black box announced 'Garmin Vivoactive GPS Smart watch for the active lifestyle.' He opened the box up and took out the all black watch.

"I just thought it could monitor your input when eating nibbles," she said saucily. Paul laughed and Sarah laughed, they fell onto the floor laughing and tickling each other.

"Mind my necklace, mind my necklace."

"Well get it off!"

Chapter 24

January 2015
Unknown Location

The old metal door hinges squeaked as he pushed against the resistance of years of neglect. The air was colder and he hugged his jacket around him and blew his hands, smacking them together for warmth. He turned his mobile phone torch on, and shone it into the darkness. 'Probably find the light switch to the side of the door.' He shone the torch onto the brick wall to the left of the door. There it was, an old round brown Bakelite light switch. Hopefully, he pressed the switch down. A weak light bulb illuminated half way down the area. 'Didn't expect that.' He could hear the sounds of either mice or rats scurrying away.

Walking into the room, he thought the size would be perfect, almost soundproof as well. This might be the place. Not far to travel either. He closely inspected the walls. There was a single socket on the right hand side, but it would be doubtful if that would work. He would have to find a way of getting electricity down here, or even a generator, that would be simplest, if the noise could not be heard outside. He would just have to avoid the times when he knew someone would be coming down here. 'I can't see that being a problem, as that is when I am working.' He walked up to the end of the room, and inspected the locked metal door. He didn't have the key for this one; he gave it a push, locked. He rammed his shoulder against it. 'That hurt' he thought as he rubbed his arm.

By the looks of the door, he presumed it had not been used for years either.

He made a mental list; generator – noise levels test out, if not what are the alternatives? Rat poison, broom to clear the room up, as it needed to be as spotless as he could achieve. 'Might have to form a plastic tent to ensure cleanliness' he thought, and WD40 for those door hinges. He retraced his steps, looked back on the room, and thought it would be perfect for him to use.

Chapter 25

46 days to deadline
10th February 2015
Old laboratory, Princess
Margaret Gardens

"Sarah is coming over Anne, can you come down please?" Jean put the phone down. Sarah and Anne appeared together five minutes later. "Well ladies we must now really concentrate on getting this batch of residents tested with the latest version of the cell based vaccine, to ensure that it works as well with that as the egg based."

"Who on earth decided to alter the flu vaccine? I presume they had no idea about our product?" Sarah asked.

"My understanding is that NICE looked at the better performance of preventing flu in the over sixty-five year olds achieved in America, and decided that even though its more expensive, it would save money for the NHS, by reducing the number of elderly blocking A & E in the winter." Anne told Sarah. Jean nodded.

"Yes, but if only they knew how much work it has been to alter the drones, and check that performance figures have not been affected." Sarah moaned.

"I know, but it was unexpected and therefore unavoidable." Jean countered. "Right, we now need to have the last batch of residents urgently vaccinated tomorrow. Sarah, have you brought your list over?" Sarah handed over the list and Jean scanned the medical notes for each resident.

"That's interesting about Cilla McIntosh, she seems to have dementia past the usual stage for inoculation. Is there a reason for her delay?" Jean enquired.

"Yes," lied Sarah, "I kept her back in case we needed someone who should react immediately, so that we would not have to wait for a result. She will be perfect to check the efficiency, as she is now at the point where the drones will activate, and as such we should get a result within the deadline. Of the final five, I would expect Gordon to react, and possible Gareth. The other two should not have heart attacks as they do not have dementia, so we can check that the drones are not activating too early," Sarah concluded. The real reason she had Cilla on her list, was that she had only just realised that Bill had held back her scans. She knew he had a soft spot for her, but she had had to come up with a trial resident to prove the case beyond doubt, and she was the only person that was advanced enough in her decline of behaviour to use. Bill would understand, although of course he would be very upset.

"This is the very hard part of using residents from next door, knowing them personally, I don't know how you have managed to do it Sarah," Anne commented. "It's the reason I don't go round to the village, I could not bear to see future subjects and get to know them as you and Bill do."

"Well you know me, I really do believe we are helping them. No one wants to suffer or see their nearest and dearest suffering. If one day there is an affordable cure, then I will be the first to celebrate." Sarah leaned back in her chair.

"Ok everyone, let's wait for the results, we really are up against it, and we have plenty of analysis still to complete and document."

Anne's bungalow

Anne sat down on her sofa, legs tucked under in a coltish manner.

Jean was due soon for supper. Anne pondered how her own problems were of the heart, whilst her dear companion had heart problems.

John set her body alight whenever he was near. It was becoming more and more difficult to ignore whilst working downstairs.

She was sure no one knew. Their liaisons were clandestine, almost like teenagers. She had even been writing in her diary the very same symbols she had used when she dated Malcolm in the 1960's; numbers one to ten. Last night was definitely a ten! It had been amazing. His tender touch and sensitivity had sent her into complete ecstasy. She had had to ensure that he showered away the aroma of her Rive Gauche afterwards. It could have been a sure giveaway, as to where he had been!

Jean ringing the doorbell brought Anne straight back into the moment.

She rose, slipped on her fluffy kitten-heeled slippers and shimmied to the hall door, just as Jean let herself in.

"Come in my lovely, Lasagne and wine are ready when you are. Sit yourself down, whilst I get two glasses."

"How are you feeling now?" Anne enquired as she came back with two large glasses of red.

"I must say I was whacked by the time I came home," Jean replied. "Did you see Bill's look – so depressed at the moment. Something is troubling him? Isobel is going round tonight to chat to him. I hope she can cheer him up." Jean slipped off her shoes and sipped her wine. "I am exhausted. An early night I think."

Anne nodded she could see Jean was whacked. Some food, some wine, and early to bed seemed best. Anne got up and went to serve the lasagne and pour some more wine.

"Today's the anniversary of Mum's death."

"I hadn't forgotten Jean. How many years is it now?"

"Eight. Doesn't time fly?"

"It certainly does."

"Do you remember those awful nursing homes we looked at for my parents when we moved here?" Jean asked as she lifted her fork full of lasagne.

"Do I? Weren't some of them awful? What about that one where everyone was sat around the edge of that soulless room? Was it the one in Pershore? Do you remember, the residents didn't even seem to have their own clothes on, let alone have the buttons done up correctly," Anne remembered.

"That one where the smell of urine and stale food was overpowering? You know, where the staff seemed to call everyone 'luv and pet' Do you remember? I am so glad we

153

found the one we did for my Mum and Dad. I could not have forgiven myself if they had been separated and neglected.

"Well you certainly did a wonderful job looking after both of them, especially your Dad. All those years you visited him, even when he hardly ever recognised you,"

"I just loved it when he did remember and we could talk about the old days, and even sing songs from some of their am dram productions. It was so sad seeing them so vacant and lost."

As Anne placed a couple of slices of Tarte au Citron on the table, Jean asked. "What is your opinion Anne, do you still think that the increase in heart attacks over the next three to five years will be put down to the 'baby boomers' lifestyle?"

"I do, I really do. Every day in the papers there is yet another survey stating that if you do this, or don't do that, you will live longer, each survey being carried out usually by some self-serving organisation. I feel that most analysis will say only that people are suffering heart attacks seemingly at an earlier age, and then a government sponsored advert campaign will be launched to say exercise more, eat more fruit and vegetables. You know the usual response."

Anne re-filled the glasses. Jean sat there slowly drinking her wine and remembering the huge toll paying for her parent's care had been on her finances, not that she cared as long as they were looked after.

Jean was gone within the hour. Anne decided to call it a day fairly soon afterwards. Sleep came easily.

Chapter 26

45 days to deadline
11th February 2015
Princess Margaret Gardens

It was the most amazing sunrise. The clouds were a deep red. Streaks from the plane trails crisscrossed the sky. What a perfect start to the day, John thought as he set off on his pre-work walk. A couple of miles set him up every morning, woke up his senses. Good time to reflect on how the current research was going.

John entered the command room, at six o'clock. Rive Gauche wafted nearby acknowledged Anne's attendance. She was busy at one of the desks. The others arrived shortly afterwards and work was underway when Major Ross noticed it was ten thirty.

"Anne, was Jean all right last night?" Major Ross enquired.

"Tired, she went home to bed really early."

"Just go and check on her, it's not like her to be late."

Anne filed her work, locked it into the office safe, and walked towards the door.

"Tell her to stay in bed if she's not well. It will not be a problem," Major Ross said passing over Jean's duplicate door keys and security code to Anne just before she left the room.

Anne climbed the two flights of stairs, being careful not to ruin her heels in the holes of the stupid metal stair treads. Obviously designed by a man.

She walked along the verandas at the back, to get to Jean's bungalow. She passed the last remaining occupied ones, all the others having been transformed internally to be the laboratory she and Jean worked in. The disguises used to make them look occupied always impressed her in their ingenuity.

Anne knocked on the glass top panel of the back door of Jean's bungalow. Jean had chosen to put up a net curtain across this panel for privacy.

"Coo-ee Jean. Are you ok?" Anne called out.

She knocked again. "Jean are you there?" She reached into her coat pocket and brought out the set of master keys and looked at the card that had Jean's security number on. She entered after working out which keys worked the two locks. The door opened. A fly zoomed past her ear and fled into the fresh air.

"Jean are you ok? It's Anne." She felt uneasy at the quietness.

Everything was in order in the kitchen. She entered and walked through the little kitchen. Its black and white Marley floor tiles spotless, the red Formica worktops cleared apart from the old kettle and toaster. She walked through the lounge where the curtains were still closed and into the inner hall, then straight into the bedroom.

The unlined thin orange curtains were still drawn, giving a half-light to the room. The unmistakable smell of lavender filled the room. Jean lay still, on her back. Her hair fanned out onto the pillow. Anne had never seen her hair loose before, only ever up in a bun.

"Jean, Jean?" Anne touched her exposed hand. Her hand was, of course, cold; why else would she have been late for work. Her eyes were closed, her lips, she could now see through the dim light, were blue. Never a beautiful woman, but now she looked so peaceful, serene even.

Anne checked for a pulse, but could tell that there would not be one. A tear escaped down her face and dripped onto the bedding. She pulled the sheet and blanket over her face. Jean had never adopted the fashion for duvets. Jean always said they were untidy. She did so like her precise hospital corners to her sheets and blankets. The pea green candlewick bedspread was usually smoothed perfectly flat.

Anne noted her watch and glasses on the bedside cupboard, together with her glass of water and tablets. The small bedside light was still on.

'Had she just lay down to sleep and been taken unawares last night?'

Anne sat down on the bed and paused to reflect on her friend's life. She stroked her hand and tears rolled down her cheeks. Putting her cold hand back under the bed sheet she turned off the bedside light.

'Good night my friend, all the best.'

Standing up she composed herself and straightened the bedding.

She looked back as she left the room. Probably it would be the last look at her companion. At least she died knowing her project was going ahead.

'No more tears,' she told herself as she left. 'Everybody will die. You are born, you live, and you die.' Let's face it, although she was only seventy-five years old, Jean had had a fantastic life, and the very best years, she always told Anne, had been living here in Malvern and being involved in the nanomedicine research. Of course we will all miss her, but at our time of life, everyone is used to friends passing. The cause of death will be needed for her research. 'Let's hope the autopsy does not show signs of dementia.' Jean had had the earlier experimental inoculation, before they had perfected the activation point of the nanobotes, and she had not been showing any signs of dementia, so it would be terrible if the nanodrones had activated early, causing premature death. This had been identified in other initial trial patients' autopsy results, and they had spent years on the technology, trying to have a ninety-eight per cent accuracy of activation. They would soon find out as Jean like all the other trial subjects would have an autopsy to see if she had had dementia, and if so, at what stage it was at. This was the most important part of their research, ascertaining the cause of death, and, if the subject had had a heart attack from the nanodrones, was the dementia at the stage where that person was incapable of looking after themselves. Was the timing of the nanodrones' activation correct? Since Sarah had been providing the residents from Peak View for the trial, Jean had been able to correctly identify the stage that the dementia was at, not just as before from the autopsy slides, but also from the use of Sarah's medical notes, as well as observations of the person around the village, and talking to their friends and partners. The research from the residents in Peak View village had made the analysis so much more comprehensive and had resulted in real fine-tuning. Sarah had been brilliant in choosing the residents suitable for the trial. Her toxicity of the plant extract was now at ninety per cent, which was activating the nanodrones incredibly accurately. However, the target was still ninety-eight per cent, and the trials had had to be reassessed due to the use of a new cell based flu vaccine carrier for the nanodrones, rather than the egg based version that all their previous work had been trialled on.

Major Ross called everyone together and passed on the upsetting news. As he walked away, his thoughts were all about the project. GCHQ had already notified Downing Street about Jean's death.

Major Ross organised the local doctor to visit to sign her death certificate. Jean would have to have an autopsy due to the nature of her work and being a subject of the trial. No foul play was suspected surrounding her death, as security had been maintained all the while for the research establishment. The local coroners' office had not been notified, as this was a job for a more specialist investigation unit. They had been carrying out all the post mortems on the volunteers in Hereford. They took slides of the brain, which were used in Princess Margaret Gardens for analysis. Isobel and her team were now experts in this analysis of brain tissue samples, and used in conjunction with surveillance notes on the trial subjects next door, together with their yearly check up test results, they were able to ascertain if the drones were identifying the action point correctly.

It was mid afternoon before her body was collected. Dr Jennings had certified the death. Jean's death would be registered in Hereford, as was usual for the trial personnel.

Major Ross asked Anne to go back to the bungalow and search all areas, and remove any sensitive material. Everything must be put into evidence bags and sealed and brought back to him. Anne was to be the only person to enter the bungalow and she needed to report back if extra security measures were needed to secure the site.

Anne set off with a heavy heart. She had not been asked by Jean to visit her home very often, as Jean preferred to visit Anne's home, as it was more comfortable and warm. She understood why Jean chose to live in such an austere manner as all her money had been spent on her parents' care in the nursing home. She had not bought new furnishing for years. The bungalow was very much the same as when Jean had moved in all those years ago, and most of the furnishings had belonged to the previous occupier or Jean's parents.

Using the master set of keys again, she opened the two security locks. Loaded down with the plastic evidence bags, she entered the kitchen. A thorough search through all the drawers and cupboards produced nothing except a shopping list. 'Bread, butter, cheese, tomatoes and milk.' Jean was not known for her varied diet. For her, eating was a necessary function. She really could not be bothered to cook, too busy with her research.

The lounge curtains had been opened, probably by Major Ross when he accompanied the doctor earlier. Anne searched the bureau, and removed all the paperwork, together with an address book, making a mental note to ask Major Ross, who was going to contact her brother?

Jean's parents had died fairly recently, living to a ripe old age. They had both donated their bodies to medical research, so Jean and her brother held a memorial service for them at the local church. Several of her parent's friends from years ago had attended. All expressed their sorrow at their passing, and when huddled in groups drinking the coffee and tea, and eating the sandwiches laid on, said that it was a shame they had survived so long with dementia.

There was a shoebox near the fireplace, full of old black and white photos, all slightly curled at the edges. Jean with her brother at the seaside in the 1940's, Jean sat on the rug in front of the fire when she was about six, stroking her cocker spaniel. Her mother carrying her as a baby, standing next to the pram with her brother sat inside looking towards the camera. Memories. Anne guessed the photos had come from her parent's house, when she had removed all their personal effects. She put the shoebox into a plastic bag, for Major Ross. Continuing into the bedroom and bathroom little was of interest; very basic toiletries, soap, toothbrush, toothpaste and face flannel. As she unlocked the small fiddly key to the oak utility twin door wardrobe. She saw neatly arranged on old wooden hangers, Jean's tweed skirts, blouses and jackets. Three pairs of clean, flat brown shoes carefully placed underneath. Anne left them in place. By the bed were the usual items; medicines, tissues and a glass of water. Anne bagged the medicines, to check against her records and for them to be checked for purity, just in case anything untoward had happened.

Anne made another note to discuss with Major Ross, was he going to have timed automatic lighting and curtain opening and closing to keep up the appearance of occupancy of the bungalow, as they were doing with the windows hiding the old laboratory from view.

Major Ross agreed that Anne should contact Jean's brother. Anne phoned him straight away. She knew he lived somewhere down south. She had found his telephone number in Jean's address book.

Jean had had little contact over the years, apart from their parent's memorials. The extended family had never understood why Jean rarely came to family events, especially after she turned sixty. Her parents had never asked questions about her work, which had made them rather emotionally distant, as neither of them had much to talk about, even before dementia and then Alzheimer's had conquered them. Her brother had not asked why she had moved to Malvern, nor even bothered to ask what she did with herself. He was so used to her saying she could not talk about her work, that he grew disinterested. Phone calls were reserved for Christmas and their birthdays. Anne thought he was retired now from a job in insurance.

Anne telephoned him that afternoon and discussed with him, that she knew that Jean had donated her body to medical science, and was he aware of the fact? He expressed surprise initially, and then said that it seemed to be logical knowing Jean's lack of occasion and pomp.

Anne suggested that they have a memorial service just as his parents had had, fairly soon, so that people could pay their respects.

Chapter 27

Deadline minus 44 days
Anne's Living Room

It was nine o'clock in the evening, Isobel was sat next to John on Anne's cream and gold sofa. Bill headed straight for the matching armchair, making claim to the most comfy chair, whilst Anne sat daintily on the large padded footstool, legs arranged carefully to the side. Sarah, Mark and Paul had to sit on the chairs from the kitchen and were dotted amongst the others. The drinks had been poured and nuts and crisps were being picked at. Anne had hung all the coats up in the hall.

"It was so unexpected, I knew she was having a problem with her heart, but she did not seem concerned. She had been working flat out," Anne expanded "as we all have, getting all these trial results analysed. When she came round the other night, she was shattered. That deadline of the 26th is so tight. It's quite worrying. Number 10 has put poor Major Ross under tremendous pressure. They both have so much to lose if we get it wrong. However, at least Jean died knowing that we were in the last stages of the project.

"She didn't have any doubts about the project?" asked Isobel.

"Why? Have you?"

"I am now quite unhappy at the underhand way the drones are going to be used. It's the lack of choice that concerns me, not the vaccine, just that the public will not have had the choice. When we started out, the nanomedicine we were developing was for people to have as an alternative to suffering from dementia, now they won't have the choice." Isobel raised her voice.

"Well we are all aware of the consequences Isobel, and yes we have concerns as to the initial impact, but let's face it, we have discussed this for years. All of us, who have been involved in the development from the start, knew of the immense benefits to not only the elderly and their relatives, but also to the country. Are you surprised that the Prime Minister now wants to save the public purse and save the NHS without all the different factions stopping the project for their own, usually commercial or religious reasons? Euthanasia is still on hold because of them isn't it, even though there are people who want to die a dignified death? The main issue is what the public will initially make of it, once they discover it's in use. This will depend so much on when they realise it. If it is in three years' time, then hopefully the politicians can show how great the impact has been and why the NHS has been able to continue to function," Anne responded, trying to keep her patience with Isobel.

"You don't have ANY doubts about not telling the public? It CERTAINLY isn't the project we started on all those years ago." Isobel stared directly into Anne's eyes, crossed her legs and folded her arms, raising her shoulders in a huff.

Isobel looked over to Bill for his support. Bill bent down to pick up his drink avoiding looking directly at her.

"Bill," she almost shouted, "do you agree with me?"

"Well," he paused. He hated conflict. "Well," he looked around the room at everyone looking at him, waiting for him to reply. "I think we have spent the last five years discussing this haven't we?"

'Not again', Anne thought.

"Isobel, you know the plan and the developments over the years as well as the rest of us. Look how many people we have followed through the trials. Sarah has reported how relieved residents have been that their relative did not suffer from dementia, that they were taken so quickly. Look at that couple that have married next door, after their partners died. Sarah tell Isobel again about them."

Sarah leant forward. "Anne's absolutely right." Sarah looked at everyone. "When we opened, we had two lovely couples, the Partridges and the Smiths. Margaret Partridge was one of the earliest to be given the drones, and not long afterwards Bob Smith was selected. Both died, as expected, and both had the drones activated at exactly the correct time, in that their partners knew they had dementia, and were worried how they would cope with their care. I had so many conversations with them, and both partners were so glad their loved ones had not suffered. Anyway, as it happens, Steve Partridge and Barbara Smith fell in love and they were our first wedding at the village. We have listened in on them, and many are the times they have said how pleased they are that they met. How pleased they are that both their partners died quickly without suffering. How they have been spared the terrible heartbreak of seeing them being more affected by this terrible disease, how inevitably they would have become their partner's carer rather than a wife or husband." Sarah waited for effect. "I certainly think our solution is without doubt the most civilised. I have no doubts at all, none at all. If I did, I would not continue to provide the plant extract to activate the heart attacks." She looked around the group for a response. Everyone except Isobel nodded enthusiastically.

"And don't forget Jean's parents," Anne continued, "both suffered from dementia and then Alzheimer's, so she knew first hand all about the suffering, the cost emotionally and financially. The worry about their care, there were so many problems for her and her parents. I shall never forget when we both visited them. Jean had been at pains for me to know how intellectual they had been. She told me that they had been leading lights in their local community. Yet, here they were, almost unaware of each other, just husks of human beings, unable to even feed themselves. What sort of life was that? All of Jean's money was spent paying for their care. She had used up all the money from the sale of their home, and because she could not bear to see them go into community care, she never spent any money on herself; it all went on her parents. It broke her heart to see them.

She used to try and visit them every day to ensure that they were being fed and looked after properly. She had such mixed emotions when they died. Is that what you want for people, Isobel? Is it? Who will care for you? Who will care for me? We don't have a Jean to look after us do we? Why do we treat animals better than humans? Why? Medical staff seem hell bent on keeping people alive longer, despite this not usually being in the best interests of us the patients. I don't want to be having my bottom wiped for me by some underpaid, uncaring care home worker."

"They are not all like that Anne," John intervened.

"I know John, but quite a lot are. The care homes can't afford to pay the staff a decent wage and the councils just don't have the money."

"My friend Rosemary has just visited," Isobel spoke "I have not seen or heard from her for years. The reason why?

She has been caring for her husband of fifty years, through dementia. She managed to care for him at home until the end. She is so proud and grateful that she was able to do that. Her marriage vows were really important to her, 'In sickness and in health.' Her religion kept her going through all the very difficult times. She felt she had done the right thing by her husband. I understand that a lot of people cannot do that, but what about all the medical advances being made in the understanding of dementia? Is there a vaccine around the corner to prevent dementia and Alzheimer's, so that our treatment might not be needed?" Isobel fired back.

"Yes I agree, but what if it goes the way of cancer treatments where, although research has provided methods and medicines to improve and extend life, these treatments cannot be afforded by the NHS. Then there is more frustration caused to both the patients and their relatives knowing they could be helped if only the NHS would fund the treatment. The NHS DOES NOT have an open cheque book, NICE are cutting back on so many life extending treatments. The way we are going to administer the drug, removes all this angst. Sudden death, at an unknown time, without any influence from relatives, or politicians, solves the problem. No need for nursing homes, no bed blocking in hospitals, GP's able to spend more time with patients, solving the problem of the shortage of trained medical staff. You know the massive benefits to both the population and the NHS. Don't forget the absolute main reason is to remove the suffering of dementia." Anne stood up, and swiped the peanut bowl and stormed into the kitchen to refill it and calm down. Isobel looked at John, who had nodded agreement throughout all of Anne's speech. 'Well he is obviously on message,' she thought.

"Anyway, I thought we had come here to remember Jean, not discuss work," Anne altered course, as she re-entered the lounge.

"I'm sorry Anne, you are right, let's raise our glasses to Jean," Isobel retorted. John stood.

"To our dear colleague and friend, Jean."

Bill raised himself slowly, stood up straight, reached down for his glass, and raised it.

"All the best to a lovely lady." Isobel turned to Anne.

"Let's hope her autopsy and slides come back soon. Obviously there will be no funeral, but we can organise a memorial service for her." Everyone raised their glasses, drank, and sat sombrely down. The atmosphere had not recovered from the argument; no one spoke or knew where to look.

"Well, must be off," said Paul.

"Gosh is that the time, so must I," said Sarah quickly gathering up her shoulder bag from the floor and walking towards the kitchen. Ten minutes later only John remained.

"Are you alright, Anne?"

"Bloody furious! It was meant to be a lovely evening, remembering the good times with Jean. Instead it was a bloody fiasco. I am so annoyed, John."

"I know Anne, sorry it didn't work out the way you planned. It's not your fault. Isobel was out of order. I don't know why she is suddenly having doubts at this late stage; nerves perhaps. Do you want me to help you clear up?" He picked up two of the kitchen chairs and began to take them to the kitchen.

"No, it will only take me a couple of minutes to clear up John. Thanks for offering."

Anne cleared the glasses and plates away, viciously plumped the cushions, and reflected on how Isobel's doubts rankled with her. Truth be known, she still was not one hundred per cent sure that people would look back and congratulate them. God forbid that the exact opposite should happen. She thanked her lucky stars, not for the first time, about the total secrecy demanded by the trials. The use of GCHQ, and the SAS had been essential to her continued work on the project. Their research being anonymous was essential to the team success, as they all faced severe criticism and worse if the inoculations failed to work as planned. The initial trials had been going for nine years now and the recent results showed the correct calibration for the national roll out. All they needed to confirm now was that the change to the cell based flu vaccine would not alter the activation point.

Isobel slammed her back door, rattling the glass panel, threw off her ankle boots and coat, and stormed into the lounge.

"Blast her, talking down to me like that in front of the others," she spat out loud. "Bloody cheek, I've had enough of her." She flung herself into her chair and switched on the gas fire. "Bloody, bloody cheek. I'm entitled to my own opinion." She picked up her address book from the coffee table next to the phone. 'Shall I call her? I've a bloody mind to do so', she thought. 'I really, really have had enough. John didn't even say goodnight with a peck on the cheek as he used to do. Anne now has it all, the project and John it seems'. She sat back and considered her options. What if the cell based flu vaccine doesn't respond in the same way as the egg based one, what then? 'March 26th, I don't think so. That would wipe the smile off her smug face, trip trapping around in those silly shoes. It's all right her and poor old Jean saying the drones should react the same, but it hasn't been proved yet has it? It could be bloody carnage.' Isobel went to reach for the landline, thought better of it, and picked up her mobile.

Chapter 28

Deadline minus 43 days
Sarah's apartment

"Well that was pretty heated." Sarah opened her apartment door.

"Wasn't it? Strong emotions to say the least. Bad timing though," Paul replied as they headed to the fridge.

"Beer?"

"Certainly could do with one." They pulled the ring pulls and stood drinking for a moment.

"Nibbles?"

"Sarah! You are so naughty! Yours are certainly better than those we have just had." He grabbed her around her hips and swirled her round, before heading towards the bedroom. "Gosh, where's the lovely candle smell, it's more like smelly socks."

"Sorry," she laughed, kicking the socks underneath the bed.

"Who cares, get 'em off."

"What my socks?" she teased. He grabbed her shoulders and engulfed her with his kisses. His hands were

171

masterly at undoing her bra, whilst she threw off her tee shirt. Her shorts button opened easily, and she stepped out of the rest of her clothes. Paul was undoing his trousers too slowly for Sarah, who grabbed him. Hard as a bullet. They fell together onto her bed, his coarse body hair against her soft downy skin. Paul kissed her passionately all over, Sarah's nipples raised in anticipation. He licked and sucked them, cupped them, examined them, buried his head in them, whilst she stroked his hair – thick and luxurious. She arched her back, and felt them grow and expand, as she anticipated what was to come. He slid down the bed, and examined her closely, stroking her hair, a natural blonde. He parted her lips and smelt the natural allure. Buried his nose and breathed in. He could not wait a moment longer, Sarah was ready. He entered her, and she muffled a cry, as he slid slowly in and out, teasing her, smiling at her. She caressed his cheeks and stroked them slowly, affectionately, and urgently. He quickened his pace, and they came together with an arching of her back. A quiet sigh, her arms limp against her still body. She was satiated, she was spent. Paul uncoupled and flopped down beside her. Ten minutes later Sarah moved on top and began kissing him. Mouth first, then his nipples, down to the flaccid tool. She licked it with an exaggerated smack of her lips, raised her head, and smiled at him. Paul's eyes were closed in concentration. He flinched, as she licked and sucked him. He responded, and she sat astride him and moved slinkily above him, kissing him all over, wherever she could reach.

"Oh my goodness," Paul exclaimed.

"Shhhh, in case they're listening."

"Good for them, they might be enjoying it also."

They lay together recovering, hugging, stroking each other. Sarah was still up for it, and tried to interest Paul, whose eyes were closed, and his breathing slow. Sarah presumed he was asleep, and crept to the bathroom.

Paul heard the shower come on, and Sarah singing a soft lullaby. That was different to normal he thought.

Paul left later on, in the early hours, creeping along the corridor to his apartment so as not to wake anyone. He was desperate to move from here and hopefully if his plans worked, he could buy their house and have money to spare. 'I just can't stand living any longer with the residents, listening to their conversations, listening to their ailments being swapped like a competition.'

He went inside his apartment, and decided to have a coffee, thinking all the time how he just could not wait to lie in Sarah's arms all night, every night.

Chapter 29

Deadline minus 40 days
The Prime Minister's Office
Downing Street

The phone rang. The Prime Minister picked up on the second ring.

"Yes Hetty, send him straight in," he replied.

"Come on in, Charles," the PM commanded. "Take a seat. Coffee?"

"Yes please, Prime Minister," Charles replied.

Martin, the PM's strategic policy manager, rose and walked to the internal phone "Coffee and biscuits for three please, Hetty." He walked back to the desk and sat adjacent to the PM. He noted how Charles, as usual, was looking very individually dressed today. He had a certain reputation for a unique way of dressing, no boring grey suit for him. Today was no exception: he was wearing his favourite sage green and lavender tweed Saville Row jacket with Jodhpur styled trousers, matching green shirt, lavender silk spotted tie and matching top pocket handkerchief. You certainly never missed Charles in a crowd; of course the most noticeable feature was his waxed moustache. Very Salvador Dali.

"Look Charles, I have brought Martin in today to help you with the election. As campaign manager, I would like you to use Martin's expertise in communication. I think you will agree with me, that his work during the autumn has been sterling?" Charles looked at Martin, smiled and with a nod of the head, affirmed the PM's opinion.

"You will need to work on the campaign together. Martin, we are going to need some brilliant posters and campaign marketing from you. I know you have already been preparing some ideas for Charles on the election haven't you?"

Martin looked at them both, and then ran through a couple of threads of a campaign that would be hard-hitting on several issues. Strong imagery was going to be the winner again.

"Now Charles, I need you to come back with your strategy formulation. This time I want a hard pound campaign, so that other parties will not be able to stand the fire power. The main focus will be-

One – Look what we have achieved.

Two – Look what still needs to be achieved.

Three -Look how we will achieve it."

The PM slammed his hand down hard on the desk, rattling the cups and smiled.

"Like James 'Ragin' Cajun' Carville said." He paused for effect. "Do either of you know what he wrote on the Little Rock wall during the Bill Clinton 1992 battle for election?" The PM challenged them with a knowing smile.

Charles sat back and looked skyward, whilst racking his brains. Martin leaned forward and said quietly "Sir, wasn't it something to do with standards of living, the economy and healthcare?"

"Full marks, well done Martin," the PM clapped his hands together and bowed his head in acknowledgement of Martin. "He actually wrote 'It's the economy stupid and don't forget healthcare', and that is what I want us to focus on, promises of further improvements to the start we have made on healthcare. Root up management of the NHS, and reforms to the pay structure at the top, and we promise to pour in eight billion, yes eight billion pounds, into saving the NHS, Charles."

Charles looked surprised. "Where are we going to find that sort of money from the budget? Where will the savings be made?"

"Charles, that's where you come in, I want spin, and loads of it. I want us to guarantee that by 2018 all Accident and Emergency departments will have adequately trained staff to cope with the demands created by the increased population and the elderly. Bed blocking will be a thing of the past, as social services will have money poured into them to enable a service that can look after the elderly and infirm, either in care homes or in their own homes, with adequate, well paid, trained staff. At the same time, GP's will be able to have additional powers to ensure that all patients can be seen within two days of asking for an appointment. This is our main message of the campaign, Charles."

Charles raised his eyebrows and exhaled.

"Wow. That's some promise, can we deliver it?"

"Charles, we can not only say it, we can do it. I have looked into this for months and know that come the next election, the NHS will be in a very strong position, so much so that that alone will win us the next election. Aneurin Bevan's vision will continue, without the need to implement further savings from NICE on the usage of the new expensive treatments for diseases such as cancer.

With regard to living standards, we must hammer home our successes, but we must continue to express doubts about the levels of immigration and the terrorist threat to national security. These issues, in particular immigration, are the key issues with our opponents and could be our Achilles heel. Come back with your strategy Charles, after you have discussed it with Martin." The PM looked up from his notes.

Charles put down his notebook, and rose from his chair. "Alan, I will be back next Thursday as arranged with my initial strategy, for your approval."

Chapter 30

Deadline minus 41 days
05.00, John's Bedroom

John turned over, and looked at Anne's soft blonde hair. It was beautiful even after last night. He breathed in, to enjoy her sweet aroma. It was so lovely to wake up with someone so beautiful in her soul and her natural beauty.

She stirred and turned over towards him. Face still made up, lipstick long gone though. Her bare thigh brushed his, and he recalled the softness of her skin on her inner thighs and how soft and downy she was. Heaven.

He lay on his back in the semi darkness, and thought back over the years. It was too early for bird song and too cold for the window to be open. He could not wait for the spring and summer; to wake up to the dawn chorus, to open his eyes to the bright early morning light. They would walk again up the hills, and take a picnic for the two of them, to lie down in the bracken, hidden from view, and to laugh at themselves, acting like lovestruck teenagers. To wear shorts and polo shirts with the sun kissing their skin would be just bliss, just absolute bliss.

How many years now, he thought? Well although he had known her for nine years approximately, he had only flirted with her for what, about seven years? She was some tough cookie to get to know intimately, despite her sexy walk and way of talking. It was very much a case of 'hands off, no touching.' A tender kiss was all she would permit for a couple of years. John laughed to himself, not like the kids today, who did not even bother to kiss. You never saw couples walking in the streets holding hands, or being cinched in a long passionate kiss. It seemed to be 'Hi, what's your name? My place or yours?'

Anne was much too much of a lady for that. His wooing took until last year when after that extra glass of wine on her birthday, she had been persuaded, willingly, to let down her guard. It took almost until Christmas before they undressed in the bedroom. They acted just like a couple of virgins. Of course they weren't but that's how it felt. He lay there and a lovely warmth spread over him, as he remembered their first tender night. The secrecy made it even more exciting. Anne had worried in case it was true that the bungalows were bugged, but John had said it was rubbish, of course they weren't. He laughed to himself, he hadn't a clue if they were or they weren't. GCHQ must have had fun listening to them if they were. They were probably horrified that two old fogies were at it, but we all thought that when we were young. If you've got it, use it or lose it, that was their motto, and he chuckled.

Anne stirred. "Were you just chuckling?"

"I certainly was my little songbird. How are you, sleep well?"

"Wonderfully, like a log. What about you?"

"Well thanks to you, I had a great night, and I slept well."

Anne gave him a nudge in the ribs.

"Ow, cheeky."

"Well we had better get up and get on, otherwise we will be late, it's half past five already." John said.

Anne turned over and pretended to go back to sleep, and then turned her head and smiled. "I know, slave driver."

John laid the breakfast table, and made the tea and toast, whilst Anne did her hair and make-up. She breezed into the kitchen, smelling beautiful. He loved her so much. He smiled at her as she walked over to the table.

"What are you working on today, John?" Anne asked as she sat down.

"We are still having problems with absorption affecting transmission strengths. Major Ross is pushing us really hard," John said as he poured them both cups of tea. "We are getting additional scientists on board to bring in some fresh input and are going back to progressing the inoculation method in addition to the skin absorption. Major Ross is looking into it with GCHQ. What about you?"

"Well I'm hopefully getting more results in today. Sarah is giving me five more trial subjects from the village today. This new cell based flu vaccine seems to be acting in the same way as the egg one, but we cannot afford to get it wrong. What did you make of Isobel the other night? I was quite riled."

"I know Anne, I could tell straight away. As you said earlier, it was the wrong time to discuss it, she should speak to you in the lab, or with Major Ross if necessary."

Anne cleared the table and started to wash up.

"Umm, that's what I think. I will tackle her about it soon I think. If she has major reservations about the results, it's imperative she tells me, but if it's a moral issue, then I think Major Ross needs to talk to her. Anyway, we must get off."

08.30 Old laboratory

Princess Margaret Gardens

Anne walked down the laboratory without her usual sashay. She was worried how Isobel was going to react to her today. Isobel looked up from her 'scope and waited for Anne to speak.

"Isobel, I think we need a frank discussion about your position regarding the trial and the roll-out, don't you?"

"Yes, I have serious doubts about the vaccine being given without client consent."

The laboratory went very quiet, Bill and Sarah listened, aware of Isobel's new attitude.

"So what do you want to do? There is no way that anything is going to change now; we are within five weeks of signing off the trials. We can't replace you at this late stage, your knowledge is indispensable and we need your analysis of these final results."

Isobel looked over Anne's head to give her time and to avoid answering. She didn't know what to say. There were two choices, which would suit her plan better? Do I string her along and continue on with the research and hopefully make it fail its deadline, or should I ask for a transfer and delay the roll out as they need my knowledge? She looked at Anne.

"Anne, I realise that this is a real problem. All I can do, is carry on, you know how I feel, but I realise that it would leave only you, Bill and Sarah to complete the trial, as we are so close to the sign off. However, if we miss the deadline then I want to transfer, perhaps to John's team. I know his team is going to enlarge, and my knowledge is equally relevant to his research. Do you mind?"

"Isobel, first of all I am so glad you will carry on. I will speak to Major Ross and make sure he is happy with the situation. You can discuss the transfer with him at the relevant time, as I will be pulling out all the stops to get this signed off on time. We are on the home straight now, and we must complete the trial."

Anne turned around, and Bill and Sarah continued with their work, looking away when Anne passed, trying to appear as though they had not noticed or heard them discussing the issue.

09.15 Major Ross's Office

"But I am not happy with that solution Anne. Not happy at all. Look, she has worked on this project for what... nine years? Why query it now, at the eleventh hour? This 'Rosemary' friend, is she a plant by a pharmaceutical company? Didn't Isobel say she hasn't heard from her for years? Why has she contacted her just at this critical time? Coincidence? Isobel has known the reasons behind all the decisions, as they were made, but no, now just when we need everyone to really up their game, she is wavering. Can you rely on her now, that's the question Anne? Are you better off without her at all? Could she jeopardise the whole project?"

Anne was quiet. It was not the response she had expected, having thought he would be happy that she had managed to keep Isobel on track.

"I just thought that as we are already one person down, that we could not afford to lose anyone else, and John would certainly be very keen to use her. He was telling me how urgently his GPS tracking was needed." "That's not in dispute at all, and her knowledge will help John with one of the two routes of administration. John could then concentrate on the transmission of the tech through absorption. However, we can only have people working on the project who are committed to it. Could you cope without her?"

Anne sat and thought for a couple of minutes.

"I need some time just to consider her workload and see if I can split it between the three of us. Can I come back to you in the morning sir?"

"I can't wait that long, I need a decision this afternoon Anne. Come back to me with an update at six please."

10.30 Command Post.

"Morning John," Major Ross said as he arrived in the command post. "Could you join me?" he continued. "I need a full update now, bring your research notes please." With that he strode forward, despite his limp, into his office.

John passed Anne in the new laboratory; she was bent down peering under her desk. He tapped her bottom lightly. "What have you lost?"

"Just dropped my pen," Anne straightened herself up. She was wearing her pencil slim skirt with a soft pink cashmere cardigan today, and looked very sexy and cuddly.

"I didn't ask you how's it going with the arrangements for Jean's memorial?" John asked as he slipped his arm around her waist.

"I'm too busy John. I'm going to ask her brother Nigel to see to it. I've seen Isobel and Major Ross this morning. I thought I had a solution, but he doesn't agree with me."

"Oh, you don't usually disagree on anything."

"Well he thinks I will be able to cope without Isobel on my team. He thinks she should transfer to you, to enable you to get your trial underway. Do you remember we discussed it last week? He has asked me to go back to him tonight with my suggestions as to how I can conclude the work without her. So I'm sat here working it out. I think if she is not fully committed then she's unlikely to give me her full attention, and might even try and scupper the trial."

"Do you honestly think she would do that?"

"I just don't know, John. Can I risk it? Well anyway I hope everyone is given permission to come to the memorial. Jean only had her useless brother, and it would be very sad if there were only a handful of people there," Anne said thoughtfully.

"I know several of our team have said they would like to go. Some of us have known her for almost ten years. Doesn't time fly by?"

"We will have to check with Major Ross who can go," John replied "Obviously he will not be able to, but I hope we can all go. I'm just off to his office now, I'll ask him."

"Sit down John," Major Ross instructed John as he entered his office.

"I hear you all got together Saturday night?"

"Yes, it was such a shock about Jean, and the timing could not be worse for their project."

"They will cope John, Anne is more than up to it."

"Of course you're right. I know Anne's told you about Isobel's attack on the project. She really was very vocal about her new objections, very bad timing. Anne was very upset. I hear that you have suggested Isobel move over to my team."

"Well Anne is coming up with plans today, and we are going to discuss it later. What are your thoughts?"

"Well there's no doubt I would welcome her expertise, and I could really use her."

Major Ross nodded and then picked up two sheets of decoded memos from his desk.

"GCHQ are reporting several developments regarding the terrorist activity they are monitoring. The need for your new GPS tracking system is ever more urgent. Just how far off do you think we are now?" Major Ross asked.

"Well, if they urgently need to track people entering Europe as asylum seekers, they could try using the vaccination transmission; it rather depends on which group of people they want to monitor. If it's the terrorists embedded with the refugees and asylum seekers pouring in, then it would make perfect sense to say to the refugees, that they have to be inoculated against diseases, to prevent epidemics such as Ebola being brought in to Britain. It could be a condition of them receiving benefits. That should not raise any queries, and would enable the British Government to track arriving terrorists.

Now regarding home grown terrorists, or rather suspected terrorists and their families, this is where the new untested version really should come into its own, if we can make it work. Currently the problem is getting sufficient absorption through skin contact, to make the signal strong enough to be monitored. We have had some success, but again it's the method of transference that is the key to it working.

Mark has been working flat out, trying to get the nanotechnology to work by transference from paper, whether its newspaper, paper cups – the type coffee shops use – or just normal paper. We think that is going to be the easiest way of subversively transferring the tracking drones to the subject.

The final method, which is now proving to have good transmission, is the moist pads solution we talked about for all travellers in and out of the country. It should be quite simple to get the public to agree to this method, by saying that the information that is being stored is just fingerprints to be stored in their biometric passports"

"Right, well we really are covering several angles, John. Let me report back and see how they want us to progress," Major Ross said.

"We can work on weeks, before a trial on the vaccination, especially if Isobel can be spared now, rather than in five weeks' time. Then I expect the moist pads will be ready. We are probably still several months away from the absorption from paper method. The early trials are proving to be difficult. Roll out will depend on how sure they want us to be that it works. This will depend on the length of the trials, and what alterations are needed. GCHQ will also need to ensure that they have the computer facilities to monitor the additional quantity of people. I understand that you have already checked this one out?" Major Ross nodded.

"Perhaps we should be getting more researchers on board now, ready for the trials. It took quite a while for

Paul and Mark to be transferred; we cannot wait that long again." Major Ross suggested.

John walked back to the lab, Paul and Mark looked up.

"What does he think?" Paul asked.

"Apparently, there is a lot of pressure at the moment. We need to look at the problem of absorption through the skin, as this covert method is going to be the most useful for the home grown terrorists' tracking. Let's put everything away, and sit down now and talk about the options again and how we can progress."

John went and got three coffees, and the biscuit tin.

"Well, we really are pulling out all the stops!" Mark said cheekily. John laughed.

"No expense spared, you know the British Government."

"Right, let's look at the implementation of this nanotech. I think we might need to roll out for trial the older vaccination method, whilst we perfect the skin absorption. Do you both agree?" John asked. Mark and Paul both nodded. "Well that was the easy part. It's going to depend on how the government finally decides to roll it out. The main initial tranche is to target terrorists, known and suspected, here and abroad. Major Ross has ruled out adding it to Anne's flu vaccine programme, mainly as it might interfere with results, but also of course as we said, that is aimed at the over sixty-five age group, hardly the target group for terrorists. I cannot see a jihadist bothering about getting flu." They all laughed.

"I still think there is mileage also in either a spray or administering it in drinks. Perhaps we shall end up with several versions, dependant on who is being targeted. Have we checked the tracking with GCHQ, are they ready?"

"Well I've been over, and they see no problem at all, as it's rather similar to their technology for mobile phone tracking," Paul commented.

"Major Ross is going to speak to those that matter about recruiting additional researchers now, I have asked for four or five as soon as possible," John confirmed.

"To live in the village?" Mark queried.

"I don't see why not; we have the room, and it's so much better for cross pollination of ideas. Do you agree?" John asked.

"Certainly."

"Yes sure," Paul confirmed.

"There is a chance we might get Isobel, either now or after their deadline date."

Mark and Paul looked at each other. Mark spoke first.

"Well, her knowledge has been instrumental in getting our ideas working, so if she was with us full time, it should speed up the trials no end."

"Sure," Paul agreed. "We know a couple of researchers from GCHQ that could enhance our team. One person I can think of straightaway would be a chap called Ahmed, who I worked with. He has vast knowledge across very different fields of research. Anti-terrorism was one of the fields that he excels in. He would be great for not only the R and D, but also the implementation. The other person is James, a good solid researcher, who sometimes just comes up with a really extreme idea, but which often has elements that can be used. They would fit in well. We really also need some specialist info, from QinetiQ. Even radar might be useful, as they did with the computer work."

"Right, I'll talk to Major Ross tomorrow, let's see if they are available. The apartments are mothballed, so no problem there. Give me their surnames, and he can get straight onto it. National Security is at risk, with the terrorist attacks at present. We need to know where these terrorists are, and we need to know soon. The other project must be put on the back burner for now. Right, before you go, let's just cover where you are on the strength of signal."

Paul talked to John for another hour, explaining how his ideas were not yet panning out.

18.00 Major Ross's Office

Major Ross consumed the information Anne had put down in her memo.

"So you feel sure you can manage without her? So with just forty days left, you feel certain that you can finalise the tests on the cell based vaccine with just you, Bill and Sarah working on it? Positive?"

"Sir, I don't think I have an option. If she has changed her stance on the trial on moral grounds, then frankly she is unlikely to assist me greatly. She will be a negative influence on us. No, I will just work harder. We've got just under six weeks and five final test subjects. One should react this week, so we can analyse her slides next week. Two others are expected to react during the next few weeks, or at least we can see why they haven't, and the two remaining subjects should not react at all. If these people react differently then we have the capacity to cope. Worst case scenario is; one, a bad reaction, not causing a fatal heart attack, but severe permanent disability: two, too early a reaction in the two residents known not to be at the stage of their dementia giving rise to care problems. If we don't have these issues then six weeks is more than sufficient time for me to ensure the sign off is safe. If we do get problems, then depending on which reaction is the problem, we will be tight right to the wire. I'll also ask Bill to check if any of our original Hereford servicemen are able to be used for trials if we need them."

"Right, tell Isobel that she can transfer today on the understanding that she may be called upon to help your trial if we have unexpected reactions. We have to meet the deadline, there is no alternative."

Chapter 31

Deadline minus 39 days
09.45 Medical suite
Peak View Village

"Hello Bill." Bill showed Cilla into the medical suite, and settled her in one of the chairs by his desk.

"I'm so sorry I'm late. To be honest I got up and dressed and sat in front of the TV, and completely forgot I was coming down to you. When you phoned me, I jumped a mile."

"Are you alright?" Bill placed his hand on her arm. "Have you eaten breakfast?"

"Oh breakfast, I'm not sure to be honest. Might have, probably have, I don't feel hungry." Bill smiled.

"Don't worry, shall we go down to the restaurant afterwards and have a snack to make sure?" he asked.

"Yes that's a great idea."

Bill thought he could check the records and see if she had been down and if so what she ate. The records were very thorough.

"What are we doing today? Another scan?"

"No, we did that yesterday Cilla. No today you are having your flu vaccinations, which we delayed from the autumn, remember?"

"Oh, that's all right then."

Bill walked over to the fridge and removed the specially selected vaccine for Cilla. He had produced a vaccination using the older strength of the nanodrone and Gelsemium elegans mix, and mixed it with the new cell-based vaccine.

"Roll up your sleeve." Cilla pushed up her cardigan sleeve. "There you are Cilla. All done. Let's go and have something to eat shall we?"

Bill felt relieved that was over with, he had calculated that she would not suffer any reaction, or at most a few days of sickness and diarrhoea. The old vaccination had not worked in trials, as it was not up to the strength required to activate effectively, so he knew his darling Cilla would be safe. The trials would not be affected, as the others would receive the current trial vaccine.

Cilla followed Bill to the door, he locked up and they sauntered off downstairs. Bill still had four more residents to inoculate, of which two were people he knew quite well as they were on his floor, and he passed them regularly in the corridors.

He decided to speak to Amanda later, and see if they were continuing to check which residents missed meals or were coming down at odd times. It was often a good indicator that people were starting to forget things, although of course, sometimes, they were just not hungry! One of Amanda's roles in the research was to find out why during her chats when she saw the residents around the village, and note it in their records.

Chapter 32
Deadline minus 20 days
23.30, A Corridor
Peak View Village

Amanda rang the doorbell, and then peered through the kitchen window in the corridor. Returning to the door, she called out.

"Cilla? Are you alright?" She was of course expecting this earlier but for some reason the vaccination had not taken effect yet. Cilla had pulled her bathroom alarm five minutes ago. Amanda had her master keys with her. She listened again.

She had become used to this now, at the beginning it had been most unsettling, and she always hoped that the heart attacks would occur outside of the village, when all she had to do was intervene with the body collection and autopsy. She had formed strong bonds with most of the residents over the years, and disliked knowing who was inoculated and who was vulnerable. This month's batch of residents hopefully would prove the case for the new vaccine, and no more testing would need to take place, with the exception of those already vaccinated over the past seven years.

Amanda opened the door and immediately the smell assaulted her nose. Rushing into the bedroom, she could see Cilla leant forward moaning loudly.

"Cilla?" she rushed over to the bed. Cilla was clutching her throat.

"Can't breathe, can't breathe. My legs have gone weak. Feel awful." Cilla managed to get the words out as she held her chest.

Amanda phoned Sarah.

"Sarah come up to number 1507 straight away, Cilla is having breathing problems. She's been sick and has diarrhoea. She's in a very bad way. Is Bill around?" She put her phone down and stroked Cilla's forehead. "Don't worry we'll sort you out pet."

Sarah burst through the front door, still putting on her jumper over her pyjamas.

"What's happening?"

"Just come up and found her like this. She is having problems breathing. Just look how badly she has been sick, and obviously has bad diarrhoea." Amanda stroked her forehead.

"Don't worry Cilla we'll sort you out." She turned to Sarah. "Could this be a reaction to the injection? It's been almost nineteen days now; I have been wondering why she has had no reaction yet. I asked Bill about it only yesterday."

Bill came through into the bedroom. His appearance was like Sarah, hastily dressed. He looked at Cilla, and as he blinked away the tears, he smiled at her. Cilla was gasping for breath, she looked at him pleadingly. Amanda started removing the wet duvet, and took it into the bathroom where she picked up Cilla's flannel, whilst Sarah and Bill checked her over and spoke reassuringly to her.

"We need oxygen. Call the ambulance Amanda; I'll get the oxygen up here from the clinic. Sarah come and give me a hand will you, it's too heavy for me to move. Come on quickly!" Bill rushed out of the room with Sarah.

Amanda watched Cilla's distress. 'Why has this gone wrong, it's the first time in a couple of years we have had any problems and never like this?'

The next hour flashed by, ambulance men blue lighted Cilla to Worcester. Sarah, Bill and Amanda were left to wait to hear what the results would be. Amanda called in a cleaner to sort out Cilla's apartment, hoping that not too many residents had heard the commotion.

Each time there was a death, it caused unease amongst the villagers. She noticed that no one questioned it, just commented on how awful it was that yet another person had passed over.

Bill sat in his apartment waiting for an update. At least she has not died, and as she didn't have an immediate heart attack, there was no reason to think she would have one now, but something had gone wrong. The drones obviously activated, and the toxin had not caused death, exactly as he had planned. He loved Cilla and could not bear to administer the new improved inoculation which used the more potent vaccine. The old version, he had used, should have just caused her to be sick as the other residents had been, before they improved it. Why was she in such distress with her breathing?

Sarah, went down to the medical centre, switched on all the lights, and began checking Cilla's file. She had been inoculated, according to Bill's records, at 10.13 on the 17th February, nineteen days ago with the latest vaccine. So why was she reacting so badly, why hadn't she had a heart attack? This was so puzzling, and so important a reaction, in these very last few days before the sign off. So many questions flooded her mind. The team would be all over the results first thing in the morning; she would have to answer many questions as to why the toxin had not worked. She had sent texts to Anne and Major Ross, so knew they would be in very early. 'Best go and get some sleep,' she thought.

Chapter 33

Deadline minus 19 days
07.00, Major Ross' office

Anne, Sarah, Bill and Amanda sat opposite Major Ross.

"Right then, where do we start? This is a major setback. Anne, when was the last time we had a bad reaction like this?"

"The breathing problem is new, but the sickness and diarrhoea was the old problem we thought we had solved. Do we think that the cell-based vaccine has altered the reaction? We must get straight onto this. Bill you know Cilla very well indeed. Do you know of anything that might have caused this reaction?" Anne asked.

Bill blushed. Amanda thought how sweet, he obviously was embarrassed that they knew he and Cilla were thought of as an item. In fact, Bill was sat there, wondering if he could bear to tell them he had used the older version of the vaccine, to avoid her dying, even though it would mess up the test results. Never in a million years did he think that she would be admitted to hospital. He needed urgently to phone the hospital after nine o'clock to see what the prognosis was. She had looked so poorly as they took her last night, and she was so embarrassed to be in such a state.

They had tidied her up as best as they could before she went, but she was too distressed for them to change her. Her arms and legs had gone limp, and she was struggling for breath even with the oxygen.

"No, I don't think she was any different to normal. We had breakfast straight after the vaccination and she seemed absolutely normal and then she went back upstairs. She said she was going to watch television. During the last two weeks she has been her usual self, which was rather a surprise as Sarah and I had expected the fatal reaction fairly quickly."

"Right, we need to get blood and urine samples this morning, to see what is going on. Sarah get onto it will you? If you experience problems with the hospital, let me know and I will get the samples organised." Major Ross instructed.

'Bill looks particularly cut up,' Major Ross noted after they had all gone. 'Let's hope that she is home today, and this is not too serious a reaction.'

09.00 Medical centre.

Peak View village.

"Cilla McIntosh was admitted last night, can you please put me through to the ward?" Bill waited impatiently whilst they located her.

"Did you say Cilla McIntosh?"

"Yes, please hurry."

"I'm doing my best," the operator said, used to taking calls from worried relatives. "Just putting you through."

"Hello how can I help?"

"Cilla Macintosh, she was admitted last night, can you tell me how she is?"

"Are you a relative?"

"No I'm her friend."

"I'm so sorry, but we cannot pass on patient's information unless you are a relative."

"I'm her partner," Bill lied.

"You need to come in, visiting is between three o'clock and seven thirty.

Bill slammed the phone down. How on earth was she getting on, all alone with no visitors? She would be so scared. This was his fault; he was now having doubts that he had done the best thing for her. Hopefully, her reaction was only temporary and she would be out today.

He had been so worried about the muscle spasms and weakness last night; as Sarah had pointed out, another reaction to the toxin was that it could inhibit the respiratory centre of the medulla oblongata and the anterior horn cells of the spinal cord, resulting in respiratory depression and muscle paralysis. This last part was by far the most worrying. What if she was permanently paralysed? What if he had caused it? He could not bear to live with the guilt. What would happen to her? She had no relatives. Could he look after her?

Bill had not given any thought since the meeting, as to how the reaction of Cilla would affect the trial. He didn't care; all he worried about was his Cilla.

09.30 Princess Margaret Gardens

New laboratory.

"This could be a really massive problem, John." Anne sat down with a coffee in hand.

"What do you think has happened?"

"Well until we get the blood and urine samples back, we can't begin to know. Major Ross is surely going to have to get permission from the hospital to release those to us, as they don't know about us at all. I expect it will take a couple of days, unless Cilla is released before then. We don't know how she is yet. All we know is that she was admitted. Sarah thought she looked as though she was suffering from possible onset of paralysis, which is one of the known symptoms of the Gelsemium elegans. We knew about it right from the start and we ensured that we either had a weaker or a stronger toxin to make sure that we didn't inflict that on anybody. Sarah controlled that so well. Do you remember all the sickness and diarrhoea that we had ages ago? What a problem. All those unnecessary health precautions we had to implement in the village to pretend that it Nora virus, to explain the sickness to the residents."

"I certainly do, the extra cleaning staff needed was quite a problem for Amanda, and the extra laundry."

"I must say I was worried about all the suffering, especially those lovely ex-servicemen in Hereford. Anyway, we have not had this problem for years, so we must presume it is the change to the cell based vaccine. We must identify the cause urgently. There is no-way we can roll out the vaccine if there is any chance at all that this will happen. It may delay the roll out for a year. Perhaps we should insist on the egg based vaccine being rolled out, as we have done all our years of testing and we know it works?"

"Is that likely? I thought there was no way NICE would change its mind?"

"The problem would be that they would need to know why there needed to be a change. I don't think they are in the loop, too risky given the project."

"Well I think you can write that off as an option then. Don't panic until you know how Cilla is, and then all you can do, if she is badly affected, is to wait for the samples to be analysed. Let's face it; if you miss the deadline so that you ensure there are no major negative lifetime problems that must be a price worth paying, despite the intense pressure you are under. Imagine inflicting paralysis on dementia patients, how would they or their relatives cope? Terrible idea."

"Of course you are right. I shall have to be patient, and talk to Major Ross about a possible delay; he will be incandescent with rage if we can't go ahead. Perhaps I should ask him to allow Isobel back onto my team? Would you mind John?"

"Well as you know, I am under such pressure at the moment. I have just read the latest Strategic Defence and Security review. Basically they are now saying the potential threat to the UK and the world is now as dangerous as it was during the years of Nazi Germany, because of the threats posed by Russia and Islamic State. The government is to do everything in its power to guarantee the safety, security and prosperity of Britons. We have to be able to respond to more than one crisis on 'multiple fronts' in the future. Well my tracking system, if we can work out how to subversively administer it, will go a long way to helping MI6 and GCHQ at least locate the enemy, as well tracking our own troops when in known enemy locations. However, if Major Ross agrees, of course you must use Isobel. Major Ross is getting requests for updates all the time now. We are up against it at the moment. Paul is coming up with some really good ideas about how the nanotechnology could be used. We need trials to commence as soon as we can."

"I think we had better not see each other tonight, sounds as though we are going to be tied up here all evening." Anne looked disappointed, but knew her duty.

"Let's meet up in the rest room for a drink and catch up later."

Chapter 34

Deadline minus 19 days
Queen Elizabeth Hospital,
Birmingham
09.00

"Major Ross, fancy seeing you here again. How many years is it? Fifteen I bet."

Major Ross nodded,

"Just over that now. You haven't moved on then?"

"No love it here, after the move from Aldershot. It keeps me in peak condition, plenty of blood and guts and trauma. Talking about blood and guts, how did your wounds heal in the end? Your leg gave us the run around didn't it?"

Major Ross laughed.

"It's fine, a bit of a limp as we expected. Your chaps did an amazing job on it – god knows what I'd be like otherwise."

"Great that's what we like to hear. Best hotel in the world here you know."

"Sure is."

"Did you continue with your PTS counselling?"

"Well to be honest, I didn't, should have, but didn't. I wanted to forget all about it, but of course it doesn't happen like that does it? The flashbacks come back to haunt you. My wife is a star; she's the one who suffers with me. When I sit bolt upright in bed at night screaming and swearing in a hot sweat, she calms me down and hugs me until the moment passes. She won't hear of separate bedrooms as she wants to be there and help me get through it."

"Go back and get some more counselling if it gets unbearable."

"I know, the times I have told my men to get it. Easier sometimes to give advice than take it."

"Did I hear you are in charge of the ORW over at Hereford? Enjoying it?"

"Well of course I would still prefer to be operational, but we are inventing some ground breaking technology at the moment."

"So is that why we are to have a civvy in our midst?"

"Sure is, our trials are completely under wraps, part of a very important Ministry trial, all very hush hush. We will carry out all the analysis but we need you to care for her and be told about any changes as soon as they occur. If her paralysis is permanent and we cannot identify why, it will have a devastating impact on ten years research."

"Leave it to us, she'll have expert care, you know that. So you need samples when she arrives? I will phone you when she arrives, and I would suggest you send someone over to collect them. It'll be more secure and quicker."

11.00 Old laboratory

"When? I see. Does that mean I can go and collect the samples myself to save time? Ok." Anne put down the phone. "Bill, can you come over?"

Bill ambled across.

"Sit down Bill. Right, that was Major Ross on the phone he's over at the QE2 hospital. They have had the notes on Cilla sent over as he requested. He is arranging for her to be transferred this afternoon to the ward, where our service personnel are treated. I would imagine for the more specialised secure care and the need for us to access her information. Our consultant is a Lt. Colonel A. M. Williams, R.A.M.C. You know the care there is second to none and she will not seem out of place, as the servicemen and civilians are together being treated on the same ward. Of course there are plenty of army doctors and specialists in war wounded."

"Why is that appropriate for Cilla?"

"Right, it appears that she is showing signs of paralysis, as we half suspected last night. Now is this temporary or permanent? We have to know immediately, as this would make a huge difference to the trial. I know you and Cilla are friends so obviously you will want to visit her. Go today and get her blood and urine samples, and then we can detect the potency of the 'Gelsemium elegans'. Tomorrow, if she is transferred today, she should be looked over by Lt. Colonel Williams. We need to come up with suggestions as how to move forward to see if we can relieve the symptoms. We must know if this is a temporary problem, which her breathing issue seems to be, or a permanent medical issue. Either way Bill, we have to seek the reason this has occurred. It is imperative. We can throw whatever resources we need at it to resolve the issue. We have less than three weeks to be sure that this new vaccine will not cause any other reactions than those planned."

17.00 Queen Elizabeth Hospital

Bill looked along the ward, left and right. He pulled back the curtain surrounding the bed he thought the nurse had said. A patient was sat on the bedpan with a nurse in attendance.

"Can I help?" the nurse barked at him.

"Oh so sorry, looking for Miss Macintosh."

"Well she's in the next bed." The nurse turned to her patient. "Sorry about that Emily."

"Well not to worry, it doesn't seem as though there is anybody out there who hasn't seen my bits now," she said with a rasping voice and laughed ironically.

"Hello Cilla?" Bill nervously opened the curtain very slightly. Cilla was lying on her back, with an intravenous drip attached to her wrist. A monitor was bleeping next to her. Cilla looked asleep. The oxygen mask hid her face except for her eyes, and she seemed to be breathing quite passively, not at all like last night. The nurse at the station had said she had arrived about three hours ago, and had been immobile since. A consultant was coming to see her in the morning, as she was settled at the moment. Bill had mentioned about needing the blood and urine samples, and the nurse was completely unaware of the authorisation being given. She would need to check. In the meantime she gave permission for him to sit with her.

Bill moved the visitor's chair closer to the bed, and examined her face closely. He held her hand, which was warm, and noted that she had quite a good colour.

As he sat there, the ward continued its usual timetable; the sounds of the food trolley coming up the corridor, then the nurses and assistants chatting around it, talking about what they were going to do tonight-the pub, going home to their children, going out to the cinema, all the usual day-to-day things that we all did. The catering assistants were taking the food to each bed. It was mostly sandwiches by the sounds of it. Cake, yoghurts or ice-cream seemed to be the choices for afterwards. Bill felt lucky he had never stayed in hospital; he hated the enclosed atmosphere, completely out of kilter to the world outside. Some of these poor patients had just flown in from war zones; he imagined how they would be feeling. Limbs blown off, lives changed forever. One minute putting their lives on the line in unimaginable heat and discomfort and the next, airlifted out back to the sterility of a hospital ward in Britain. Wives and husbands hastily gathered in the hospital, lives changed forever. The prospect of no longer looking up to them, more likely to be looking after them, at least in the short term, until they were rehabilitated, had prosthetic limbs fitted. Heroes, heroines, everyone one of them.

Yet here was Cilla, all because of him. He had not been able to concentrate all day. He had caused this, it was entirely his fault. If he had used the latest version of the vaccine at worst Cilla would be dead, but she would not have had to face the prospect of being looked after 24/7 due to paralysis. How many months would she be in hospital? Would she ever come home again? Could she face the prospect of being stuck inside an institution, with no fresh air, or hearing birds sing for the rest of her life, confused with her dementia and unable to move? The everyday quiet of your own home, your radio, your television choices replaced by the sounds of chattering nurses, trolleys, beeping machines, the snoring and chest clearing of others. Not being able to get up and walk around in the middle of the night. All decisions made on your behalf- when you eat, when you have a cup of tea. Visitors overstaying their welcome, chatting endlessly about Mrs so and so down the road, who you did not know or worse still care about. Visitors children and grandchildren being talked about, when you didn't know them either. Feigning interest to be polite. Visitors who had never been to your home, but now loved to visit, supposedly to keep you company in hospital. Awful.

"Would you like a sandwich? We've got cheese or ham?" the nurse smiled at Bill.

"Cheese would be lovely, thank you."

"White or brown? Cup of tea?"

Bill chose the white and a cup of tea. Of course the nurses were wonderful; it was just that being independent was so different to being cared for.

"She's been sleeping ever since she came in. Are you a relative?" the nurse enquired.

Bill wondered how to respond, and simply said that he wasn't but was involved with her medical test and was waiting for permission to take blood and urine samples.

"I'll check to see if the permission has been granted, after we finish settling the others. OK?" With that the curtain closed, and Bill resumed staring at Cilla, and stroking her hand.

He got home after eleven o'clock in the end, as it took ages for them to find who had given permission for Cilla's samples to be released. He had carefully carried them to his car, as though they were gold dust. Bill couldn't think straight, what would they show? He thought they would show the strength of the Gelsemium elegans but not which vaccine had been used. He didn't think Isobel or Sarah would find him out. He had wept a few tears during the day over causing Cilla's distress, and now he just had to sleep, ready to face whatever tomorrow threw at him. Hopefully they and the consultant would work out a way of neutralising the toxin and, or the drones. Perhaps she would be fine tomorrow and today's angst would have been unnecessary?

Old laboratory

07.00 Princess Margaret Gardens

Anne arrived even earlier today. Major Ross had sent her a text late last night to say Bill had the samples, and he had stored them overnight in the fridge in the medical centre in Peak View; Bill would bring them over at 7am today. Sarah was already in and was waiting for Bill. She was going to test them first thing for the levels of the toxin. The testing would take her all day, but Anne was so anxious to find out the cause of Cilla's paralysis that she just could not stay at home any longer.

Today, hopefully, the consultants at the QE2 would feed back all Cilla's data since her admission yesterday, to add to the research. Sarah had thoroughly checked the three remaining trial subjects who were vaccinated at the same time as Cilla, and no reactions had been noted.

Isobel was working with John today, so Anne decided she would not speak to her, unless she felt that it was really necessary. Bill walked in and passed the samples over to Sarah. Anne walked over to them.

"How was she, Bill?" she asked.

Bill shuffled his feet, and looked down.

"Not good, not good at all.' He looked up at them both. "She seemed more peaceful, but she cannot move, she was on a ventilator obviously. Whilst I was there, she showed no improvement. They are obviously turning her to keep her comfortable, lovely nurses, really attentive. Standards are so much higher in there being services staff. I was very impressed."

"Right Sarah, straight onto it then. I shall be here, just keep me informed all through the day. This is a big one, a really worrying development. I'm just going to speak to Isobel, despite thinking today I would not bother her, but I have just had an idea that might relieve some of the symptoms, or at least is worth trying. If you need me, I will be in the new lab. OK?"

Bill and Sarah had already started to unpack the samples, and were preparing them for loading into the test equipment.

08.09 New laboratory.

"Well it's worth a try," Isobel agreed, "we have never tried it before, but quite honestly, it's our fault, so rather than just concentrate on why she has reacted, it's worth trying to ease her symptoms whilst Sarah and Bill continue with the analysis."

Anne walked down to the Command Post and through into the office.

"How's it going Anne? Are we onto it?"

"We just could not have expected this reaction. It's one we have never had before. Bill and Sarah are testing the samples. I have had an idea in the meanwhile. Could we get them to give Cilla blood transfusions to weaken the level of the toxin? I've spoken to Isobel, and we think there is a chance the effects could be lessened. What do you think?"

"Well if you both are in agreement, I do not see any reason why not to. It will not affect our trial at all. I am due to speak to her consultant this morning, and will ask him then to arrange it. He, of course, is totally unaware of what the medical trial is, only that it is top secret and for the Ministry. All he will be able to do for us is pass on his observations, and give an opinion on the likelihood of permanence to her current state. I understand none of the other residents vaccinated have any side effects. Why was only one person affected? What was different? We cannot roll out the product if there is any likelihood of a repeat performance. This is a deal breaker Anne. We must get to the root cause and solve the issue. We have just over two weeks now, we must not fail."

Anne walked slowly out of the room and back up to the rest room. 'What on earth caused this?' she thought for the hundredth time.

Chapter 35

Deadline 16 days
14.30, Queen Elizabeth hospital

"Hello Cilla," Bill took her hand and patted it. Cilla lay there, all the machines working for her, as they had done for several days. She had shown a very slight improvement with the blood transfusions, but was still paralysed. Bill had not been able to come up for two days, as he was working flat out with Sarah, on the cause of Cilla's problems. He found it impossible to work on the testing, knowing he had caused it. Also, knowing that all the testing in the world was not going to identify the reason, and that they could progress the trial to roll out without Cilla's problem repeating itself.

Sarah had not found the link to the older version of the toxin. Isobel had kept up with the results of each test, and had asked him some uncomfortable questions, which made him wonder if she suspected anything. So far, Anne was still worrying about the results, even though none of the other trial residents had shown any reaction.

Bill had been checking on their scans and results, to see how close they were to the nanodrones activating. He thought one of the four, Derek, would get a reaction any day now; his scans and his behaviour were suggesting that his dementia has progressed to an inability to cope. This would reassure the team that everything was as it should be, and probably they would put Cilla's reaction down to an allergy to the vaccine. This did not stop Anne going through all the previous years of data, and comparing results and side effects over the years. She was working 24/7 and burning herself out.

Cilla flexed her finger, Bill looked at her, had she just moved?

"Cilla, it's Bill. How are you today? Are you comfortable? Sarah sends her love." There was no reaction. He sat there desperate to help her. It was still too early to say if she would ever move again. Her consultant was not too positive about it happening, but it was difficult for him to appraise the situation, as he could not be told about the trial.

Bill stayed an hour, and when he left he felt all alone, empty and desolate.

16.45 M5 Motorway.

He drove home slowly, his mind a million miles away from the traffic roaring past him in the outside lanes. Tears flowed down his stubbly old face. Every now and then he swiped his folded handkerchief across his eyes to mop them up. What on earth was he to do? His darling Cilla was not responding and it looked certain that her situation was not going to change. What had he done? What was going to happen to her? There was no way he was going to let her stay alone in hospital. Could he look after her? How could he, he was not young any longer, would he have the strength, the stamina? He drove on, it was getting dark, and the oncoming car lights were beginning to bother him. Could he have her at home in the village if twenty-four hour care was provided? Was that likely? Social services were stretched to breaking point, and he knew that home care visits were being limited to fifteen minutes several times a day, just to ensure the basics were provided.

Cars zoomed past him; he looked at his speedometer, fifty miles per hour. He used to zoom along at ninety miles per hour years ago, but his reactions were getting slower and he felt safer at fifty.

What about asking Major Ross if he could get funding for Cilla? That would be a brilliant solution and Cilla could live with him, if his apartment was adapted and they funded twenty-four hour care. Bill thought about how he could keep her company, talk to her, change the television and radio programmes to keep her amused. Feed her, and possibly get her taken outside, even if it was only downstairs in the village into the garden. That would be great, as last he began to feel positive. After all, he reasoned, it was the trials' fault she was paralysed; Major Ross could hardly refuse could he? They were spending millions on this research project, surely some could be diverted to Cilla?

Bill turned off the motorway and drove towards Malvern. Traffic was really heavy at this time of day; he sat in the queue waiting to be able to turn left at the roundabout.

He must speak to Anne and see what she thought. The car driver behind tooted his horn impatiently at Bill not merging with the traffic. Bill pulled away and drove on.

By the time he was back in the lab it was six thirty, but everyone was still hard at work. He walked down the lab, to Anne at the far end.

"Hello Bill how is she?" Anne asked.

"No change."

"Oh dear, I am so sorry." Anne felt for Bill, but also was increasingly worried that they were no nearer to finding an explanation for her paralysis.

"Anne I need to talk to you in private about Cilla, could you find time tonight before you go home?"

"To be honest Bill, it looks like another late night tonight. Let me just finish these tests, say give me an hour ok?"

Bill walked back to the village, he needed to sit down, have a cup of tea, and think exactly what he wanted to ask Anne.

An hour later and Anne and Bill finished their conversation.

"I really do not think he will authorise it, as we have not funded any care for others affected by the trial. I will certainly discuss it, and recommend that in this particular case, we fund her care. Let me ask him tomorrow, and I will let you know immediately afterwards."

"Anne I am pleading with you to do your best, I could not bear it if she was left locked into her world physically and mentally without me having done all I can to help her."

Anne touched his hand.

"I know, leave it with me Bill, let's see if he will make an exception.

He walked over to his desk, and found the files of two more trial subjects who had passed away, both from the previous vaccine. The autopsy notes were being sent over for analysis. One test subject had been an ex-serviceman from Hereford and the other one from the village. Because they had had the egg based vaccine, their records would be updated and kept, just in case they reverted to that vaccine again any time in the future.

Chapter 36

Deadline 15 days
08.00 Major Ross' office

"I don't think that will be possible Anne, it would form a precedent, especially if we are going to sign the project off and production is going to start. Going forward if it became public knowledge, and others were affected in a similar way, God forbid, then the government would have to fund the same care for everyone else. You know how these government departments are, you cannot set a precedent." Major Ross leant back in his chair and looked directly into Anne's eyes.

"But surely it should be years before anyone has any knowledge of the nanodrones."

"Well we hope so, but I know it will not make any difference to getting that sort of expenditure signed off."

"Surely it will cost more to pay for her to stay in hospital or in a nursing home?"

"That isn't how these departments think, common sense is not used I'm afraid Anne."

"He is going to be devastated; I think you know how close he is to her."

'To be honest Anne, she is not likely to live that long, and I think Bill knows that really. Let's be positive and hope we can find what has caused the paralysis and get her back walking." Major Ross stood up, Anne realised the discussion was over, how on earth was she going to break the news to Bill? He would be upstairs waiting for her.

She walked slowly up the stairs and crossed the hallway. Bill immediately approached her the moment she entered the lab. As he nearer her, he could tell from her demeanour that the answer was negative. Tears welled up in his eyes. Anne took him by the arm and guided him to his desk, and sat him down.

"I'm so sorry Bill, although Major Ross really wants to help, he is quite clear that the authorities will not set a precedent, even for us."

Bill looked down into his lap – it was the worst possible news.

"Do you mind if I just go home for an hour, to clear my mind?" he croaked.

"Of course not Bill, I understand." Bill rose and shuffled out of the lab.

Bill's apartment

He picked up the kettle, and filled it with water, and turned it on. The tears poured down his face, his shoulders heaved with the sobs. He sat down on the kitchen stool to steady himself.

As soon as he had made his tea, he went and sat in the lounge and looked through the window and thought. He knew what he felt he must do, it would be a kindness, an act of courage to save Cilla any more humiliation, and he must do it on his next visit. There was no way she would get better, the vaccination had been the cause and nothing was going to change it now. He had caused it and he must resolve the situation. He sipped his tea slowly, and thought how he must prepare.

Chapter 37

Deadline minus 6 days to go 14.00, Queen Elizabeth hospital

"Cilla can you hear me?" Bill whispered into her ear. The nurses had reported that despite the continuing paralysis, they thought she could hear, and they had had the occasional movement of her eyelids when they spoke to her.

"Cilla its Bill. How are you doing darling? Can you blink, just to let me know you can hear me?" There was no response at all; the ventilator continued to breathe for her, her monitors continued to bleep. Bill looked around him at the ward; several bays had the curtains enclosing them partially allowing an after dinner snooze and to give a little privacy, only a couple of beds were fully visible to him from his view point. Neither person lay facing him nor were there any nurses around.

Bill reached inside his jacket, whilst keeping an eye out at the ward. Just as he was about to take out the hypodermic syringe, a buzzer went off. He jumped, and froze, quickly replacing the syringe inside his jacket. A nurse came onto the ward, and went over to Jack's bed.

"Yes Jack alright? A bed pan? Of course, give me a minute." She disappeared off the ward. Bill's heart was pounding. He talked to Cilla again. He talked about anything he could quickly think of. The nurse returned and waited for Jack to finish using the pan.

"Hello Bill. No change then? It's a real mystery to us, looks like either a chemical or an allergic reaction to something. Are you any the nearer at your end to the problem?"

Bill confirmed nothing was known yet.

"I got a message to say she might have been responding a bit recently."

"Well I haven't seen it myself. We want it to happen so much, that sometimes we might read more into a move than there is."

"Nurse."

"OK, coming Jack." With that she disappeared behind the curtain and then off to the sluice.

Bill sat there alone again. No one was around, now was the time to act. He reached inside his jacket, feeling carefully for the syringe. He brought it out, hiding it between his jacket and the side of the bed, with his back to the ward. Expertly removing the shield from the needle, he prepared the syringe for use. He looked at Cilla.

"Cilla, forgive me," he whispered into her ear as he reached for her arm.

Suddenly Cilla's monitor alarm blared forth, right beside his head. He stood up with shock. 'What the hell caused that?' He quickly pocketed the syringe. His heart was pounding, his forehead throbbed. He had to sit down.

Another nurse walked fairly smartish to the bedside.

"Cilla, what are you doing my luv?" She looked at the monitor, and pressed the reset button.

"Don't worry Bill, her monitor has done this several times today. We'll have to get it looked at." She checked all the readings. "No problem Cilla, damn silly machine playing up again. It must have given you both heart attacks!" she laughed. Then happy everything was working again, she left Bill recovering from the incident. She turned and came back "Bill, Cilla's samples are at my desk for you when you go. OK?"

Bill sat down and put his head in his hands, and waited for his heart to calm down. He began shaking. He looked at Cilla and left quickly and went outside the ward, and into the visitor's unisex lavatory in the corridor. Locking the door, he sat down fully clothed on the toilet, unable to stop shaking. Internally he was calling Cilla's name, over and over again, unable to get over what he had almost done. He sat there for what seemed like hours, until the door handle moved for the second time.

"Anyone in there?" the voice called.

"Yes, just give me a minute," Bill rose and looked into the mirror, smoothed his hair, and ran both hands over his face. He opened the door.

"Sorry, upset tummy," he said to the waiting stranger as he passed him.

"No problem mate," the stranger said as he disappeared into the toilet.

Bill stood there not knowing what to do. He suddenly remembered Cilla's samples and retraced his steps to the ward, and collected them.

"You all right, you look a bit shaken up?" the nurse asked as she handed them over.

"I'm fine thanks." With that Bill left, in search of the solace of his car.

16.30 Old Laboratory.

"Oh Anne, Bill's been in with Cilla's samples, he's gone home for a small nap, he looked knackered. OK? Said he would be back about six, and will work through this evening," Sarah said. She certainly wasn't coming back later; she had a night of 'nibbles' with Paul that she was looking forward to. Some things could not be put on the back burner for work!! She suddenly thought of Cheng, 'I do hope he is getting everything ready for us.'

Chapter 38

Deadline minus 4 days
Old laboratory

"Good morning Isobel," Bill smiled weakly at her.

"Bill,' she acknowledged him with a small nod of her head.

"Will you be back in John's lab next week?"

"It will depend if we have signed off this project. John is expecting me. He is hoping to trial the GPS inoculation this week. In fact, what would you think about being one of the first test subjects? You would be perfect with your travelling to the hospital so often. They are inoculating ten Regiment staff tomorrow; can I see if John could use you?

"Well I don't see why not. Your tracking won't kill me will it?"

"No of course not. That would be great, I'll speak to John and get that organised. I was hoping you would come round tonight if you have time, perhaps for supper. I've got a couple of things I want to discuss."

"Oh lovely. What time?" Bill was rather surprised as Isobel seldom asked anyone back to her home.

They arranged for him to go round at seven thirty. He was not sure what she would serve, but presumed it would be comfort food. She really had piled on the pounds since Jonathon's day. She was looking much older than her age now. Mind you, he thought that he had never dressed his age either, in fact he had always looked older than his years. Both of them were dressed for comfort rather than style, it had to be said. Isobel smiled to herself when he accepted, she felt sure she would get him to agree to her plan, he would have little choice.

19.30 Isobel's bungalow

"Come on in, let me take your raincoat. It's horrible out there tonight."

Isobel hung up his coat, and adjusted the saucepan of potatoes simmering on the hob. "I've just cooked something nice and easy, as time was short, hope you don't mind Bill. Bought it from Waitrose. Smoked haddock fillets and I've got some veg and mashed potatoes. Alright?"

"That sounds wonderful to me. I haven't had a decent meal since Cilla went into hospital. By the time I've worked over, and then driven up to see her, I've no time to cook, been living on takeaways and rubbish."

Isobel drained and then mashed the potatoes, and plated up the meal, putting the plates down quite firmly on the table, before sitting down and staring at Bill.

Bill took a mouthful of food.

"So what do you think about Cilla's progress Bill? Are you surprised how she reacted to the vaccination?"

Bill continued to look down at the table, not wanting to make eye contact.

"Well I'm not sure."

"Oh I think you know far more than you've told anyone Bill Matthews." Isobel's tone of voice had changed.

"What do you mean?" Bill frowned, taking another mouthful of food.

"Now that I have been working with Sarah on Cilla's results, I think that I know why it all went wrong Bill, don't you?"

Bill was shaken; he didn't think anyone would have worked it out. The deadline was only four days away, and they were still talking about not signing it off. Anne was telling him, that the PM might go ahead with it anyway if only one paralysis had occurred. They had written off Cilla's reaction, as one of those things and the roll out was too important to worry about whether a very small percentage could be affected negatively. How could they say that? How could they say Cilla's agony was not to worry about, even though of course knew why she had been affected.

"What do you mean?"

"Did you use the old weaker toxin with the new cell based flu injection?"

Bill was stunned that she had worked it out. Should he admit it? He took a mouthful of food, to give him time. He chewed his fish very slowly, still looking down at his plate.

"Well Bill, did you? I think you did, that would be the only cause that I can think of. You can tell me. You know my feelings about the roll out," she smiled at Bill. "Another glass of wine?"

Bill accepted, and continued eating.

Isobel looked at him and knew she was right. Her plan was going to work, she just knew it.

"Are you going to tell anyone? It was unforgivable; I was only doing it to save Cilla dying from the nanodrones. I could not bear to lose her yet," he looked over to Isobel. "Well that hasn't worked has it? She's in a much worse state now, dementia and paralysis."

"I had worked that out. You know how much trouble you will be in when they find out, don't you?" Isobel paused to let Bill take in her words. "Now I think that I can help you solve this problem. I won't spill the beans, if you let me help you. Let me tell you what I was thinking." Isobel leaned forward and began to explain her plan.

Chapter 39

Deadline minus 2 days
Command Post

"John," Major Ross called.

"Yes Major."

"Where is Anne this morning?"

"Now you mention it, I haven't seen her today. Is she upstairs in the old laboratory?

"I am a little worried," Major Ross, replied "She is bringing me the final analysis today. Anne said she would come in especially early as it's all down to her now. Just go and find her would you John? I know you're very busy, but the pressure is really on today and I need to see her urgently."

"Of course," John immediately turned and left the room. He flew up the two flights of stairs, out into the reception area and walked straight over to the old laboratory. Bill and Sarah were engrossed in their research. He could see Isobel's boxy shape at the far end and headed straight for her.

"Isobel."

"Good morning John, how are you?" Isobel touched her hair and smiled. She was dressed as always in her polyester cream trousers, with a non-descript blouse, same gold locket poking through, and beige flat shoes. Her glasses could do with a polish John thought.

"Worried. Have you seen Anne this morning?" he said quietly.

"Sure have, she was in earlier, not sure where she was going afterwards, but she picked up the analysis she had asked me to prepare, and headed out of the door. I presume she has gone down to the new laboratory. Why?" Isobel brushed a speck of dust off John's jumper. John looked down and checked his jumper, before looking her in the eye.

"Major Ross has not seen her yet, and needs her analysis urgently."

"Sorry, can't help you. If I see her, I'll let you know."

Isobel turned back to her work, leaving John to go down to the new laboratory.

"Hi Mark, seen Anne?" John asked as he entered the laboratory.

"Nope not today," replied Mark.

Strange John thought. She had been arriving so much earlier now that the pressure was building, ever since Isobel's transfer and Cilla's health issues.

Perhaps she has a migraine and has gone home. He headed outside. As he rounded the corner of the first block of bungalows, his stomach churned. Let's hope she is just resting; perhaps she came over feeling unwell, and has headed home. She certainly had been in great fettle last night, even though she was, of course, tired. He had stayed rather late; perhaps she was just whacked out. He quickened his pace. The back door was open, slightly ajar.

"Anne. Anne?" he called out softly in case she was resting. "Anne, are you there? Anne its John."

He strode straight through to her bedroom. The bed was made, curtains open, dressing table in order. He could smell the remnants of her Rive Gauche perfume. Perhaps she was in the bathroom.

"Anne, Anne, are you there? He gently knocked the door. "Anne," he eased the door open. Nothing, everything was in order. He felt her flannel, her towel, and her toothbrush. All had been used today, all damp. Where was she, where on earth was she? "Anne," he shouted, "Where are you?" Well she obviously had got up, got dressed and gone out. Where was she? What about breakfast, had she eaten? He returned to the kitchen. Everything was in perfect order. He could not tell if she had eaten, she always cleared away. There were flowers in the vase on the window sill. He looked around. Wait a minute, what was that on the floor under the table. He reached down, and picked it up, turned it in the palm of his hand. A button, a cream veined brown button. Where would that have come from? It looked like it came from a man's cardigan. Well it was certainly not his, as he could not abide cardigans. He put it on the kitchen table.

He suddenly thought about her lab coat, was it still here? He rushed back to the bedroom, tore open her wardrobe. It was still hung up, pristine and white. How come? Isobel said she had seen Anne. Wouldn't she have it with her? Where on earth was she? He could feel panic rising. He half walked and half ran back to the main building. He dashed down the staircase to the Command Centre. Major Ross was studying a sheaf of yellow papers. He turned quickly.

"John?"

"Can't find her," he blurted out, getting his breath back. "Her back door was open. She isn't there. I checked all the rooms. Nothing seems amiss at all. It's spick and span, all in order."

"Well what are your thoughts John?"

"I just don't know. Last night she was fine, tired because of the hours, but fine, not showing signs of stress."

Major Ross just looked at him, taking it all in.

"Isobel said she had seen her this morning didn't she? Ask her to come down straight away," Major Ross ordered.

John phoned the old lab. He paced the room, whilst waiting for Isobel to appear. Then he heard her steps on the staircase. The door opened, and John walked right over to her, accompanying her back to Major Ross.

"You asked for me, Sir?" Isobel asked.

"I heard that you have seen Anne this morning. When and what was she doing?"

"Yes, it was quite early; she came into the laboratory, picked up my summary of the analysis, scanned through it, and then left with it. She was only there about ten minutes, maximum."

"We can't locate her, she is not in the facility nor in her home. Do you have any idea where she might be? Do you think she has gone out? Did she mention anything to you?"

"Nothing, she just came in, picked up the summary and left. She might have gone to the shops I suppose."

"She would not go out without telling us, and certainly not to the shops, that's for sure," said John defending her.

Major Ross looked at both of them. "Right, I want you both to go back, and without making any obvious fuss, search all areas for her. Bearing in mind that Anne seems to have the summary with her, this has massive security implications. It is essential that only the three of us know about it. Do you both understand? John, will you please check the new laboratory, and all the rooms underground, plus the perimeter of the grounds. Have a look at the bungalows and make sure she is not in another one. Isobel, please check all the old laboratory areas, rest areas etc. Come back to me the minute you either find something or have finished your checks. We are looking either at abduction, or she has left under her own free will."

As they left the room, Major Ross dashed off a report, coded it and placed the yellow paper into one of the caskets, and sent it down the communication tube. The reaction should be swift.

Chapter 40

The Prime Ministers' office
Deadline minus 2 days

The phone rang in the PM's secretary's office.

"Patch me through to the PM. Top security issue." No explanation was needed. This was the direct line to GCHQ.

The PM lifted the phone on the second ring.

"Yes?" He listened carefully, frowned, and ran his left hand through his hair.

"What has been organised? Is The Regiment onto it yet? Do we suspect this researcher?" He listened again. "Well I need to be kept fully informed." He put the phone down, and leant his chair back, stared up at the ceiling, and sighed. 'Oh my goodness he thought, oh my goodness. This could be a disaster, a major disaster.' They only had two days left before the button was to be pressed with the pharmaceutical company. Worse still, what if the dossier was in the wrong hands and the cat was out of the bag. Everything hung in the balance now.

Princess Margaret Gardens.

Command Post

Isobel returned first.

"What have you found?" Major Ross asked.

"Nothing, nothing at all."

"Think Isobel, what frame of mind did she seem in when you saw her?"

"I didn't notice anything different about her at all. She didn't have her lab coat on, but there again, it was early and she was looking at the report."

"Thank you. Go back upstairs, continue with your work, we are now possibly without a team leader, and we have only two days to complete this report. Take charge until we find Anne. Can you cope? Do you need any help? I will expect you to report directly to me for the rest of today. You must not make any comment to anyone, not even John about Anne. Do you understand?"

"Of course, Sir." She turned and smiled to herself. She was in charge of the project, fantastic. She left the room and went back to her desk, passing John on the stairs, as he rushed past her.

John's worried face told Major Ross everything, the minute he saw him.

"No luck then?"

"Nothing Sir. Her car is in the car park, in its usual space. No signs of a struggle anywhere. Everywhere just looks as normal."

"The Regiment are already sending over a team to search her home. They should be here very shortly. Just leave them to it John. Go back to the lab, and carry on with your project. The deadline cannot be extended, so by tomorrow night, we need to have the final decision."

Princess Margaret Gardens.

Car park.

A large white van drove into the car park. Four men got out and got dressed in what looked like painter's whites and unloaded step ladders and tool kits, with rolls of plastic, and walked over to the back of Anne's bungalow. They were in very good spirits, pulling each other legs, joshing and joking as they went back and forth to the bungalow, unloading the van. The ground outside was checked for footprints. The door was opened and further checks for footprints were made. The all clear given, they entered and closed the door. Each one dispersed to a different room. Forensics taken, areas checked for clues. Items bagged, no matter how unlikely they were to be of use. Not a word was said, just in case the rooms were bugged. Finished, they locked, left the bungalow, and sauntered along the pathway, and disappeared. They waved as they left to the non-existent Anne.

"Back soon," one of the men called.

Major Ross's phone rang. He answered and listened.

"Just the button?"

"Footprints?" He listened. "Have you cleared the site? I want two to return to base with the bags for analysis, but the other two to stay in the area until stepped down."

The New Laboratory

John's phone rang.

"Be right down Sir."

"Right, we still have no idea what has happened. Have you thought of anything?" Major Ross asked John as he entered the room.

"I have thought through all the scenarios," John replied, "and think it can only be that she has been kidnapped. I don't know by whom, it's got to be someone who does not want the trial to go ahead or who wants a ransom. I just know that Anne would never sell us out; she totally believes we are doing the right thing. She's put years into this research, and fully backs the way of introducing the nanodrones. I know that she's confident about the results, and is right behind the project. She was concentrating on Cilla's paralysis and the death of the last test subject."

"Could that have unsettled her?" Major Ross asked.

"Perhaps, but she is such a professional, I really don't think so. She certainly didn't discuss it last night when we ate. I feel one hundred per cent positive that she hasn't stolen the research. That she has not sold us out. Who would know we were here? The security has been so tight all the way through. All links to the product via the pharmaceutical companies, or unions etc. should show up Boston or Cambridge, anywhere but not here."

"GCHQ are checking everyone, UK and foreign based, known to them at present." Major Ross informed John. "We do have the new intake of staff so they are being checked out at present. Their backgrounds and contacts are being looked into again – the usual in the circumstances."

Major Ross did not mention the apartment bugging being monitored.

"OK, we have to continue with the final report. I need you to take over the whole project John. With Jean gone and Anne missing, I have asked Isobel to transfer back and work as lead researcher today with Bill and Sarah. I need you John, to take over until we have Anne back. Worst case scenario, you will have to put your name to the final report. I've got all the data here, I need you to go and read all the latest test results, as we do not seem to be making any headway with the cause of Cilla's paralysis, talk to Sarah in particular about the analysis she is doing.

Tomorrow is the last day that we can give the go ahead for this project this year. Go and read the up to date information. The repercussions are just off the scale if it is incorrectly calibrated. It appears than only Cilla has had negative results from the cell based flu inoculation, so is this an allergic reaction? We are still outstanding the autopsy of the other resident who died last week, he was not expected to die from the toxin as his dementia was very early days. So again, what did he die from, was it natural causes? If the nanodrones are actioning too early or causing debilitating illnesses, I would not ask you to sign this off until you were certain, however the politicians may take the risk in which case I might have to as well."

John felt a sense of foreboding; he picked up the report and headed to the office. Major Ross had given him the access code for the computer programme. He settled down for what he guessed would probably be several hours' work. Could he manage to make sense of it all in time? He would need Isobel and Bill's input.

Major Ross sent the current situation update by canister to GCHQ. Let's hope we find Anne today, he thought as he returned to his office.

The tracker team had been deployed and feedback received. It was confirmed that Anne, wearing her kitten heeled shoes and another person's footprints, had been tracked. It looked by the shoe size that the other person was a small person and they had walked to the car park. The tracks went dead there. Obviously this looks like she and the man left by car. The ground had been scuffed, so they are of the opinion that Anne may have been pushed into the car. Major Ross decided not to worry John with this information.

Chapter 41

Deadline minus thirty-nine hours
09.00 25th March
Unknown location

"Stay there, don't move."

Anne stood stock-still. Breathing slowly, remaining outwardly calm. 'Keep up the pretence,' Anne thought. Her survival instinct was on super drive.

Anne spoke slowly in as low a voice as she could muster.

"Why am I here?" Anne asked. "What do you want with me?" Her heart was thumping so hard she could hear it.

There was no answer. Moving her fingers, she touched something behind her. A brick wall perhaps? Damp, cold and gritty. Her abductor was moving around the area, dragging something bulky towards her. He was having difficulty with it. The noise seemed to rebound around the walls. Where on earth was she? The cumbersome sounding object was dropped finally in front of her showering her legs with dust. She coughed.

"Sit," came the instruction.

"Did I hurt you?" Anne asked "Only you scared me when you grabbed me."

No reply again.

She gingerly extended her leg, and connected with something in front of her. Its surface gave a little bit. She lifted her foot and lowered it onto something soft and about twenty centimetres high. Well it seemed as though it might be soft at least.

Anne carefully bent her knees, bound by her tight pencil skirt. She knelt down slowly, her knees sinking into the soft surface. The manoeuvre was very awkward with her hands bound behind her back. Anne was not very supple nowadays, her knees and hips did not respond as well to the glucosamine tablets as when she was in her sixties.

"Please can you release my hands?" she asked in as kindly a voice as possible. "My shoulders and arms are really hurting."

No response again.

The surface she was kneeling on felt springy. A bed mattress she wondered? 'Oh please God may it be clean.' She could not bear the thought that it was soiled, stained, smelly or used. 'Please let me see the state of what I am knelt on.' The blindfold irritated her. 'Please release me,' her inner voice screamed. She heard the abductor move about again. A sour smell of body odour wafted towards her. It was making the situation even worse. The smell reminded her of her father's old nylon shirts, which when ironed, smelt just like this. He was brought up before deodorants and would not use them as he thought they were not manly. The shirts were used for years because they never seemed to wear out. The smell was pungent, and it never washed out, stuck like glue in the fibres.

She thought immediately of John. His hygiene was impeccable, he always wore freshly laundered clothes, and always used deodorant and aftershave He was a real gentleman. She was missing him so much already. He would sort this out, no question about it. He would take command. Had he already noticed her absence? What was he doing? Major Ross must also have realised something has happened; he must have missed her by now? She was due down with her final analysis at six o'clock.

The abductor was moving again.

"What do you want with me?" Again she tried to project a calm demeanour. She did not want him to feel threatened by her, to agitate him, so that she might put herself in more danger than she could already be in.

The smell became stronger. She felt him moving behind her. She had remained kneeling. Suddenly he pulled at the rope around her wrists. He was untying them, thank goodness.

"Shit," he said under his breath as he struggled with the second knot. The rope came away. Her hands shot down to her side, but he grabbed her right arm before she had a chance to rub her wrist. Her shoulders ached, and were stiff and sore. Her left arm was still down by her side, loose. Too late, he grabbed her wrist and brought it forward. Both wrists were tied together again. Well at least they are less painful in front of me. Anne leant forward, put her hands on the mattress and lowered her hips until she was sitting down, with her legs to one side.

It had become quiet again. Was he staring at her? Then she heard his footsteps going towards the door. The door was opened and she heard him go through it, and shut it before locking it.

'Oh, oh my goodness,' her body began shaking, her heart raced. She was alone. 'Where? Why? How long for? Calm down, calm down. Breathe slowly. Come on, calm down. You are not hurt, you are alive. What is the worst that can happen – no don't think about that.'

She listened. Nothing. She listened again. Her ears had become like huge satellite dishes, straining to hear something, anything. Nothing. No traffic sounds, no other sounds at all, not even birds chattering. Where on earth was she? It certainly smelt as though she was in a large empty space. A factory? Perhaps she was in a basement?

She sat there, and tried to remember all that had happened today. Answering the door of her bungalow, after she had popped home for her lab coat, she had a blanket thrown over her head and she was immediately forced to walk outside. She thought they headed to the car park, and then a car door was opened and she was pushed into the car foot well. The space was very narrow, and her tight skirt made it really difficult. The car had rocked her from side to side around bends. She did not think she was in there long, was it perhaps ten minutes? Her panic had been off the scale, her breathing quick, and her mind in chaos.

Abducted? Kidnapped? How great a danger was she in? When it stopped, she had to be helped out and then she remembered being pushed as she walked over long hummocky grass, along a gravel path, down some steps, that felt uneven like brick. How many steps had she come down? Sufficient to take her down to a basement? It would explain the lack of noises. Why was she here? She had not been roughly handled. Why did she not make a fuss when she was blindfolded? Why had she been so compliant – fear? Surprise? Anne thought of all the things she should have done. She should have slammed the door of the bungalow, she should have shouted; she could have sat on the ground so she could not be pushed along.' Why was I so stupid? So compliant?'

"Stupid woman," she shouted out loud. The words echoed around the room. "Stupid, stupid woman," she cried out again. The tears welled up, and then flooded down her face. 'Well, that will ruin my foundation won't it? Stop it!'

She mopped her face as best as she could by using her tied wrists.

'Think of all the good things. Right, I have shoes on, I am dressed, and my hair and makeup are done. I have had breakfast. A shame it had not been late evening, as at least I would have had a couple of glasses of wine.'

Anne calmed down and waited, and waited for something to happen. Her hips and knees were so uncomfortable. Time passed really slowly.

A noise caught her attention. Footsteps. Footsteps down the steps. A pause, then the door lock was being opened.

"Hello," Anne spoke. "Hello?"

No reply. She could hear the door closing and footsteps closing in on her. Another pause, then the footsteps changed direction, away from her?

She could hear what sounded like a plastic carrier bag being opened. The footsteps returned to her.

"Food," the abductor spoke firmly. She heard and then felt something being put onto the mattress.

"Can I please have my hands untied and my blindfold removed? Please? I promise not to look at you. My wrists are hurting so much, can you at least let me eat, even if you tie them up again afterwards? I will not move. I am an elderly lady, I'm not going to hurt you," Anne pleaded. She raised her tied wrists in front of her, pleading.

Cold fleshy hands took hold of her wrists. My goodness was he really going to untie them? The rope was loosened. Rubbing her wrists, she could feel the imprint of the rope in them, they were sore. She remained still. The footsteps grew quieter as he left her. The door opened, and closed with the key once more turning in the lock. Waiting a few moments, Anne reached up to remove the blindfold. She pushed it up off her eyes, and over her head. It was just a length of torn white cloth, probably from an old shirt.

The room was very gloomy. A weak shaft of light emitted from the tiny window high up on the opposite old bare brick wall. She looked around the room.

Paint cans littered one corner, all stacked haphazardly. There were dozens of them. The other corner was full of old gardening tools. They all looked neglected. Old hoes, soil colanders and terracotta plant pots stacked in leaning piles, with broken shards of terracotta on the floor. A very old wooden ladder, paint splattered from many years use, was slung from a couple of hooks along the wall, underneath the window. Cobwebs and dirt covered most things, clearly visible even from this side of the room.

Cobwebs. Oh my goodness – spiders! Anne had a fear of spiders, not as bad as when she was young and would scream in distress until her mother came to remove even the smallest of spiders. Her father used to laugh at her. Nowadays, it was only large bodied spiders that bothered her, really only because they moved so quickly and she could not bring herself to kill one. Let's hope they were hibernating, if they did such a thing.

Anne sat there and pondered where she was. It certainly looked like either an old garage, or basement of a large house. Malvern, if she was there, was awash with Victorian houses with basements. She now noticed stacks of old car tyres. She could not tell where she was. The window was most likely at garden height, meaning she was in a basement, rather than a garage. The floor seemed to be dirt, dry where she sat on the mattress, with damp, mossy brick walls on three of the four sides. The door was old and wooden, wide, solid and heavy looking. Most of the paint had peeled off years ago.

She suddenly remembered the mattress she was sat on, she looked down to inspect it. Thank goodness, it was old but clean, no stains in the middle. She breathed a huge sigh of relief; it would have been too much to have had to lie on a soiled, stinking mattress. Her eyes landed on the plate and glass on the floor next to the mattress.

She picked up the plate; it was china, with a pattern of roses on a white background. A doorstep of a sandwich sat squarely on it. The bread was springy white and hand cut, from a crusty loaf. Well buttered, with Brie and tomato slices inside. Really nice looking and well made, obviously by someone who had a robust appetite. Normally Anne would have dainty sandwiches, but the mornings' stress had increased her hunger. She used both hands to pick it up, as it was so thick. Taking a careful bite, and then satisfied to its taste, she consumed the lot very quickly. 'Gosh that was good'. She felt revived, almost cared for. Who would make such a lovely sandwich? Her abductor had smelt so badly, but had brought a pretty plate and a really decent sandwich. What an odd combination. The glass was full of creamy milk, and she drained the glass slowly. 'That's nicer than my normal skimmed milk,' she thought.

She sat there and looked at the empty plate and glass. Now another worry surfaced, the milk had set her bladder off. When had she last been to the bathroom? How long should she wait, perhaps someone would come soon and release her. What could she do if no one came?

Anne looked around the room. Nothing obvious. She looked again – what about a paint pot?

She listened first to make sure no one was coming. No sounds. She raised herself from the mattress. Her hips and knees were stiff and sore. She moved her hips from side to side to loosen them. Her skirt was going to be a problem, tight and calf length. 'Just have to cope. Get on with it Anne,' she told herself.

Listening out all the time, she tiptoed over to the paint pots. Were there any with loose lids? She wanted a large paint pot, easier to use she reckoned. She carefully moved some, nervously checking for spiders all the time, in the semi darkness. Dusk was approaching and it would be totally dark by four o'clock. She found two very large tins; both had lids on, but felt virtually empty, or most likely had dried up paint inside. What could she use to open the lids?

She crept over to the garden tools and saw what she thought might be the handle of a hand fork or trowel. She pulled it, trying really carefully not to let anything fall and make a noise. She stopped and listened again. Nothing. The hand trowel came free of the other tools. That might do the job. She tried the first paint pot lid, its rim twisted as she tried to prize the lid off, the old paint was obviously holding onto the lid. Anne kept trying for a few minutes. It moved just a bit, giving her hope. She tried all around the rim, raising the lid slightly with each easing, until eventually it released. She lifted the lid off with the trowel, being careful not to get paint on her fingers. As she thought, old dried up paint inside. Right that would do.

246

Anne had never been good at squatting. When she had travelled abroad in her youth, and had come across the dreaded squat loo, she had decided the best way to cope, was to remove her knickers and trousers if she was wearing them, and then put them on again afterwards. She used this ploy now. Feeling terribly exposed, what if her abductor came in now? She used the tin, and then put her underwear back on in seconds, pushed her skirt down, and put the lid on the tin. 'Thank goodness for that.'

She felt rather pleased with herself, as she tiptoed back to the mattress. The lack of water and toilet paper was going to be a major headache if she was here overnight. She just was not used to poor hygiene. Anne was so fastidious about it that she often felt like tapping people on the shoulder to remind them to wash their hands, instead of letting them head out of the public toilets with them touching the doors with their dirty hands.

She was too old for all this, feeling all of a sudden a victim. She was not in control of the situation, unable to solve the problem. Anne was not used to this. She was the person always in command, solving problems for herself and everyone else. Used to being a spinster, she coped. She was proud of her coping ability. Now, she had no control. Tears came to her eyes, and then progressed slowly down each side of her face, she tried to keep her head up high, to keep her composure, but it was all too much for her. She allowed her chin to drop, and she looked down at the floor, heaved and sighed, and the tears just flowed.

She sobbed. She wallowed in the situation. Then just as suddenly, she found her inner strength. 'Anne, you just take control. Stop wallowing. Stop this minute! It will not improve the situation at all. Goodness what a sight you must look now. I bet my mascara has run? What must I look like?' She held her head up high. 'Just get on with it,' she told herself briskly.

247

Anne knelt down on the mattress, carefully folding her legs, trying to find the most comfortable position for her hips. The trouble with sitting cross-legged was, although it offered a little bit of comfort, with her skirt up to her thighs, it was just too cold. She thought back to her junior school days, when in assembly everyone had to sit cross-legged. Good old days. 'I wonder what everyone is doing now?' Anne had resisted the trend to look up on the Internet about long lost friends. It would be difficult to discuss her life now, so it was easier not to try.

She so wished she had worn trousers this morning. She had not as John always admired her in her tight long pencil skirts, with her kitten heels helping her swing her hips attractively. Always giving a little more wiggle when she saw John, and hoping he was watching. I love it when he calls me 'songbird.' 'Come on John, come and find me, rescue me, I need you, I need you so much. The operation really needs me, what on earth have you done today?' The deadline was in a less than a couple of days. Would they have got the Regiment involved yet? And GCHQ? They must realise I am missing. Surely they are looking for me. Who was GCHQ monitoring? The abductors? Have they had a ransom demand?

All she knew about her abductor was that he was older, and was sweating profusely, probably from the adrenalin, appreciated good honest food, was looking after her and did not seem to be going to hurt or threaten her. 'Was he holding out for a ransom? How much and from whom? 'It would certainly not be from her family, as she didn't have anyone now. 'From the government? 'Who would know about her role in the trial? She was sure that she was fully protected by tight security. Had her security been breached? Did someone know about Princess Margaret Gardens? She sat there continuing to go through different scenarios. She became aware of time passing. No one came. She realised she was getting very cold, and weary. She pulled her cashmere cardigan around her, and curled up in as tight a ball as she could muster, to try and keep warm.

She woke to the sound of footsteps coming near her. Where was she? Curled up on what? She opened her eyes; it took a short while to remember where she was. It was very dark, and then the light was switched on, a very dim light. Oh no, she had removed her blindfold, would she be in trouble? She closed her eyes quickly, and pretended to be asleep. 'Do not breathe quickly, keep calm.' Something was draped over her. It felt soft, warm, and clean smelling, wonderful. Something else was put carefully on the mattress. Her plate and empty glass were picked up. The door was opened, the light switched off, and then the door was closed and locked. She listened carefully, opened her eyes, moved her head, no one was there in the gloom. She was alone.

She had a new duvet over her, it was without a cover, but was a feather duvet, it draped around her exquisitely. What was the other item? She looked around and saw a large tight plastic bag; it was instantly recognisable as a pillow. Brand new. Clean. Bliss. She unwrapped it.

Her abductor obviously did not wish her any harm. She pulled the duvet tight around her, and carefully placed her head onto the pillow, closed her eyes and slept, spiders forgotten.

Chapter 42

Deadline minus seventeen hours
07.00, 26th March
Unknown Location

The weak sunlight woke Anne. The light strained through the grubby window, casting a shaft of light across the duvet. What time was it? Her watch confirmed what she thought. Seven o'clock. She sat up quickly. She felt terrible. She fluffed her hair into shape. Running her tongue over her teeth, they felt disgusting. She would have rubbed a finger over her teeth, except her hands were dirty. Worse was to follow, she stroked her cheeks and chin. Stubble. This was all too much. Her best-kept secret was her beard and moustache. Every morning, straight after her shower, she sat in a bright light to pluck all offending hairs away, and then shaved. She would die, if anyone, anyone at all knew about her moustache and beard, especially John. The shame of it was too much. Again, she felt her chin; at least five strong hairs resisted her stroke. Then she noticed something on the duvet, small droppings, and a quick look confirmed her worst fears. Mice droppings! She flicked the duvet up, to throw them onto the floor. She sat back horrified; a mouse had crawled over her in the night. 'Oh my goodness'. Think positive, at least it was not rat's droppings, she laughed, things could always be worse. She had not heard the footsteps, and the door opening startled her. Was she going to see who her abductor was?

Chapter 43

Deadline minus eighteen and a half hours 05.30 26th March Princess Margaret Gardens

John arrived early at 5.30am. He had not slept. Where was Anne? Where was his songbird? Was she safe? He had spent hours reading her notes and the analysis on the computer. Isobel had uploaded the complete file to him. He knew all about the toxin being administered covertly. They had all been shocked, but over the weeks and months, they had all discussed the issue. It had been accepted that this would be the only way the government could ensure the cost cutting needed to save the NHS and also, more importantly to them, that suffering was going to be reduced for all those affected directly or indirectly by dementia.

He could see how the general public would see all the benefits and in the main welcome them. Yes, it would have been great, if they could have had the choice to have the nanodrones, but the fear and arguments were the same as for euthanasia; that relatives could put pressure on them either to 'fight on' with their illnesses, even when the person had had enough pain and suffering, or relatives wanted them out of the way, to free up their inheritances and their time spent caring or visiting them. Choice would mean very difficult decisions needing to be made, once people were declining in health. When was the right time to decide when to have the nanodrones? If done covertly, then none would be faced with the decision. The main problem, of course, would be the unions, the pharmaceutical companies and religious groups. All of them had a lot to lose.

The pharmaceutical company producing the vaccine, surely knew that they were going to be the facilitator of this? They must have signed a gagging order, and most likely would be charging a vastly increased price to cover part of their other losses from selling the vast array of medicines for the elderly.

John thought that his research on communications was sensitive, but this project was a ticking time bomb for the government if it went wrong!

He had heard all the discussions, all the pros and cons, particularly when Isobel had had a go at Anne the other night, about the repercussions. He agreed with Anne though, that all that was happening was that people would die earlier, before they had had to endure possibly years of decline, mainly being looked after in nursing homes at huge expense and often not with very good quality care. Relatives would be spared years of heartbreak. Surely this was a good thing?

'It took me ages to get an appointment with the doctor last week, ten days before I could see him,' John thought. 'Ridiculous, something has got to change. The system is in meltdown, something major has to change. This has got to be the way that will succeed.' He pressed on studying the research.

Major Ross' Segway was shown as being on its way. Ten minutes later the Command Centre's door opened. Major Ross strode in straight to John.

"Just come from a meeting this morning at Credenhill, John. GCHQ have been listening to all likely sources of abduction. The Regiment have been searching disused premises locally. No news yet, John. Nothing is showing up at all. There has been no communication from anyone about her disappearance. No ransom, no leaks to the press, we are all at a loss at the moment." Major Ross walked over to his office. "Did you finish reading the data? What do you think? As far as you can tell, do you think the maths for the calibrations seems ready to go? Major Ross asked. "What comeback have we had about the paralysis situation?"

"I have spoken to both Sarah and Isobel this morning, and they are still completely unsure about why it happened. It can't just be written off as a possible allergic shock, if we are to roll out this trial. The problem is not knowing, how likely others are to react in the same way. Tests are being carried out today, on our instruction, to see if Cilla is allergic to any other substances. We should get the results later today."

Outside Princess Margaret Gardens.

Mark, Paul and Bill walked towards the reception doors.

"Is something up?" asked Mark.

"Everyone seems really jumpy and on edge," Paul confirmed.

254

Bill nodded. "The pressure is really on to get our project signed off in time."

"Are they going to be able to do it?" Paul asked Bill.

"It will be a bit tight, but Anne will do her best. You know the problem with Cilla is unresolved and also the other test resident who has died early. Results are still being sought for him, to make sure he has died from natural causes," he replied.

"It had better go through as Sarah has produced the toxin in production quantities. Been working her socks off." Paul said.

They all entered the main reception area and Bill went to the old laboratory, whilst Mark and Paul, turned right to enter their doorway.

"Did you notice his eye? Looks a little sore don't you think?" Mark asked Paul.

"Didn't really notice to be honest," Paul replied, as he used his security pass.

Bill walked down the lab towards Isobel, at the far end.

"How is she?" Isobel whispered, whilst keeping her eyes on her research work. Bill looked around, saw Sarah and then raised his eyebrows, and nodded towards the exit.

"Let's go down to the rest room," Isobel said, putting her research papers into her desk and locking the drawer. She followed Bill, out into the reception area, and then to the rest room. The room was empty. They checked out the ladies and gents toilets, before they spoke.

"She seems ok. She's keeping calm at the moment. I took her a duvet and pillow, so that she's not cold. This had better work Isobel. It was the scariest thing I have ever

255

done in my life. I used that burka I told you my mum had for that am-dram production, this morning. Anne had better not have a clue that it's us. We will be in such serious trouble if she works it out. I know we are only keeping her for a couple of days, but it's still kidnapping. Anyway she needs some toiletries. I have raided mine, together with a towel and toilet paper. I am going back at twelve. I don't think John or Major Ross will miss me at that time, they will think I've gone for lunch for a change. It should only take me half an hour to drive there and back. We are going to release her, aren't we? I think we might have to drug her to move her, if we can't let her escape herself. She was just so surprisingly compliant when I took her. I think she just could not comprehend what was happening. I don't think we'll be as lucky next time," Bill updated her.

"Sssshh!" Isobel said putting her finger to her lips and then quickly disappeared into the ladies' toilets, locking the door. Bill took his leave hastily, just passing John as he entered.

Chapter 44

Deadline minus fifteen hours
09.00, 26th March
Basement – unknown location

She had eaten her breakfast of cornflakes and a croissant. She had drunk from the flask of tea that had been left together with another rose patterned china cup and saucer and the matching milk jug. The burka had really shocked her. She could see the black casual shoes and the bottom of his trousers. Her request for toiletries, most importantly toilet paper, was listened to in silence, and his reply,

"Twelve o'clock," was spoken in a deep 'put on' voice before he turned and left the room. The paint pot was used again. She had better get another one ready for later.

Walking over to the cans, she looked for mice droppings and spiders. Plenty of woodlice under each paint pot; she had no problem with them. After setting up another can, she walked over to the window and stood on her tiptoes. The window was much too high up. What could she stand on? Hang on a minute, her brain suddenly kicked into gear. 'Get back in control Anne.' There was the old ladder which was slung on wall brackets under the window, surely if he was not going to be back until twelve, she had loads of time to try and escape.

She walked over to the door and put her ear to the wood. Anne listened and could not hear a thing, apart from a car going past. She walked quickly back to the ladder. Was she strong enough to lift it? She reached up onto her toes and lifted one end off the wall hanger. She dropped the end immediately. Gosh it was very heavy. The ladder had caught her cardigan and snagged it. 'Bloody hell.' She loved this cardigan. Anne caught her breath. She then went to try and lift the other end from the other hanger. The angle of the ladder was now 45 degrees and it meant she could not lift the other end off the wall hanger. Anne needed to rest the loose end higher up. She looked around. Car tyres? Eyeing them up, she thought a pile of three tyres high might do it. She walked over to them, yes they might do. She picked one up, and thought that it was not too heavy. She rolled it over to the window wall. Her skirt was now getting filthy with dirt, moss and cobwebs all over it. She brushed her skirt in a vain attempt to clean it. She brought two more tyres over and with a struggle and several attempts, she managed to balance one above the other.

'In my heyday, I wouldn't have had a problem at all. What was the time?' she checked her watch. 9.30am, she had plenty of time. She managed to lift the loose end of the ladder up sufficiently to balance on top of the stacks of tyres. The other end came off its hanger and thumped down onto the floor, causing the tyres to topple as the ladder clattered loudly down, hitting her hard on the ankle and also hurting her wrist. She collapsed in pain. She sat down on a tyre and rubbed her ankle. Had anyone heard the noise? She sat still for several minutes and no one came.

Well at least the ladder was off the wall. The next question was did she have the strength to move such a heavy old long ladder?

This was going to be difficult; she had never manhandled a ladder before, never needed to. It was really heavy, and long, and incredibly difficult to manoeuvre. She made several attempts, but could not manage to get the one end high enough to rest it onto the window sill. There must be another way? She looked at the tyres again, and finally came up with an idea. If she could make two piles of tyres, and balance the ladder across them like a platform, she might be able to stand on the horizontal ladder and see out of the window. She stacked the tyres into piles of three, and with great difficulty, managed to get the ladder across them like a bridge. It was exhausting and Anne was sweating both from exhaustion and adrenalin.

'All I need to do now, is climb up on the tyres and balance on the ladder.' She pulled her skirt right up to her hips, showing off her still shapely legs, and kicked off her kitten heels. Very gingerly she clambered up the tyres and tried to balance on the ladder rungs. The rungs hurt her bare feet, and then the third rung she stepped on, creaked – 'Oh please don't break'. Would it hold? She was so scared. The piles of tyres were so unstable, and her legs shook.

She managed to balance long enough to slowly stand upright. Her legs started trembling, as she tried madly to grab hold of anything to steady herself. Anne could just see out of the window, her eyes were level with the lowest part of the glass frame. She saw that there was a garden wall on the other side of a garden. Where was she? The ladder was beginning to slide. Anne jumped down, and immediately regretted doing so, her right ankle jarred as her weight landed on it. She bent over and rubbed it quickly. Her skirt was still up around her waist. She brushed the dirt off her feet and slipped on her shoes.

'The platform is too low; I will never be able to get out of the window at that height. I've got to make it higher?'

For the next ten minutes, Anne built the tyre piles higher, to five each side. She figured that she could now rest the ladder on top of the tyres and then fix it onto the wall hangers so that it would lay flat on top of the tyres, giving her a firm platform to reach higher up the window. She struggled to build the tyres higher, and then get the ladder back up, but she persevered. Once everything was in place, she pulled on the ladders' front edge to check its security. 'Firm, thank goodness'. She checked her watch again. 'Still fine for time,' she thought. Now that she reckoned the ladder was safe, she looked around for something to break the glass windowpane. She looked amongst the garden tools. The old hoe, with the long handle looked ideal. She picked it up, and used it as a crutch to help her climb the tyres again. Once on top, she looked out of the window. There was a Malvern stone garden wall curved around two sides of the front garden. Mature shrubs surrounded the lawn. She noticed the street lamp was a Victorian gas lamp. She was in Malvern! There were only two places in Malvern with the old renovated gas lamps left. She would know where she was, if she could get out of here. She carefully lifted the hoe, until she held it like a javelin. Clinging to the windowsill, she drew back her hand, and thrust the hoe towards the glass. The old thin glass shattered easily, making an enormous din as it fell to the floor. She quickly enlarged the hole using the hoe. Shaking her clothes carefully, she tried to remove the shards of glass from them, checking her hands she worked quickly expecting the sound of breaking glass had attracted attention. She had to try and get herself through the window. She had no idea how far the drop was, but it didn't look far, from the angle she was looking. She pushed down on her hands on the windowsill and gave a little jump. 'Have to try harder,' she thought and tried again, putting more effort into her jump. 'Must believe I can do it'. She landed with her stomach on the window frame, half in and half out of the window. She noticed both hands were bleeding. 'Just get on with it Anne.' She wiggled her hips forward and her body moved through the opening a little more. Her head and upper body were now through, and she quickly checked what she was going to land on, just as she slipped completely out. Landing on a grassy bank, she quickly stood up, no time to think about what hurt. She looked around her. 'Where should she run?'

She could hear someone shout from inside the basement. Her escape had been heard.' Quick! Run!' She ran towards an old wooden gate at the end of a curving gravel path. The gravel was murder on her stockinged feet; she jumped sideways onto the lawn and ran on the grass until the last moment at the gate. Her ankle was really hurting, but she couldn't slow down, as someone was running along the path behind her. She flung open the low gate, and ran out onto the tarmac pavement. She quickly sized up the main road in front of her, and the Common opposite. She knew exactly where she was. She was only in Malvern Link. She turned to the left. An elderly couple walking up the road, on the opposite side, looked over at her. She quickly pulled her skirt down over her thighs. They just walked on, talking to each other and looking back at her.

She was on the corner of a road junction; a car was pulled up waiting at the junction to turn left onto the main road. She ran towards the car on the drivers' side shouting.

"Help me, help me!"

The driver opened his window.

"What's up, luv?"

"Please, please help me." and she rushed around the front of the car and got into the passenger seat. "Drive, just drive." She implored. He looked at her, and turned left out onto the main road.

"Thank you, oh thank you." She kept repeating, looking behind them to see who was following. Just then she saw the community hospital entrance on the left hand side.

"Oh pull in here, pull in here!" The driver pulled in, and she jumped out just as he reached the car park barriers.

"Thank you!" she shouted back as she ran full pelt into the reception area.

She ran up to the reception desk. The room was deserted except for two patients waiting on the red sofas near the consulting rooms and two receptionists sat waiting at the reception desk. She looked around and said to everyone,

"Please, please help me." They looked blankly at her.

Her hands were dripping blood, she had no shoes on, and her tights were all torn. Her clothes were snagged and dirty. Where on earth had she been? Everyone just stayed where they were and looked at her, trying to take in what they were seeing.

Anne kept looking towards the main entrance doors, checking if she was being followed. She decided to take action, she must hide. She ran around to the back of the receptionists' desk, and crouched under the desk overhang, by the receptionists' chair legs. Whispering,

"Help me, help me."

The older, stockier receptionist picked up her phone, and said

"Mr Chapman, can you come straightaway to reception. We have a situation; an elderly lady is here, in great distress." She put the phone down.

"It's alright luv, you are safe here. You're safe," she repeated, "Calm down. Would you like a cup of tea?"

Anne just turned to face the desk wall, trying to hide herself from everyone.

She heard the internal door open and quick footsteps coming towards her.

"Where is she?" a young male voice asked.

"Under the desk here," the older receptionist replied.

She heard the sharp click of his shoes around the desk, and she felt the proximity of his legs.

"Hello. What's your name?" he spoke in a commanding but soft voice.

"Anne King." She spoke to the desk wall, afraid still to turn around. "I've been abducted and need your help."

"I see." Anne could not see him look at both receptionists. The other patients were still sat on the sofas, observing what was going on. They looked at each other and the young mum shrugged her shoulders, as they couldn't work out what was happening.

Mr Chapman stood up and put his hands on his hips. What was he to do?

"Where is home Anne?"

"Princess Margaret Gardens," replied Anne.

"I see." Mr Chapman knew of the retirement bungalows. "Well Anne, why don't you come with me, and I will get one of the nurses to look at your hands?"

Anne recoiled "No, I'm being followed. I've been abducted, you must help me."

"I am sure, Anne, that we can ensure your safety. Just come with me, and we will look after you."

Anne could sense that he was being patronising. He obviously did not believe her.

"I am Anne King, and I am a research scientist, working in Malvern. Please phone QinetiQ and tell them to let Major Ross know I'm here immediately. National security is at risk."

"I'm sure it is Anne," he said as he looked at the elderly, dishevelled lady underneath the desk.

'Dementia,' he thought. 'I think we might need to admit her, and after her hands have been dressed, we can contact social services. '

"Let's just take you to the minor injuries department, so we can see to your hands. Take my hand, I'll protect you."

Anne thought the only way of getting out of here was to go with him. She rose. Gosh! Was she stiff and in pain! She stood up, as straight as she could, keeping a very close eye on the entrance doors. She held her head up high, with her shoulders back and followed the doctor across the large open reception area, checking all the time the main entrance doors.

"Gillian, let them know we are coming over," the consultant asked the receptionist.

The two patients followed the proceedings with great interest, without saying or doing anything. Anne walked past them. She was feeling a little calmer now. 'Let's get my hands dressed and then I'll get a taxi', she planned.

Just then there was an almighty commotion at the entrance doors. They were flung open and a lady in a white laboratory coat came flying in. She ran straight up to the reception desk.

"Have you seen an elderly lady, in a dishevelled state in the last couple of minutes?" she panted. Both receptionists looked towards the minor injuries unit door, where Anne, with a look of horror, was just disappearing.

"Yes. Do you know her?" Gillian replied.

"Oh thank goodness, she has just walked out of the home, straight through a glass window that she smashed. Is she alright?"

Gillian picked up the internal phone. "Mr Chapman, we have a lady here who knows Anne"

"I will be straight out."

"The consultant who is looking after her will be out in a minute."

Isobel, in her lab coat, stood there waiting. Her heart was pounding. The door to the minor injuries unit swung open and a young, very smart man walked towards her.

"Hello, I'm the Manager of Princess Margaret Gardens retirement home. I hear that Anne got as far as here. She really is very tiring. Her dementia is getting worse, this time we are going to have to transfer her to the secure unit. I am so sorry she has bothered you. Is she alright?" Isobel looked Mr Chapman directly in the eye.

"Just very scared, talking about abduction," said Mr Chapman.

"She does that, every time she thinks she has been abducted. Usually thinks she is a researcher. It's a funny old disease isn't it? Where do they get these ideas? I am so sorry she has wasted your time. I will take her back with me, and get our nurse, Maggie, to look after her. You did say she had hurt herself?"

"Yes, her hands are bleeding. If you can wait, we can see to them straightaway."

"Oh I wish I could, but we are just about to have an inspection. Don't worry, we can see to her cuts. If there is any problem, then my nurse will bring her back down, when she is calmer. Is that alright?"

Mr Chapman thought for a minute, but seeing how desperate the manager was to leave, he thought it should be fine, as they would have trained nurses at the home.

"Fine. I will just ask the nurse to accompany her to your car."

"Lovely.' Isobel fought back her impatience. She went to her car, which was parked on the double yellow lines straight outside the entrance. She would be better able to get Anne into the car, out of sight of the reception area parked there.

Gliding her across the lobby, the male nurse pushed the wheelchair out into the car park and down the path to Isobel's car. Anne saw Isobel.

"Oh Isobel, thank goodness it's you. This is Isobel from the bungalows, she will look after me," she said to the nurse.

The nurse handed the bare footed lady to the manager in the white coat.

"Goodbye. Look after yourself," said the pleasant nurse to the old lady, as she was helped into the back seat of the car.

Isobel pressed the internal door locking mechanism.

"Just in case," she said to Anne.

Anne sank back into the car seat, and relaxed. She looked out of the windows at the normality of life passing by her. The shoppers, the dog walkers, everyone just going about their everyday lives, totally unaware of the stress and danger she had been in.

"Isobel, has Major Ross got the SAS involved yet? You will never guess, I've only been down the road. I hadn't a clue where I was, until I got out. I can tell him exactly where I was kept. It's been terrible. I haven't been hurt, except when I escaped. My hands aren't bleeding so much now." She turned her hands over to see the palms. "I think I have a little glass in them, but we can soon get that out. Obviously Major Ross will want a debriefing. Tell me how is the trial going? Have you managed to explain Cilla's paralysis and what about the other person's results? Have you been in charge? Has John got involved?"

Isobel looked straight ahead and kept driving. Princess Margaret Gardens was only five minutes down the main Eastnor Road. They turned left and pulled into the car park at the back.

Isobel got out and opened the back door for Anne. She slid across the seat, and stepped onto the gritty car park.

"Ow!" she reacted as the grit hurt her bare, sore feet. Isobel walked alongside her, holding her elbow, and said nothing. They drew nearer the back veranda. Anne saw the back door to her bungalow. Home at last. She immediately thought about changing her underwear and clothing and having a lovely shower. Isobel's hand took her arm gently and guided her away.

"Anne, sorry we cannot go to your home yet. Major Ross wants to debrief you straightaway. He might also want all your clothes for forensics. He has asked me to take you to a room away from everyone as we haven't told anyone that you are missing."

Anne looked at her. 'Oh. I suppose that makes sense,' she thought. She allowed Isobel to guide her to a muddy overgrown path at the back of the car park. She had never noticed it before, as it looked as though it went to the scrubland between them and the new Peak View Village car park.

"Where on earth are we going, Isobel?"

"Apparently there is a door to an unused room here at the back. I think it is part of the tunnel system. Don't really know. I am sure this is where he meant. I've got the key," she said as she showed Anne a large rusty key and put it back in her pocket.

They walked the few yards down the incline, with overgrown brambles and nettles overhanging the path. Her cold feet were now really sore and muddy. They walked down to an old wooden door, set in an arch of brickwork. Isobel knocked no answer. She reached inside her lab coat pocket for the key, retrieved it and put it in the lock and opened the door. It creaked open to show a completely dark void. You could smell the damp, and feel the earth floor. Isobel found the light switch, and switched it on. The bare bulb lit up the brick tunnel, empty except for a couple of old tables, Anne recognised from the old lab.

"Anne wait there, and I will go and let Major Ross know you are here. Won't be long." Isobel left the room, and locked the door behind her.

"Just in case there is anyone around," she explained.

Anne sat down on the table. 'Should have asked her to bring me some warm clothing and shoes,' she looked around her; it was obviously a tunnel that had had a brick wall constructed at this end with a doorway, but she could not see where the tunnel went, as it disappeared around a corner about 50 yards away. It was extremely cold, she started to shiver.

She stood there and, thought over the day's events. Major Ross would obviously need to know everything. Hopefully then she could go and get a bath and clean herself up and pluck her chin, after her hands had been dressed. She ran her fingers over her chin and jaw line. 'Oh my goodness, I cannot wait to sort this out. I expect Major Ross will want me straight back in the lab. We must be getting near the very end of the time limit.' Anne's bladder was bursting, despite not having had anything to drink for what seemed like hours. She could wait; it wouldn't be long now.

Isobel walked at a brisk rate into the reception area, wiping her shoes on the mat, to get most of the mud off them. She crossed to the rest room and went into the ladies' toilets, and after checking no one else was there, she quickly washed the rest of the mud off her shoes in the basin, she dried them under the hand dryer, putting them on just as someone came into the room. She waited a minute, and then came out of the toilet area and found John making a drink.

"Coffee?" John asked, shaking the jar." I was coming to find you for those last test results. Major Ross has gone to find Sarah."

"No problem. I have just had a bite to eat, have you eaten yet?"

"To be honest Isobel, I don't have time, perhaps later on, when I have finished the report." John stepped nearer to her and whispered, "Have you heard anything about Anne yet?"

"Nothing at all, what do you think? Do you think she has gone off with the dossier?" Isobel offered.

John stared back at her with a jolt.

"Absolutely not, no way would she sell us out." He was amazed that Isobel even thought that was a possibility.

"See you in a minute then John." And at that Isobel left the room and walked slowly back to her desk.

Chapter 45

Deadline minus eleven hours
13.00, 26th March
Command Post

Major Ross picked up the phone.

"Yes?" He listened intently "Really, how long ago? The hospital, what the Malvern hospital? I see. You didn't confirm anything? OK. Thank you." He placed the phone back into its cradle. Well it sounded as though it could be Anne. 'Why isn't she back here then? Who collected her? Is she all right? It sounds as though she has been injured. Where on earth has she been? Well it seems as though she has been held against her will, certainly not stolen the dossier. Right, let's find her,' he immediately sent a coded message to GCHQ, asking for help, and then he phoned his men at the Regiment.

"Are our men still here? Right, we have had a sighting at the Malvern hospital. Get a dog unit down there straight away. Keep it quiet. Let's have it look like a dog walker. See if we can pick up a trail."

He replaced the phone.

16.00 The Tunnel.

Anne was now getting very cold. Her feet were the worst, and her hands were also now very sore, although the bleeding had stopped. She cradled them on her lap, palms upwards, protecting them from harm. She was worried about the dirt getting into the cuts. Where on earth was Major Ross? 'I am desperate for the loo, and to get my hands seen to.' She screamed to herself.

At last the door reopened, and Isobel appeared.

"Major Ross is so sorry Anne, he has to deal with an urgent response to Whitehall about the trial. They are really pressing him for the go ahead. He and John are working on your final analysis now."

"Why doesn't he come down now? I can finish the report in about an hour. My final analysis is complete except for the last death and Cilla?"

Isobel ignored the question and put down a small plastic bag, and a bottle of water.

"He asked me to bring you some food." Anne picked up the bag, being careful of the glass in her hand. The bag contained a packaged cheese and ham sandwich.

"Thank you Isobel. Can you open the pack please, my hands hurt."

Isobel came over, and took Anne's hands, turned them over and looked closely in the dim light.

"I think we should dress your hands Anne, while we are waiting for Major Ross, I will go and get some kit. OK?"

"Thank you Isobel, I really would appreciate that. Can you also bring me a coat I am freezing and something for my feet?" Isobel opened and relocked the door.

'Why does she still do that, surely I'm in no danger here?'

Isobel walked back to her desk.

'Not sure if I can go back soon,' she thought. 'Perhaps Bill could go?' She was still very mad at him. It was his fault they had had to move Anne. 'How on earth could anyone be so stupid as to leave her with her hands untied in a room with a ladder? Bloody mad!' Now they had the problem of having her here. 'What on earth are we going to do now? 'Plus Anne was injured, which Isobel had never wanted or planned. They had hoped to just keep her away from the trial long enough for the deadline to pass. 'I wonder if she has worked out that I am involved. Did the burka hide Bill enough for her not to recognise him? How are we going to get out of this?' She phoned Bill and asked him to come up to the lab. She wrote a note. Ten minutes later Bill was there.

"God you stink Bill, go home, wash and change your shirt."

"I'm so worried," he said.

She passed him the note, and then he screwed it up and put it in his pocket as instructed.

"Just go home first and change, everyone will wonder why you smell."

"I will. Where is the first aid kit?" Bill asked.

Isobel passed over the door key to the tunnel. Bill turned, and nodded. He walked quickly down the lab, quietly removed the first aid kit from the wall and left the lab.

Anne felt better for the sandwich and water, but really needed the loo; she crossed her legs as tight as possible. Just then the door opened, she jumped with shock. Was it Major Ross? Instead Bill came in; she could see the first aid kit in his hand.

"Hi Bill, did Major Ross send you?"

"Yes Anne. Are you all right my love? You look as though you have had a really bad time. Let's have a look at your hands. Isobel thinks you might have some glass in them." Bill reached for her hands, looked hard at them and then opened the first aid kit and started the fiddly and quite painful job of removing the shards of glass, and then dressing her hands.

"Bill, can you tell Major Ross, I really must see him now. Plus I really need to go to the toilet. I just cannot wait any longer. Can you tell him?" Bill nodded but did not look directly at her, as he walked slowly to the door. He then turned around and looked back at her then lowered his chin and left the tunnel.

Once more she was on her own. Her thoughts were in turmoil. She was putting two and two together. She had not really noticed before the age spots on Bill's hands, but just then, as he dressed her hands, she had noticed them. 'Were they the same as the person in the burka? Surely it can't be Bill? He was so benign, so innocent and kind? If it was Bill then why? What were his motives? After all he was here looking after her now? Why? Was Isobel in on it? Why

274

would they abduct her, after all these years of working and living cheek by jowl? What was going on? How much longer before she could go to the loo? At least her hands were now comfortable, clean and bandaged.

Bill walked slowly away from the door, up the muddy path, but instead of going to the laboratory, he walked to the car park and opened his car boot, taking out the two Waitrose plastic carrier bags. Closing the car boot, he checked that no one was looking and he walked quickly back down the muddy path, avoiding snagging his cardigan on the brambles. Checking again that no one was around, he reopened the door and entered the gloom.

Anne was now sat on one of the tables. Her face told of her puzzlement at Bill's return so soon.

"I have bought a few things for you Anne." He passed over the two carrier bags. "How are your hands now? Major Ross says he is still too busy to come over." He lied unconvincingly.

She looked inside the two bags.

"This is my shopping list from when I was in the basement isn't it?" She turned to Bill, "Bill? Surely not, why? Why on earth would you abduct me? What the hell's going on Bill?" Bill turned away from her.

"I'm so sorry Anne, so sorry. You were never meant to get hurt. Isobel just wanted you out of the way, long enough for the trial to be delayed, and then the earliest roll out would be next autumn."

"Isobel? What difference does it make to Isobel?"

"She hopes that the delay will affect the way of administering the vaccine I presume."

"So why are you involved?"

"She's blackmailing me Anne. It's all my fault Cilla is paralysed. All my fault, all my fault." Bill looked away.

"Your fault? Why on earth is it your fault?"

"I used the old toxin with the cell based vaccine, it's the reason she is paralysed."

"Why on earth did you do that?"

"I didn't want her to die, I wanted her to live even if she had dementia, and I expected her just to suffer from sickness and diarrhoea, that's all. The toxin obviously changed its strength with the new vaccine. Anne, she is the only person I have ever loved, except for my parents. I had held onto her CT scans and exchanged them to prevent her from having the doctored flu vaccine, but Amanda noted that Cilla was showing classic symptoms and told Sarah, who worked out what I had done. She urgently needed a test subject for the deadline to prove the case and told me she had no option but to use Cilla. It's entirely my fault. After Cilla was paralysed, Isobel worked out what I had done and has forced me to help her delay the sign off, by kidnapping you until after the deadline. I had no option but to agree to her threats, otherwise she was going to expose me to Major Ross."

Anne eased herself off the table, wincing as her ankles and feet touched the ground. She hobbled the couple of steps over to Bill, and put her arms around him and hugged him. Bill melted into Anne, his head on her shoulder, hands down by his side; tears welled up in his eyes, as he looked vacantly into the distance. Anne pulled away from him and held him by his arms, and looked directly into his eyes, then hugged him again, patting and rubbing his back, as though he was a small child.

This touching scene was suddenly shattered, as Isobel flew through the door, and slammed it shut.

"Bill, what the hell are you doing? What on earth is in those carrier bags?" she screamed as she rushed over to them. "She knows doesn't she? She knows." The pitch of Isobel's voice rose even higher.

Anne held onto Bill, and she continued to stare at Isobel. In a low, smooth voice Anne slowly said, "She does." She paused, nodded her head and repeated, "She does."

Isobel stood rooted to the spot; Anne could see she was working out what to do next. Isobel turned and rushed back to the door, went out and locked the door again. Muffled steps could be heard as she ran up the path.

She and Bill separated and just stood looking at each other, taking in the situation. They looked blankly at each other and at the locked door. Bill frowned.

"I think I have joined you Anne."

Anne nodded.

"I think you have."

Anne managed to get up onto the table again, taking the weight off her damaged ankles and feet. She rubbed her ankles, and winced. Her feet were freezing, and she suddenly realised she was cold to the core. She started shivering.

"Anne there's a big bath sheet in one of the bags." Bill came towards the table and started opening one of the carrier bags. He pulled out a huge dark brown bath sheet, and wrapped it around Anne's shoulders. She looked at the carrier bags, she remembered asking for toiletries, but most importantly, toilet paper, and two large bottles of water. She was desperate for the toilet, but now Bill was here.

"Bill, I am so sorry, but I am desperate for the toilet. What can I do?"

Bill looked around; the tunnel disappeared around the corner. He walked to the bend. Around the corner the tunnel was pitch black. He could not tell how long the tunnel was. He looked around but there was nothing except the two tables down by Anne.

"Anne we are going to have to make do. I will take the other table down to the bend, and place it on its end to form a screen. You will have to go down there, and squat behind it. Don't worry; I will stay up here, well out of the way. Use the paper sparingly, as we do not know how long we will be here."

Anne looked apprehensive, but was desperate; she hugged the bath sheet around her as she slid off the table.

"Bill you are so brilliant, let's move the table straight away please."

Bill took hold of one end, and Anne the other. Anne made sure she did not catch the dressings on her hands, as her hands were really sore. By putting the table on its end, it provided a six-foot high screen. Bill left her to it.

Anne came back after ten minutes.

"Better?" Bill asked.

"You cannot believe it. I'm so glad you bought those things for me."

She asked Bill to pour some water onto her fingertips, being careful of her dressings. She rubbed her fingers together as best she could, and dried her hands on the bath sheet.

"We had better keep most of the water to drink, Bill."

"I had felt so bad about you being in my basement. I knew how clean and tidy you are, and I knew how you would be suffering. I wish I had brought the duvet with me. It is so cold here, and if we are still here tonight it will be worse. I do think that Isobel is bound to come back with something for us, don't you?"

"Do you? What do you think Isobel will do now?" Anne asked.

"I have no idea, she has changed so much and I no longer know what she is thinking."

"Why did you get involved, Bill?"

Bill looked down, put his hands in his pockets, and hunched his shoulders.

Anne eased herself back onto the table and waited.

"Isobel had been talking to me in recent weeks, about her deep reservations about the inclusion of the nanodrones into the flu jab. Ever since her friend Rosemary came to visit her, and had spoken about how she had looked after her husband until he died, and how Rosemary felt it was her duty and privilege."

"Yes she told us, don't you remember, at my house?" Anne replied, "But that can't be the only reason surely?"

"She kept telling me, how when we all started here, the nanomedicine was to be an opt-in option for everyone who wanted it. She was proud to be one of the top researchers that would develop a product that would provide a choice for people dreading the onset of dementia; a technology that removes making a decision about calling it a day. You know all the reasons Anne."

"Yes, I understand, but I just don't agree."

"She had asked me several times, if I agreed with her. The night before your drinks party to remember Jean, she came round to my home, and spoke for over two hours about it. I told her all about Cilla, and how we just clicked straight away, I just know she is the woman for me, I just know it. She is so kind Anne, and quite quiet, just like me. We have had drinks together every evening since we met at the village bar. Of course I realised that dementia was beginning to take hold very early on, but I thought if I could prevent her having the nanodrones, I might be able to look after her. I have asked myself, could I be her carer? Have I got the stamina, and the patience? Quite frankly, did I want the burden of looking after her once her mind has gone? I reckon I would have been fine, until she no longer knew me and recognised me. Now I have to think about what will happen if she remains paralysed, Major Ross doesn't seem willing to help fund her care so I'm thinking of selling my parent's home."

"Your parent's home?"

"Yes, that's where you were yesterday, in the basement."

"That explains the lovely crockery."

"Yes my Mum always had lovely things, always very pretty and feminine, sent my Dad around the bend sometimes though."

"Oh I had no idea. Was it you who put me there?"

Bill nodded shamefacedly.

"I never could bring myself to sell it after Dad died there; he never got over my mother dying in the car accident."

"Oh Bill, when did that happen?"

"Oh fifteen years ago, next month. She should never have been driving at her age, but she would not be told. In her prime she had been a very accomplished lawyer, and she did not take kindly to being told what she could and could not do. Dad died later in his sleep, from a heart attack."

Anne let this information sink in.

"I have paid a gardener to keep the garden in order since then. I doubt I will ever move there. So I could sell it, then Cilla could have years of quality home care in the village, I could care for her. It was my fault Anne, my fault that she's helpless. "Isobel knew what I had done. So she devised a plan. Jean had just died, so you were the only person capable of giving the go ahead for the project, for the production of the flu vaccine. We thought if we could delay your decision until after the deadline had passed, then the earliest implementation would be next year. With the General elections due in May, if the PM loses the election, or has to form another coalition, then in all probability the whole scheme will be shelved." Anne nodded, as this was the reason there was such a rush on at the moment.

"I never wanted to hurt you Anne, please believe me." Tears welled up in his eyes again, and he walked over and touched her arm.

"I just hoped if we abducted you to my parent's house, we could keep you there a few days, and then release you, and you would never know we were involved. It never occurred to me that you might try and escape. I think that I thought if I fed you, and made sure you were as comfortable as possible, you would stay, and then my plan was after the deadline had passed, just to leave the door unlocked and you would walk home. You would not know who had kept you, and all would be well. Isobel wouldn't need to tell anyone what I had done to Cilla, and she would get the vaccination delayed.

"Surely I would want to know who owned the house I was kidnapped and held in?"

"It didn't cross my mind Anne. I don't know how to kidnap anyone, for goodness sake. Isobel had a right go at me for leaving the ladder in the basement. Now I don't know what will happen. Major Ross has asked Isobel to be lead researcher reporting to John until you are found."

Anne could not but help a gasp of breath escape at the mention of her lover John. Her heart ached knowing how worried he would be about her, and also the work involved trying to catch up on all the research.

"They are continuing the report, and Sarah is working flat out to resolve the paralysis problem. I think Major Ross is praying that you are found today. He trusts you Anne, and he really wants you to sign off this momentous research."

"Oh my goodness Bill, it is so important that I get back to the lab today. What can we do? Where do you think this tunnel goes? Should we try and walk to the other end?"

"I don't know Anne, I have never been down here before; I didn't even know this place even existed. Shall we try? There is no light round the corner, do you want me to go on my own, Anne?"

"Oh my goodness no, I couldn't bear to be here on my own. Let's see how far we can get."

Anne again eased herself off the table, and took Bill's arm, to try and keep as much pressure off her painful feet. They shuffled down the tunnel, going around the corner, and past the table screen. Anne was embarrassed by the smell. Bill made no comment at all, thank goodness.

The light from the only bulb was fading now they were round the corner; in front all they could see was a black void. It really was very scary, Anne never had liked the dark, it was not knowing what was there that frightened her. This was going to be a real struggle.

"Let's walk down the side of the tunnel, so we can follow the brick wall Anne." They moved to the left hand wall. Anne kept stepping on debris, each time she winced it upset Bill, who held her arm ever more tightly.

"I am so sorry, Anne. Do you want to go back, I can go on alone?"

"No, if we can get out, I want to get out as quickly as possible."

Just then her ankle was brushed by something scurrying by. Anne jumped and screamed.

"A rat, Bill there are rats!"

"I expect there are Anne, we shall be fine. Oops. Are you in some water?"

"Yes, it's freezing, let's hope it doesn't get deeper."

"It's so much worse for you Anne, I am so sorry you left your shoes behind. I so wish you had your lovely shoes on."

Anne could not help laughing, "If I did they would be ruined, and I should be so upset."

They continued moving forward. The water only got as high as the top of their feet, but it was so cold, and they were walking in slippery sludge. Anne was now getting very seriously cold, she was shaking and her teeth were chattering, as she continued on.

"Are you sure you don't want to go back?"

"No, we must get out," Anne said.

A few more metres and they hit a wall in front of them.

"This must be the end wall," Anne said as Bill felt in front of him, and moved to the right. About five feet along, Bill cried out,

"There a door Anne, a door." Bill knocked it with his knuckle,

"It's metal Anne, metal." They ran their fingers over it, trying to find the lock or handle.

"I think I can feel the keyhole, Bill."

"Let me feel." He put his hand on Anne's arm and followed it down to her hand.

"Yes that is definitely the keyhole. Let's feel on the floor to see if the key has dropped out." Bill swept his hands and then his feet around the base of the door, through the muddy water, the brick dust and the debris. Nothing. He banged the door. It echoed loudly and sounded as though it was quite thin. Anne also banged it, until she thought about her bandages. Then they both started shouting. Ten minutes went past, and they could not hear any response at all.

"Where do you think this goes, Bill?"

"Well it obviously carries on as a tunnel. Could it be part of the tunnel system that Major Ross takes to Credenhill? If it's an old railway tunnel, there are quite a few disused tunnels in Malvern." Bill thought out loud.

"Well look, we know that Major Ross comes every day at precisely the same time, what about if we don't get out tonight, we come back in the morning and shout our socks off?" Anne suggested. "Yes, that's the answer, and with a bit of luck, if the report is one day late, it can still be actioned."

Anne felt her mood lighten as they had made a plan. She almost felt as though she could skip back, but her feet and ankles certainly would not agree.

They walked back; it was easier going towards the light, as they could see what they were treading on. It took only minutes; it seemed half the distance compared to walking into the darkness.

As they neared the upended table, Bill suggested Anne walk on, so he could relieve himself. Bill was very sensitive to the situation and made sure she could not hear him, as he wet the wall. Zipping himself up, he walked back to the other table, which Anne had once again managed to sit on. She was looking at the soles of her feet, and brushing them clean,

"How are your feet?"

"Painful and freezing cold. Never mind we will be out of here tomorrow. She tried to raise her legs onto the table so she could wrap the bath sheet around her legs as well as her body.

"I am so cold Bill."

Anne reached inside the carrier bags, and rummaged through to see what else was in there. She found the toiletries and the water.

"Bill, do you want some water?" He took the bottle and had a sip and then passed it back to Anne, and without a thought she also shared the bottle.

"Do you think Isobel will be back?" she asked.

Bill just stood and thought.

"Why don't you come and sit down on the table, Bill?" She looked at her watch. "It's 6.30pm."

Chapter 46

Deadline minus seven hours
17.00, 26th March
Path outside the tunnel

"Bill bloody Matthews, Bill bloody Matthews." Isobel threw her hands up in the air. What on earth were they going to do now? What on earth was she going to do now? She wanted the money, she wanted it so badly.

She rushed into reception and straight to the ladies' toilet, removed her shoes, washed them as best she could, and dried them. She paused and looked at herself in the mirror. How on earth had it gone so wrong? What do I do now? She stood and stared for a few minutes more, at a loss for a solution, hoping her reflection would come up with an idea. We are in real trouble now. What will happen? How on earth can I let them go now, but what on earth can I do? Just wait until after the deadline tonight and let them out. I shall be arrested for abduction and worse.

Isobel heard the rest room outer door open. She waited a couple of minutes, and when she heard the fridge door being opened, decided to go back in. Paul looked up.

"I've just found time for a bite to eat," Paul said, lifting a tub of pasta salad from the fridge. Isobel left the room without saying a word, and walked in a daze to her desk. She sat down and picked up paperwork, and pretended to look at it. She then saw the note.

'John needs you now, please come straight downstairs to Major Ross' office.' She flushed red.

Do they know about Anne? Her heart pounded. Had they found out? Oh my goodness, will the police be there? She sat down and tried to compose her thoughts. She needed to get her story straight. Perhaps she should just do a runner, but where to? 'Oh my goodness, this is it! Oh well better go and face the music. Act natural, it might not be what you think.'

She walked slowly past the other researchers, into reception and down to his office. Was this it? Had they found her?

"Gosh Isobel, I could not find you," John greeted her as she walked into the Command Room. "Great news! We have been given an extension until 13.00 hours tomorrow. Sarah is certain the death is natural causes, so we only have to understand Cilla's problem. Sarah's checking to see if it's an allergic reaction. I've had the results of the last four residents from Sarah, and I think you have the autopsy results haven't you? I need you to work with me here for the rest of the day. I need your analysis of these results, so I can fully understand the data, and make one hundred per cent sure, that the calibration is as correct as humanely possible. It could be a late night Isobel if Anne is not found tonight. Presumably you haven't heard anything about Anne?"

"Nothing John. Let's get on then." Isobel had to turn away. She tried to suppress her relief, no-one seemed to know anything about Anne, and Bill didn't seem to have been missed yet. "I'll just go upstairs and get all the results. OK John?"

"Mmm, yes Isobel, you do that," he said distractedly as he re-read the notes on the screen. Isobel flew up the stairs and back into the ladies. Closing the door behind her, she waited until her heartbeat slowed. 'That was close! I hope I have made the right decision. I'll go and get the notes and hope I can persuade John that the results are not clear'.

She re-joined John and they started the checking of the summary sheets, and Isobel tried to forget about everything else.

Major Ross sent another wodge of yellow pages to GCHQ. He had to update them every half an hour on the progress, both of the trial analysis and the search for Anne. The tracker dogs had only found a link to Anne at the hospital, from the automatic car park barrier to the reception area, and treatment rooms. Princess Margaret Gardens brought nothing new due to her scent being everywhere. The helicopter had been circling the area, the heat source camera checking all the woods near the hospital, and up on the hills. Nothing was found. The ground search area was being extended, to include outhouses, garages, and all other likely areas she could be being hidden. The Regiment had sent additional men over.

The need for secrecy was fast disappearing, as the deadline was approaching.

The Prime Minister's office.

Alan picked up the phone and dialled home.

"Sorry Lucinda, I'm not going to be able to make it tonight. Will you apologise to Cameron and Lucy. It really is important that I'm here."

"Oh dear Alan, I know Lucy has gone to a lot of trouble for us. Supper sounds fabulous."

"It really can't be helped. You go, Angela and Tom are going aren't they?"

"Yes, but…" Lucinda started.

"Look there is bad news about the trial, the date may not be met, and you know how important it is to me. This really is serious; I would be bad company even if I could make it. Give my love to the kids, see you later." The Prime Minister put the phone down, and pushed the chair back. One o'clock tomorrow had better be sufficient time.

Princess Margaret Gardens

Isobel and John worked on long after everyone except Major Ross had gone home. Major Ross had ensured they were provided with food and drink, so that they did not have to leave the office.

By ten thirty Isobel, was shattered. The events of the past two days were catching up with her. She had tried to cast doubt on the results, but John had not agreed with her analysis and felt sure that everything had been done to ensure accuracy of the calibration. A decision about Cilla's symptoms was pending.

"Right Isobel, unless Anne returns tonight or tomorrow, then I am happy to put my name to this report and authorise production. The politicians must be told about the reaction of Cilla, if we have no definite answer to her problem. They can then make the final decision. Let's go home. Do you fancy a drink?" John asked.

"John, I am exhausted, I'm off to bed. I will be back at 6.30am tomorrow, is that alright?"

"I can't ask for more Isobel. I shan't sleep whilst Anne is still missing, in fact I'm going for a walk to see if I can think of anything that might shed any light on where she is." His eyes misted over. "I cannot imagine what I'll do if she is harmed." Isobel did not look at him, but left the room.

"Are you off now, Isobel?" Major Ross queried.

"Yes Sir, I need to rest, I am exhausted," Isobel replied.

"John can you update me now, so I can send details to GCHQ."

They both disappeared back into his office, whilst Isobel left the section.

Chapter 47

Deadline minus 3 hours
22.00, 26th March
The Tunnel

"Are you ok Bill?"

"Yes, don't you worry about me? Why don't you lie down on the table, and I can cover you up with the towel."

"What about you Bill?"

"I will sit down on the floor and try and nod off. I don't think Isobel will come back, do you?"

"Let's go and bring the other table down here, and you could at least lie down on a clean surface," Anne suggested.

"That's a good idea Anne." They both walked carefully up to the corner, and retrieved the table.

"If we turn it upside down, it won't rock about. The underside of the top is probably cleaner also," Anne suggested. They positioned the table a little way from Anne's, next to the wall.

"Shall we turn yours upside down, Anne?"

"Oh no, the rats might walk over me!"

"I just don't know what on earth is going to happen to us? It's such a good job we have your water. Tomorrow we will try shouting and banging on the door from 6.20am onwards; let's hope it is the tunnel to Credenhill.

Bill moved and sat on the upturned table, with his back against the wall and Anne lay down on her side and draped the towel over herself.

They were both deep in thought.

Anne could not sleep. She was very cold and frightened. The table was impossible to sleep on. She had tried lying on her back, on her left hand side, on her right hand side, on her front. Each position just hurt a different part of her body. She heard Bill's heavy breathing; his head was bowed forward, asleep. She tried readjusting herself yet again. The table wobbled again giving her such a feeling of insecurity. She looked at her watch in the dim light. 04.26. Not too much longer to wait. She gave up trying to sleep and sat upright and eased herself quietly off the table. Hobbling to the corner of the tunnel, with the towel draped around her shoulders, she hoped this would be the very last time she would have to squat. She felt very positive that they would be found today. The deadline would have passed last night. The decision would have been made, whatever that was, and she could not influence it now. There was no longer any reason for Isobel to keep them there. She eased her skirt back down and went back towards Bill.

Bless him, he had keeled over and was lying on his side, luckily still on the tabletop. She looked more closely. 'Was he ok?' She quickened her pace. Getting closer Anne thought he looked odd. 'My goodness, I don't think he is breathing.' She bent down and felt his pulse, whilst putting her face down to his mouth to check his breathing. He wasn't breathing. 'Oh my goodness, he's not breathing!'

"Bill, Bill," she shouted in his ear. She shook his shoulders, he was a dead weight. "Oh my goodness, oh my goodness," she cried out loud. "BILL!"

'CPR – what am I meant to do? 'She thought back to her training years ago. Compress the chest to what tune? What tune?' She panicked. 'Nellie the Elephant, that was it. Nellie the Elephant.' She hauled Bill onto his back, placed her hands, one over the other, fingers entwined and using the heels of both of them, started pressing down on his chest. She was unsure if this it was the correct place, on his chest, but heck it would have to do.

"Nellie the Elephant packed her trunk and said goodbye to the circus" she panted out loud as she compressed his chest. She repeated the words, and then "Off she went with a trumperty trump, trump, trump, trump." She reached down to feel his neck, still no pulse. She listened for breathing, none. She repeated the compressions. "Come on Bill, come on. Cilla needs you, Cilla needs you Bill, come on." Tears welled up in her eyes. 'Please don't give up Bill.'

Anne did not give up, she repeated the compressions for at least half an hour, but no matter what she did, Bill remained the same. He was dead. The stress must have been the final straw. 'He wasn't that old was he? Seventy eightyish? That was nothing nowadays.'

She leaned back on her haunches, checked her watch, it was 05.24, less than an hour before Major Ross passed by. 'Better go down the tunnel at six o'clock to make sure she started early.' Let's hope my hunch is right.' Anne took the towel off her shoulders and covered Bill.

Chapter 48

New deadline minus seven hours
05.00, 27th March
Major Ross's Office

Major Ross woke with a start.

"Harry? Harry?" He had been calling out.

Ross had been in the middle of one of his traumatic flashbacks of his war. He was covered in sweat, the nightmare was always the same, always had the same ending, every few nights. His wife understood when he lashed out in bed. He died every time; his men were wiped out every time. Despite initially having years of Post Traumatic Stress counselling, the nightmares and flashbacks remained. He wiped the saliva from his chin. He had managed about three hours sleep he reckoned, in his office chair.

After John had left at 23.30, he read his summary and recommendations. The PM had extended the deadline to 13.00 today. All the services had been searching for Anne since last evening. News had come in that the tracker dogs had found the house where Anne had been held. They had found her shoes in the basement and saw the broken glass and blood outside.

GCHQ were getting all the information about who owned the house. The dogs did not pick up a scent between the house and the hospital after the road junction outside the house, speculation being, that she had hailed a passing car.

Interestingly, the basement had an old bed mattress with a new duvet and pillow on it, together with a rose patterned plate, bowl, teacup and saucer. It certainly looked as though she had not been mistreated. A cloth was found on the mattress that suggested either a blindfold or a gag, and a rope was found nearby, but both seemed clear of blood. All these samples had gone back to Credenhill for analysis. Swabs had been taken, and now the hunt was on for other DNA samples. It certainly seemed to clear up any suspicion that Anne had sold them out. It must be abduction. Who and why were the questions now. Who was the lady who had collected her from the hospital? Apparently she said she was from Princess Margaret Gardens, so she knew who Anne was all right. Where on earth was she now and would they find her this morning? Let's all hope she is safe.

A canister dropped into the collecting basket from GCHQ. Major Ross rose and deftly opened the it, and put the paper into the decoder.

TOP SECRET

House address, confirmed ownership.

Mr & Mrs K Matthews.

Deceased.

Council tax, electricity and gas bills all paid on time by cheque. Minimum charges for services, suggesting house not lived in.

Major Ross reread the note. Deceased. Who paid the bills?

He needed to know now, what was the connection to the project. Was there any connection, or could it be another reason completely? Did the owner have a connection to the abductor, or was someone else aware the house was empty?

Chapter 49

New deadline minus eight hours forty-one minutes 04.18, 27th March Isobel's living room

Isobel paced her living room, up and down, up and down. She just did not know what to do. Was she certain that she disagreed so totally with the nanodrones being put into the flu vaccine without patient's knowledge, that she was prepared to sell them out, to risk even her freedom? To go to prison if necessary for her principles? Could she persuade Anne and Bill not to report her? Was that likely? What if they could not be persuaded? She just knew she did not have the necessary vitriol to kill them. She could not even kill bloody spiders. Could she leave them to die in the tunnel? Would they be found first, could she bear the thoughts of them starving to death?

Last night had been torture, knowing she could not go to them because of John and Major Ross insisting that she continued to work. Were their deaths preferable to the hundreds that will die, not having made the choice to have the injection that would end their lives earlier than necessary?

She paced back and forth; the questions had been going round and round all night. 'Another cup of tea? Oh heck, I need some wine.' She opened a bottle of red, and poured a very large glass full. It went down in a few gulps. 'My God that feels good.' She poured another. She looked at her watch, 04.18. What were the options?

Her contact had promised her substantial money for the trial results. She had resisted for a couple of years. When that pharmaceutical company lost the contract for the flu vaccine, they upped the money offered. It was so tempting. She had always hankered after time to travel, and also the company of a silver surfer, after all John had resisted all her advances; she needed to travel first class to meet the right type of high flyer. She wanted a high achiever, a go-getter, not a loser like her Jonathon -.someone to spend whatever time she had left with. To have fun again, to laugh, and to have a love life again. She could pay off her debts and be free. To have someone interested in her, and her thoughts. She would take time with her appearance and spend some money on herself. She knew she had let herself go. She was mousey, safe, wearing old-fashioned, easy clothes that needed no thought whatsoever, and washed easily. She never went anywhere to dress up. 'Well that can all change'. With the money, she could also retire in luxury, buy a house, a nice car, and travel first class worldwide with the money they offered.

She had been contacted yet again the day before Jean died. She had met the contact in a Malvern shop, and they promised her an amazing amount of money if the trial was postponed past the deadline by two months. The contact would not explain why two months, but she surmised it was because of the disbanding of Parliament prior to the election, and that meant no decisions could be made until after the start of production for this year's vaccinations.

The money would give her everything she desired. Perhaps the technology could be introduced on a voluntary basis next autumn? She presumed the company would bid for that contract.

She had worked on this project for nine years. She had loved working for Jean, but was jealous of Anne and John's relationship. They thought no one knew, but it was so clear to her. She had noted the clandestine visits overnight, the looks, the taps on the bottom, John's nickname for her, 'Songbird'. Her husband Jonathon had never called her a pet name, and John certainly did not call her anything other than bloody Isobel. Jean and Anne had overshadowed her all through the years of research. She had been top dog previously at Cambridge, but Jean and Anne were streaks ahead of her. She always seemed in the second league for everything.

The contact told her that payment would be after two months, and only if the contract for the nanodrones being incorporated into the flu vaccination contract was not signed.

So many decisions and time was running out.

Chapter 50

The Tunnel
New deadline minus seven
hours
06.00, 27th March

Anne left Bill and started down the tunnel, round the corner into the darkness. It was different this time; she knew it was not far to the end. The water did not worry her this time, or the possibility of rats and spiders. She was on a mission.

She had checked her watch around the corner in the light. When she reached the metal door, she counted to ten and then started shouting and banging on the door, listening all the time for any noise from the other side. Anne shouted and banged, continuously for half an hour. This was her only chance to get out and she went for it. Anne was exhausted, she was crying, her energy was spent but she kept at it, kept going.

"Hello, anyone there? Major Ross, its Anne. Hello, anyone there? Help! Help! Major Ross its Anne."

She had to get out, had to see Major Ross, and needed to see John. These thoughts kept her going, on and on. Her arms ached, her throat hurt. Anne was not going to give up.

She stopped and listened for several minutes – nothing. She leant against the tunnel wall. Perhaps someone had heard her and was coming with the key. What should she do now, what about the other door? It was nearer to the car park. 'I must try there. '

She walked more slowly this time, back down the tunnel, past Bill and to the wooden door. The time was 07.30. Her wrists and palms were tender, her throat dry. Better get some water; there was still half a bottle. She went back to the carrier bags, and then returned to the door.

She raised her fists, and began all over again.

Chapter 51

Command Post
Seven hours prior to new deadline
06.00, 27th March

It was 6am when John walked down the two flights of stairs wearily holding onto the bannister, ready to greet Major Ross on his arrival. He had not slept all night, tossing and turning until about 4am and then fell so deeply asleep that when his alarm went off, it was almost impossible to wake up. He fell out of bed, and it took three coffees to wake him up.

He entered the command post, to be greeted by Major Ross.

"Morning, John."

"You are early, Sir."

"Didn't go home, too much going on here, caught a couple of hours' sleep. There have been developments in the night, John. They found where Anne was kept. It was the basement of a house just up the Eastnor Road, opposite the Common. It appears from the items left there that she was looked after well, and it certainly looks as though she was abducted. No great force applied apparently. The window was broken and her shoes were nearby, with blood on the glass and window frame. Are you all right, John? Sit down." Major Ross continued whilst John took it all in.

"They tracked her to outside on the road, where she must have got a lift to the hospital. What we don't know is, who collected her from the hospital, and where they have taken her. Don't worry John, they will find her. The helicopter was out, did you hear it?"

"Yes, I stood outside and watched for as long as it was there. Presume they did not find anything?"

"No, but that is good news, as she hasn't been dumped, so we think that she is likely to still be alive."

"Oh for goodness sake, she had better be." John's head bowed as his shoulders dropped and he breathed out heavily. He sat back upright after a minute and bit his lip "Who owns the house where she was kept?" he asked.

"Well GCHQ report it belongs to a couple that died years ago – a Mr and Mrs Matthews?"

"Matthews? Might be a coincidence but Bill's surname is Matthews."

"Is it?" Major Ross absorbed the information. "Bill Matthews, eh? Where is he at the moment?"

"Well I expect he is at home, having breakfast probably."

"Just go up and get him would you John? We must explore every angle. Just don't say why we want to see him."

John walked up the stairs. He was thinking that Bill was the most unlikely suspect going. Bill kept his head down, and was deeply engrossed in the flu trial. Why would he be involved?

It was cold outside, must be minus three degrees, there was a frost on the grass. It was still dark, a dog howled in the distance as he rounded the corner to Bill's bungalow. The bungalow looked as though he was not up. John hammered his knuckle on the glass door panel. No sounds from inside. He knocked again and waited. 'If Bill was not in, where was he? I'll try the new laboratory, but it would be unusual for him to be so early.' It was still only 06.40.

Command Post

New deadline minus five and a half hours

"Well John, where is he?" Major Ross asked the minute John appeared.

"Cannot find him anywhere, he does not look to be home. Shall I take the master keys and go in and look around?" John asked.

"Yes." Major Ross thought about letting GCHQ know, but then decided to wait until John came back. For all they knew, he could have gone out for a walk.

"I'll get someone down to the house now, in case he is there."

Command Post

New deadline minus five hours.

"Bed is made, house all in order, no one there." John reported back at 7.05am.

"Right, time to take action, this makes no sense. John, am I right that Bill is one of the researchers to have had the nanodrones' tracking inoculation from your trial?"

"Yes, sir," replied John. In all the excitement he had forgotten that some researchers had had his GPS tracking.

Major Ross went over to the decoder and sent an urgent request for the location of Bill Matthews, who was on the GPS tracking trial, to GCHQ.

"Well at least we will know very quickly where he is. Using the tracking today, will be the first time in reality that it has been used. Let's see how quick the response time is, and how accurate. He was on the initial trials wasn't he? The signal strength was weak then, but hopefully strong enough." Major Ross enquired.

John agreed and sat down to wait. At 07.00 there had still been no response. He got up and made them both a coffee.

07.04 a canister dropped into the collection basket. They both dashed to it. Major Ross opened it and put it in the decoder.

TOP SECRET

Bill Matthews.

Location shows, Princess Margaret Gardens. Eastnor Road, Malvern, Worcs.

An Ordinance Survey map reference was shown.

"What?" they both exclaimed.

"Right, he is here John, I think we need to be careful, something is very wrong here. Let's get the tracker dogs in again. I think we need back up, as I just don't know what we are facing."

Chapter 52

The Tunnel
Five and quarter hours to the
new deadline
07.45, 27th March

Anne sat down on the table exhausted. What now? It was 07.45, Bill was lying on the floor covered with the towel. Her throat, hands and arms were screaming with pain from the exertion of hitting the doors.

Perhaps Isobel would come with food. She was going to be astounded by Bill's death. Will the shock be enough for her to release me?

Anne sat there and stroked her cheeks and chin. She could not stop touching her growing beard with her bandaged hands, which were filthy now, and so painful. All the hammering has caused them to bleed again, and she had got blood over her skirt and cardigan. She was so cold, and had nothing now to wrap around herself, she had even considered taking the bath sheet from Bill, but could not, that seemed disrespectful. When she breathed out, mist appeared.

Chapter 53

Isobel's bungalow
Four and a half hours before
new deadline
08.30, 27th March

Isobel struggled with the two catches on her back door, squinting and moving her head from side to side, and up and down, as she tried to focus on them. Just as she managed to open the door, she remembered the carrier bag and the full wine bottle. She grabbed them both off the table and swerved back to the door, holding onto the door jam for support, and then launched herself along the path.

Fighting the urge to be sick, she lurched across the car park and over to the muddy path. Ignoring the brambles, she part slid and part stumbled down the slope before falling against the brick wall of the tunnel entrance. She heaved, bent over and then threw up. Wiping her mouth with her sleeve, she then reached into her cardigan pocket for the key. The urge welled up again and she bent forward and regurgitated some more. 'That feels better.'

'Two bottles had been too much,' she thought. Her feet and trouser legs were splattered. She squinted at the door and then the keyhole, and tried to focus. She fell back against the wall.

Isobel tried to get the key into the keyhole three times and on the fourth valiant attempt succeeded. Turning the key, the door fell open with Isobel attached.

"'Ello Bill," she drawled. "'Ello, Anne." She noticed something on the floor, but saw Anne and tried to walk straight towards the table she was sat on. Anne could smell the booze and vomit, even from the table. When Isobel was near she launched the carrier bag at Anne, who grasped it, and then regretted using her hands again.

"Breakfast, well sort of, I couldn't find anything in my cupboards, it's all I've got. Where's Bill?" she peered around. "Where's Bill?"

Anne looked in horror at Isobel. Her hair was all over the place, a bottle of wine in her hand, absolutely 'drunk as a skunk.' Isobel wobbled and hung on tight to the table's edge, causing it to lurch sideways. She gave Anne a malevolent and sickening smile.

"Where's Bill?" she demanded.

Anne looked at her and could not decide in that moment if she loathed her or felt sorry for her. She decided not to answer and instead picked up the carrier bag. Looking inside she saw an opened packet of biscuits, a bag of peanuts, a jar of jam, a pot of yoghurt, and half a packet of cheese. The only thing to drink was a bottle of red wine.

"It's all I had, Anne. Sorry," Isobel slurred, still looking straight down to the floor. "It's cold in here Anne, it's very cold in here. Don't know how you stand it. You have even taken off your shoes. Why's that Anne? Did they hurt?"

309

Anne still chose not to reply, she obviously was completely out of it, and past reason. Isobel fell forward onto the floor, landing on her hands and knees, and then fell over onto her side, before scrambling to a sitting position with her back against the table leg. She reached for the bottle of wine that had escaped her grasp on the way down. She brushed the dirt from the top, undid it, and downed two large swigs.

"Good stuff this Anne, brought you a bottle. Have some, it's lovely."

"Isobel, you have had enough, leave it."

"Had enough?" she shouted, "Had enough, I sure have Anne, I've had enough of you and that dozy Bill. Where is he?"

Anne did not respond, instead she reached inside the carrier bag, and took a couple of biscuits from the packet. Digestives, they would do, she was starving. She ignored the wine, and drank a small sip from the remaining bottle of water, before eating two more biscuits.

Isobel remained slumped and was twittering on to herself about never enjoying working for Anne, about her work never being good enough.

"Do you know Anne, I don't own a bean, not a bloody bean. All these years of work and don't own a bean. Nothing, zilch, nowt."

Anne looked down at Isobel's head, bent forward over her knees, totally oblivious to the obnoxious sweet sickly smell on her lap.

"That bloody Jonathon, do you know what he did Anne? Do you know?" She took another swig of wine. "He bet, he bet away all our bloody money, all the bloody lot. Fucking pillock. Nothing left, nothing Anne, can you

310

believe it? Where's Bill?" Isobel paused from her ramblings, raised her head and looked around "Oh my goodness, I'm going to be sick." True to her word, she was, all over herself. The smell was almost enough for Anne to get off the table, however her feet were so cold and painful, she winced, looked away and remained seated.

"This wine's bloody good, Anne, go on have some. Do you know it takes away all your worries, all away?" She swung the bottle to check how much wine was left.

"What shall we do, Anne? What shall we do?"

"About what Isobel?"

"Now, about now. Where's Bill?"

"Why don't we all go home Isobel? I could put you to bed, and look after you?"

"Do you know why we didn't have children, Anne? Can you guess why? Bet you bloody can't. We were half brother and sister, that's bloody why. I loved Jonathon so much." Tears welled up in her eyes and dribbled down her cheeks. "I loved him so much. Dad left his Mum when he was a baby and took him with him to live with my Mum. I came along three years later. I always loved him, I did Anne, and then we fell in love. Passionately, oh very passionately. Dad had died by then, and Jonathon and I were at Cambridge Uni. We shared digs, it made sense, and then when his Mum passed away, we got married. Only my Mum knew. That's why we never had kids Anne. I thought I wouldn't mind, but I did. I BLOODY DID." She shouted before sitting quietly. "I so did," she mumbled, before raising her head and saying vehemently. "So now here I am, widowed, childless, with no money, and no one to love me. No one. Not like you and John, I know about you two. So I don't need bloody looking after by you. I want some handsome silver fox to tuck me up. That's what I want.

311

That's what they have promised me. They did, you know Anne, they did, a fucking silver fox for me. He's going to be suave, athletic, sun tanned and rich enough to really look after me, to care for me, to love me, really love me. I'll give up this bloody fucking research and go and live somewhere beautiful, warm, perhaps an island and be pampered. No bloody taking anymore shit from you and John. Oh no. I'll do nothing and be looked after, all the rest of my days. With a lovely beach house, and with beautiful clothes. I'll visit the best beauty salons, have a total make over, lose weight, have my teeth done, just like those film stars Anne. Just you wait. Bloody wonderful."

"Who's going to organise this, Isobel?"

"Them that's who, them – she promised."

"Who promised?"

"Her down at the shops, she promised." Isobel finished the last dregs of the bottle she was holding. "She did."

"What have you got to do?" Anne asked, already suspecting the answer.

Isobel was distracted "Is Bill at work? Is he?"

"That's right Isobel, he left early today." Anne lied. Isobel had still not noticed Bill's shoes peeking out from under the bath sheet, three metres away from her.

"Oh good, he needs his work. He's bloody good at work, bloody shit at everything else. Do you know he left you with a ladder, a ladder?" She emphasised. "He is so thick. Where is he?"

"At work."

"Bloody good job, he's useless at everything else. Bloody useless." Her words trailed off and she sank further down the table leg.

"Shall we go home Isobel?" Anne suggested. "Give me the keys and I will get you home to bed."

Isobel did not reply. Instead she reached down for the now empty wine bottle.

"It's gone, all gone." Isobel complained. She turned the bottle upside down to prove it. A dribble escaped onto her trousers, landing amongst the vomit. "Oh dear what shall we do? You know you cannot leave, don't you? You will have to stay here forever. Don't worry Anne, I will feed you. Go on eat some cheese, it's lovely. Bill's missing out, fucking gone off to work hasn't he, that's all he's good for, work. Left me to deal with you, he has, left me to deal with you. What shall I do Anne? You know I shall be rich, if you don't approve the trial Anne. Rich. Fancy that. She promised you know, promised. Can't wait, I've been dreaming about what I'll do. I have you know. Come the summer, I can buy a house, my very own house, not here, somewhere lovely, and big, very big."

"Why don't we go home, and then I can help you?" Anne tried again.

"Help me, not fucking likely. I'm going to find a man to do that, I am you know. Need no help from you. Anyway you've got to stay here two months at least, that's what she said. Two months."

Anne looked down at Isobel, and looked to see if she could see where the door key was.

"Give me your wine Anne, pass me your bottle." Isobel held out her hand to Anne.

Anne passed it down. Isobel opened the screw cap and took a swig then, wiped her mouth with her sleeve. She was bound to pass out soon, Anne thought, and then she could escape. She opened the peanuts and ate a handful. Her hands were so sore; since Isobel had lurched in she had

313

forgotten about them, but now they throbbed. Isobel looked up at Anne and saw she was cradling her hands.

"Did Bill look after your hands Anne? You weren't meant to get hurt. Even though I despise you and your research, you weren't meant to get hurt." She slumped back down the table leg.

Anne looked towards Bill's body. She wasn't the only one hurt. The strain had obviously been too much for him. What a fiasco! All these years of research, all the secrecy, all being threatened by Isobel. She looked at her. Was she asleep? Anne carefully moved her freezing cold feet. Isobel did not move. Anne very slowly and carefully lowered herself onto the floor. The table wobbled, Isobel stirred. Anne steadied herself against the table, and noticed her ankle was even more swollen.

"Where's Bill?" Isobel murmured and passed out again. Anne very slowly bent down and looked at Isobel's hands and then her clothes. Where was the tunnel's door key? Isobel's hands were empty as far as she could tell. Her cardigan, which had two patch pockets, was unbuttoned and would be easier to check, but her trouser pockets would be a problem. Anne gently patted her cardigan pocket on the right hand side; it only had tissues in it. Isobel stirred.

"Bill's at work, that's where he is, Anne," she mumbled.

Anne waited, and then patted the other cardigan pocket. Empty. For heaven's sake, if it's in her trouser pockets, I will never get the key out. She very carefully lifted one side of the cardigan and looked at her right hand side pocket, she could not tell if the key was inside, as her trousers were black, and the light very dim. She bent down and very, very lightly used her bandaged hand to feel for the key. Nothing. Just then she heard a noise from outside, she stopped dead in her tracks. What if Isobel had accomplices? Would they

314

hurt her? She froze and listened, a bead of sweat rolled down her forehead. All she could hear was Isobel's heavy breathing. Must have imagined it, or perhaps it was a dog.

Outside the tunnel.

Three and half hours to new deadline

Wham Jam looked around, he could see the door from his prone position in the gorse bushes on top of the tunnels' bank. He tightened his respirator, adjusted his night vision goggles (NVG's) and pulled down his Kevlar vest. He pictured in his mind what he had to do. It had been agreed that a ballistics breach on the door hinges would do the job. Arnie, like the whole of the Counter terrorism wing (CTW) assault team was dressed in his black kit, and was on the bank the other side of the overgrown path, also looking down towards the wooden door. Arnie was carrying the Enforcer battering ram, and was primed, ready. Bomber was above the bank, above the tunnels air vent, which he had located and cleared sufficiently to be able to drop the flash bang through.

Far inside the tunnel, Sam was pinned against the tunnel wall, behind his protective shield, about ten yards away from the metal door which he had already primed with the shaped charge.

"Ok Sam? Ready?"

"Yep boss."

"Stand by, stand by…GO, GO, GO!

Chapter 54

05.35, 25th March 2015

Scenery; back gardens with the washing hung forlornly out to dry from yesterday, toys strewn amongst the long grass of the tiny terraced gardens, kempt lawns with borders dug ready for the summer invasion of bedding plants, canals, industrial estates, and field after field of pasture, with animals waiting for the sun to rise, all were passing incredibly slowly. Sarah was huddled with her head against the glass of the train window, checking the reflection in the window to see if anyone came near her. Was she being watched? She was hugging her large shoulder bag on her lap. In it was everything she would be taking with her – her whole life in just her trusty bag.

She had heard the helicopter last night, and seen John watching outside to see if they were finding anything. Was this to do with her? She could not wait any longer; the time had come to leave. The early morning milk train to Paddington would take her to the Heathrow Express connection. She did not think they would miss her until she was on the flight. All her research was on her computer and backed up. She knew not to trust the Internet, far too risky.

The thought of Cheng, and her new life made her stomach lurch. This was really it. This was the moment that they had talked about last August in China, as they lay next to each other the night before coming home on her last trip. His gentle nature, and kind thoughtful ways, were so different to all the men she had been with before. He really cared for her. Despite all her bluster and confidence, she wanted to be loved, to be cherished and valued, with someone who would look after her, forever. Cheng had never given up on her, even when all hope seemed lost that she would return to him, he had believed.

The terrible time he had had when his parents' lives were threatened had passed with Paul's information, but she was aware that she had caused that problem. She should never have tried to seduce him. It was just a lark at first. Thomas was off limits, but her interpreter would be just another conquest. But the weeks had gone by and she found that it was much more than that; it was a truly wonderful relationship.

She sat back and thought about her new life. God it was going to be so different. Everything was so different in China; it was going to be so exciting, even though she would be defecting. Her Mum and Dad might never speak to her again, they were going to be so disappointed in her. It was bound to come out at some time how she had betrayed her country. Would she ever see them again in person? Tears welled up, just as there was some movement down the carriage. She jerked upright.

"Tickets please, tickets please," the train guard walked down the aisle, checked the couple sat four rows ahead of her and then headed towards her.

"The ticket office wasn't open," she explained.

"That's alright love you need to pay the full fare then. Paddington?" he held out his hand for the money. Sarah passed over her card and sat looking out of the window whilst he entered the details.

"Pop your pin in here then lass." Sarah's mind was all over the place. 'What was her pin? Oh yes' she remembered and entered it, and was given her receipt.

The guard continued through the carriage.

"Tickets please, tickets please." He slid back the connecting door and left Sarah's carriage. She relaxed and stared vacantly out of the window again.

"Tickets please, tickets please."

"Hi, sorry the ticket office was closed."

"So I hear, where to luv? Paddington?"

Helen smiled at the guard.

She would have to pick up her car later.

"That's right, my friend was going to catch this train, have you seen her yet? Very distinctive hair, blonde long and curly.

"Sort of bushy?"

"Yes, that's her. Is she on the train?"

"Yes, in the front carriage."

"Thanks. I'll go and find her." The train slowed and an announcement came over the tannoy.

"Next stop – Evesham. Next stop, Evesham."

Sarah stood up at the last moment and jumped off the train. She had quickly bundled her hair into a beany hat and was now hugging her shoulder bag as she dashed to the station exit. She had moments before seen Helen on the train. Helen continued to look out of the train window, and was looking vacantly at the station buildings, unaware of Sarah's quick exit. She was planning on her interception before Moreton-in-the Marsh, having phoned her contact that morning. Agents were in position ready to take Sarah off the train.

Sarah's heart was racing, thumping in her forehead, as she rushed outside. Helen looked casually out of the other window, and saw someone in a hurry dashing down the steps, and resumed looking along the carriage. She would make a move in a moment, when the train started up again. The train's engine started to increase in volume, and they started slowly to leave the platform. Helen looked casually along the platform at the departing people. 'Probably all off to work,' she thought.

Sarah jumped into the back of the only waiting taxi.

"Where to luv?" Sarah leaned forward and told him where to go.

"It'll cost you!"

"Company expenses," she said, as she leaned back, and checked Helen had not followed her.

"We have her in sight, we have her in sight." The agent spoke into his jacket microphone, putting his foot down on the accelerator, his car purred as he started to follow. It had been a very early call this morning. To be frank, he was not expecting anything to happen. Sit and wait and see if a young lady exits the station and follow her, were the instructions, along with Sarah's photo and description. Evesham was not exactly a hot bed of terrorism; he was not expecting anyone at all. It was probably another false start. Still it paid his wages. His wife would be pleased; they had just booked their summer holidays and could do with some extra money.

Sarah noted the black car following, and thought she would keep an eye on it. The driver looked like any other old man, glasses, hat, she could imagine he was wearing driving gloves. Her taxi left the A36, and joined the M5 motorway at Tewkesbury. The other car was still behind her, but several cars back now. The motorway was very quiet, and the early morning frost was allowing the car tracks in the fast lane still to show.

"They didn't grit the road again last night. Dangerous, these blooming cut backs will be the death of someone soon," her taxi driver proffered.

Sarah muttered an acknowledgement and carried on looking back at the car behind them. At junction ten, the car left for Cheltenham, and Sarah relaxed. Just an early morning commuter as she suspected. 'What was Helen doing on the train?' She had come up in her car at the weekend. 'Catching a plane to Zurich again? Did they suspect her? Oh my God, what if she was following her?' She had seen it in the films, but her training didn't cover that at all, despite what she thought when she joined them. Major Ross had been too involved with Anne missing.

Surely those helicopters were hunting for her. 'What on earth was happening?' There had been a security clamp down during the last four days. It was a good job she had copied her info beforehand. Why did all this have to blow up at the same time she had decided to leave? She still couldn't bring herself to say defect. Still, it's probably taken all their minds off her work for the time being.

Mark and Paul didn't seem affected. Paul seems to have got away with it. He had been looking at houses for them again this last weekend, and really had thought he had found one. He had booked a visit with the estate agent for tomorrow. Poor old Paul; he was going to be heartbroken. He'd never forgive her, and why should he? When he found out she was a double agent, and he had been used, he would be broken hearted. She felt really bad for him, she was not sure how she had managed the last few months to keep up the charade, but Cheng's future and hers relied on it. She had given Paul all of the money, telling him to hide it, and they would share it when the time was right. At least he would have plenty of money now.

Cheng had told her about how they had been promised a fabulous apartment with three bedrooms in the best part of Guangdong, which Cheng said was amazing. His parents would of course, live with them and then there was a spare bedroom when they needed it. She hoped that would not be too long. Her biological clock was ticking, thirty-three years already. She refocused her view out of the window.

"Where are we now?"

"Just past Junction thirteen."

"Ok, thanks. Can you go a little faster please?"

"Got to think of my licence luv, cannot afford to lose it."

Sarah sat back. She felt safe at the moment, not many cars on the road, it was still very early. Most cars looked like typical business commuters, single male drivers, in a typical reps type car. Lorries, of course, were trundling along in the slow lane, causing their taxi to have to move out to the fast lane, when the lorries overtook each other.

Sarah failed to notice, the car tucked behind the van following them.

"Bloody stupid car, just came from nowhere. Look at the fool" Sarah was sat bolt upright, her nerves and senses on high alert. Leaning forward straining to see who was in the car.

"Is the driver on their own?" she asked.

"Bloody silly woman by the looks of it. What the hell does she think she is doing, tearing past us, and now

321

slowing down again? She's been behind that van for ages, where the hell is she going?"

Sarah looked at the speedometer, seventy-two miles per hour.

"Just overtake her, overtake her," she shouted. Just then the buzz of a helicopter could be heard coming from behind them.

"Quick take this next junction, take this next junction!"

"To Cribbs Causeway?"

"Yes," Sarah shouted.

"Are you in some sort of trouble lass?" the taxi driver looked worriedly into his rear view mirror.

Sarah thought quickly.

"Er no, but she might be my partner's ex-wife. She's been stalking me for ages. The police can't seem to help. I am so scared of her."

"Leave it to me luv." And at that he swerved at the very last minute onto the M4 slip road, leaving the other car driving off to Cornwall.

"How's that? It will take her ages to turn round, and then we could be anywhere, the M32 is just down here, so we could be heading for Bristol or London. She'll have no chance. You OK?"

"Yes, thanks. Thanks." Sarah sat back and quickly tried to work out what to do. She looked up; the helicopter was nowhere to be seen. 'Probably just a traffic 'copter you silly fool' she thought. Definitely been watching too many spy films.'

"How far is Bristol airport?" she asked.

"I'll put it in the sat nav, hold on. Don't come this way much, it's usually Heathrow or Gatwick for my airport runs." He fiddled with his sat nav dials.

"It says here, quick route thirty one minutes. How's that luv?"

Sarah was busily checking her phone for fights.

"Let's do it. Bristol airport it is." She leaned forward and stared out at the motorway signs. Immediately, they veered over to the inside lane, and off onto the M32. 'Where should she get a plane to?' Paris? Dubai? Wherever.' Money was no problem; she had a stash with her. This was going to take much longer than she thought. Cheng would be waiting at the Guangzhou Baiyun airport. She would have to phone him when she got off the plane. Could she risk a short text? No one would know if she kept the message brief. Quickly she texted 'Go home' to Cheng. That should be sufficient.

Ikea's blue and yellow building whizzed past on her right hand side. 'I wonder if they have Ikea in China?' she thought. Bye bye English weather, English skies, bright and blue, when not cloud covered. Bye bye old-fashioned city centres. Guangdong was modern and new. Shops, nightclubs, everything was fresh and new. They would have plenty of money to enjoy it. Wow, they would be so happy, snuggled up together, no more hiding their passion, raising their family.

"We're almost there, just got to turn right here, and drive down to the terminal."

"I need to just be dropped off, just drop me off at the entrance. How much do I owe you?"

"Not sure I can luv, I think we have to drive to the express drop off area."

"Now listen to me, I will pay you extra, just drop me off right by the entrance. Now how much do I owe you?" The taxi driver told Sarah the fare. "There is an extra £50 OK? Just do as I say, and drop me off, I do not want to be seen going in there OK?"

"Whatever." The taxi driver looked into his rear view mirror. 'You do get some strange fares.' She was definitely on edge. Who knows what she's been up to' He pulled up right outside, ignoring the signs. Sarah leapt from the taxi, slamming the door and walked very briskly into the terminal. She had never been here before, so looking up at the boards; she saw she needed to go upstairs for departures. She needed to buy her ticket first, by the looks of it.

She stopped and looked at the departures board. Where on earth could she go? Paris? Munich? Amsterdam? That's it Amsterdam. The flight was a KLM one and was due to leave in one and half hours. Surely they would have direct flights from there to China? Anywhere in China would do. She walked as calmly as she could muster to the desk. She waited patiently looking around constantly. She could wait no longer.

"Excuse me, I am in a real rush, would you mind if I skipped in first?" Sarah flashed one of her most endearing smiles and tossed her hair at the smartly clad businessman. He stepped aside.

"You are so kind, thank you." Sarah spoke directly to the counter staff.

"Amsterdam, next flight, is that possible?"

"You're in luck, just two seats left. How many suitcases?"

"None today, just a meeting and back later," she replied.

"Oh do you want a return ticket?"

"No, not sure how long I shall be. Thanks."

Sarah completed the purchase quickly and taking her boarding pass, hoiked out her passport, and rushed to the escalator, running up the steps two at a time. A family of four were blocking her way.

"Excuse me, excuse me," said Sarah as she pushed past.

"Some people haven't got any manners have they?" She heard the mother say as she passed them. She looked back to see if anyone was taking any notice of her. The policeman, who was walking around downstairs, wasn't looking at her. Helen wasn't here, she felt sure she would not be following her. She was probably at Heathrow now. Just keep a look out though and act normally. 'Slow down a bit girl.'

Outside the entrance two cars with flashing lights screeched to a halt. Helen and three others jumped out of the cars as they stopped. All four of them ran straight into the ground floor area. One man peeled off to go through to security. One man went straight to the ticket desk, whilst Helen and the other woman ran along the check in desks. Surely this is where she was heading. She doubted she would be heading for Temple Meads train station. She was bound to try and fly out from here. To make sure, the other car of agents had gone there just in case.

She had phoned in to get Temple Meads train station checked for her, as soon as Sarah's taxi had swerved down the M4 slipway and then veered off to the M32, heading towards Bristol centre. They had been driving behind the madwoman driver, who had pulled out suddenly. She didn't think Sarah had spotted them following her. The helicopter had been diverted, to avoid detection, once it had radioed in the taxi's position. If she was flying out from here, where would she go? She could go anywhere, as there were no direct flights to China by the looks of the departures board. Where would she go? She must find her quickly.

Helen was bursting to go to the loo. She had just been going to go, before walking down the train, to find Sarah and confront her with all the evidence, and escort her off the train at Moreton–in-the Marsh as arranged with her boss, when the train guard asked why her friend had got off early.

"She paid to Paddington. Did she forget something?" Helen had just nodded and phoned for instructions immediately. The next station was Moreton so it was easy to grab the car and drive off, with two other cars following. She was now desperate, but she would just have to wait.

"It's Amsterdam, Amsterdam," Helen shouted into her phone, one of the agents had got the flight information from the ticket desk. Helen and the other two ran up the stairs to Departures. Showing their passes they rushed through Passport control and security checking, out into the concourse, by Duty Free.

"Right, two of you down to the gate, we'll go around the other areas and see if we can apprehend her beforehand. OK?" Helen commanded.

Sarah was just coming out of the toilets entrance, when she saw Helen. Sarah had changed into trousers and put her hair back into the beanie hat again. She quickly retraced her steps into a toilet cubicle.

'Change of plan,' she thought. Her heart was pounding so much; she sat down on the toilet and leaned forward to recover. 'Oh my goodness, am I going to make it?' This could end here. I am so scared, so scared'. She took deep breaths, and put her head down further. A couple of minutes passed. The doors of the cubicles were being hit. 'Helen?'

"Chardonnay, stop that this minute. Stop the fuck did you hear?" She heard the mother chase the naughty girl as she continued to bang the doors. Another couple of minutes passed, and the family left the toilet block. Sarah opened her cubicle door, and peered round. The area was empty. Quickly she went to the entrance and looked out. She couldn't see anyone from here. The lift doors nearby opened and she shot into the lift, as the couple pushed the pushchair out of the door past her.

She pressed the ground floor button, and waited for what seemed an eternity for the lift to descend.

The doors opened, and an older couple faced her. The man was holding the handles of the lady's wheelchair, waiting for the lift to open. She exited around them and looked to her left. She could see the entrance door she had come in through, to the left of the W.H. Smiths concession. She looked around and joined a family who had just arrived back from holiday, by the look of their tans. They walked straight outside with their trolley and two children in tow.

Sarah dashed to the right where she could see the taxi rank was. She sat quickly in the back of the first taxi, leaned forward and said.

"The Chinese Embassy. London."

"It'll cost you my darling."

"Yes, I know," smiled Sarah.

Helen gathered them together. "Well have you checked everywhere? She's missed the flight. Go and check the whole building. Abdul, go to security and ask them to check the CCTV, we've got to know where she is. You two take the first floor, and I will go downstairs and check there. Let's go."

Two hours later.

London.

Sarah stood on the doorstep of the Embassy. It had cost her a fortune to get here, but she was two steps away from safety. She reached into her bag, and pulled out her phone, and took a photo of the Embassy and sent it to Helen.

Helen's phone pinged.

'Bye bye, doubt I will see you again, sorry to have missed you. Sarah. xx'

Helen stared down at the phone; she was going to have to explain the cockup.

She would not be the flavour of the month or to think about it, the year.

"Home boys, she outsmarted us." She showed them the text.

As Helen walked away shamefaced, she wondered how the Princess Margaret op was going.

Another agent drove her back to Princess Margaret Gardens. What on earth was Major Ross going to say? All those years of research, would Sarah really jeopardise the whole project, would she? Would they still be able to roll out the nanotech flu vaccines? Had she also taken the GPS tracking research?

Chapter 55

Inside the Tunnel
New deadline minus one hour
12.00, 27th March

Suddenly a torch-sized object fell from the ceiling. The blindingly white explosion together with the tumultuously loud noise of the flash bang paralysed Anne and Isobel A moment later, a huge muffled explosion could be heard from around the tunnels bend, simultaneously, a shot rang out and the wooden door crashed open.

The room filled with men in black, carrying their twelve gauge shot guns, illuminating the area.

"What the hell?" Sam shouted as he ran through the shattered metal door. On his left hand side, large drums were exploding and bursting into flames. The room was filled with them and stacks of cardboard boxes. His feet crunched on broken glass. On his right hand side it seemed to be like a chemistry laboratory set-up.

"What the hell?" he shouted again. The flames illuminated the tunnel. Where on earth was he? Bomber had briefed him that the tunnel was almost empty. Where were the hostages? He used his guns laser to check the room out. Empty, no-one there. He moved forward, through the poisoned air, grateful for his ST10 respirator and kit. He saw a metal door in front of him. He pressed the pressel on the stock of his gun, and spoke to Wham Jam.

"Primary door breached, second door in front of me, confirm your loc. stat."

"Hostages secure, further door to our South, confirm same door," Wham Jam replied.

"Yes, same. Is it possible to get into cover? Confirm." Sam asked.

"In cover, breach when ready," replied Wham Jam.

Wham Jam, Arnie and Bomber waited for the explosion, as the metal door around the corner was blasted off its hinges. A flurry of paper snowed down onto the floor.

"Hey Arnie, are those bank notes?" Bomber picked up a handful.

"They fucking look like they are. We've raided the Bank of England by the looks of it," Arnie replied.

Sam came round the corner and joined them.

"Nice of you to join us!" Bomber said.

"What the heck is all this money about?" Sam said as he picked up a handful. "There's another room back there. Full of chemicals and looks like money. Let's get out of here."

The tunnel

New deadline minus half an hour.

12.30 27th March

John looked at her and sobbed. Tears just flowed down his face. His breath came in short bursts from the exertion of running from the control room to the tunnel. Major Ross had told him what was happening the moment he had been notified by the Regiment. He had immediately designated Johns' bungalow as the assault units holding area. They had both got upstairs just as the assault team entered the tunnel. He could not believe Anne had been so close to them.

He looked at her feet, which were bleeding through the encrusted mud. Her tights were torn to shreds and half way up her legs; her hands were even worse; bloody and bandaged. Her clothes were filthy and snagged. Her skirt ripped. Her face was such a mess, mascara all down her cheeks, lips blue. The paramedics had just put her neck in a brace, and carefully, fully supporting her neck and body, lifted her via a body board, onto a trolley stretcher. Pushing it up the muddy path was difficult, so they lifted it, and John moved the overhanging brambles out of their way.

"My poor songbird, my poor songbird," he kept repeating.

Major Ross stood by the ambulances in the car park. John accompanied the stretcher to the rear open doors, and watched as the stretcher was pushed in.

"Well John, how is she?"

"They say the effects will wear off soon."

"Trust me John they will. I can assure you."

"Where are they going to take her?"

"They are going straight to the QE2 in Birmingham. You know we have a forces medical staff unit there; I have had treatment there, after my problem. When ready to go onto the ward, they will be in side wards fully protected 24/7."

John had not even thought about Isobel, so upset was he about Anne. She was being loaded into the other ambulance as they spoke. "Bill?" he suddenly thought.

"I am afraid he is dead, John. He was covered with a towel, so it looks as though it happened before the raid. No one else was inside, so we need to know who else was involved. Was he murdered? Isobel smells terribly of drink and vomit. We need to find out what on earth went on in there?"

"Anne and Isobel should be able to tell us soon. Do you want to go with them John?" Major Ross asked.

"What's happened to the assault team?

"Looks like there is a chemical factory in the tunnel. They have to be decontaminated."

"Chemical factory??"

"John, it's just one surprise after another." John could not take it all in.

"I just need to go down and finish signing off the report; we will have just made the deadline." John replied.

"Ok John let's go now, whilst the crew are packing up. We had got half way through, so it should only take a few moments. Let's go. You know where the hospital is John?"

"Yes, been there before," he replied.

Major Ross's Office

Five minutes to new deadline.

"Well John, that's it, whatever the result, you and Anne's team have done their best, their very best. Let's hope all the research, all the pain and suffering, all this mess has been worthwhile. Let's hope we will all look back on this, and be proud, very proud of what we have all achieved."

John looked at him, and had no more time to think about the trial, his only thoughts were for Anne.

"Sorry have to fly, must go to Anne." John left the room, taking the metal treads two at a time, for the second time that day.

John drove along the motorway, with all the events of the past few days, crowding his mind. 'How were Anne and Isobel, what on earth had happened to them?'

What was the chemical factory all about?' There were just so many questions to be answered.

'I just need to get to Anne.'

Chapter 56

Two months after the extended deadline Glossa, Skopolos

Anne turned over gingerly, protecting her bandaged and swollen ankle from the bed sheets. She cast off the bed linen, suddenly hot. John stirred and turned to face her. The low early morning sun highlighted Anne's hair, casting a halo around her face. She smiled at John, who caringly stroked her cheek.

He had lain awake for two hours, listening to the early morning sounds of Glossa waking, high above the harbour of Loutraki. The baker opposite their front door, had already loaded up his small narrow van, and left for the first delivery of the day. Captain Yianniss's house was a traditional Greek house, clinging to the hillside in the small village. The narrow pebbled lane right outside their doorstep was pedestrian only, unless you were local and knew better. It wound its way up the steep hillside from the village centre and the church, whose bell was tolling now, calling the locals to early Morning Prayer.

Yesterday afternoon had been quite a struggle for Anne, the airport, and ferry journey had not helped her ankle. John had taken their suitcases from the taxi at the bottom of the hill, one at a time up to the house, whilst Anne sat on the bench in the village square and took in the local colour. John had had to ask a lovely local man where the house was, as the map they had been given was so basic, it had been impossible to find. Giannis had not only helped him find the house, but had also helped Anne up the hill, holding her elbow to support her. He turned out to be a local fisherman, and so kind and spoke quite good English. His enthusiasm was contagious and brightened Anne's demeanour.

The front door of the house opened straight into a large room, which turned out to be the only bedroom and sort of boudoir. After a tour of the house, they had fallen into bed, exhausted, leaving unpacking their suitcases until the morning.

John decided to get out of bed and inspect the veranda next to the bed. It was very narrow and quite basically built out of wood. So narrow in fact that it only just managed to accommodate two folding wooden chairs, with a small wooden table between them in a row against the whitewashed wall. There was a small wooden door at the far end. Wonder where that goes? When John opened it he was amazed to find the smallest en suite ever, with a very small washbasin, and a toilet with only just enough space to be able to sit down. If you looked down you could see the four floors drop to the lane underneath, through the floorboards.

"Anne, you won't believe what I have just found." He walked back to the French doors and repeated. "Anne come and see what I have found. "Anne groaned and turned onto her stomach and looked at John.

"Do I have to?"

"Yes, you really must come and look," enthused John. Anne slowly unwrapped herself from the bedding, and hobbled across to the doors, and just stood there and sighed.

"Isn't this the most perfect view? And smell that freshly baked bread. Fantastic." She looked out to sea. Looking down to the harbour, she could see traditional village houses, a church, gardens growing fruit and vegetables, with chickens scratting around the edges. Local thin cats promenading along the walls and the lane below and then way down the hill by the harbour wall, the fishing boats.

"I wonder if Giannis is there this morning? We must buy him lunch to thank him." The sun warmed her, and she just stood and took in the atmosphere. The sea shimmered happy and bright with the sunlight. This place is just so peaceful, so homely and so Greek.

"Come, I must show you what I have found," John urged her. He held her hand and walked her to the end of the veranda. "Go on, open that door." Anne looked at John.

"Is this a trick?"

"No, just open it."

"That's amazing! I have never seen that anywhere else, ever."

"It will be very handy, especially with your ankle, at the moment."

It turned out later that this was how most of the old village houses had coped with adding bathroom facilities to their old traditional structures. They had spent their first morning, pointing out every house they saw with the same feature. Each house had added the bathrooms in different ways; often it just looked like a wooden shed had been added to the upper floors of their homes, dangling it appeared precariously in mid-air. Ingenious he thought.

John leaned against the veranda railing, the baker's bread smelt wonderful. It was one of the reasons he had woken up early this first morning; the smell of bread baking seemed to envelope the area. He hadn't minded the noise of the loading of the van. It was a lovely local sound, the sound of a village waking. The early season's morning sun, already warm on his skin, and the light was so incredible, bright, bouncing off the sea at the bottom of the hill, way out to the islands dotted in the azure ocean. His thoughts were like a travel agent's blurb, but that is exactly how it was here, magical. The village was waking up; local people could be seen through their windows and verandas preparing breakfast, and collecting produce from the various pocket sized vegetable plots in their productive gardens. Their cockerel's crowing echoed around the hillside, and the occasional choking sounds of the two-stroke engine of the local fisherman's van, as it wound its way up the hill, stopping to sell today's catch. He could be heard shouting out his presence as he wound up the hillside from the harbour.

John looked down at the tiny swimming pool over the track behind their house, the sun caused azure blue and while ripples over the water. It was theirs for the time the house was under their occupancy. Bet it was still quite cold John thought, as it was only May, and the pool was unheated.

John used the veranda bathroom, to see if it was suitable for Anne. It would certainly mean they would not have to trek down the four floors to the basement bathroom in the night.' It certainly wasn't discreet!' John thought, as the thin wood did not shield anyone from the goings on. 'Fresh air though,' he chuckled.

"It's ok Anne you could do your teeth and hair in there quite happily." He told her as he came out, squeezing through the door.

Anne moved her knees so John could pass the chair she was sat on, on the veranda.

"Anne, would you like a lovely cup of tea?" John asked.

"Yes please," she smiled. John began the descent to the kitchen. The house was very traditional, which is why they had chosen it, the steps were wooden, narrow and steep. Holding onto both bannisters, John thought it was almost like going down boat steps. Anne would need to be very careful. The kitchen on the third floor down was at the same level as the dirt track and swimming pool. He opened the window shutters and the backdoor, which lit up the whole of the small room. A cat strolled past the door, on its early morning mission. It looked up at the noise John was making and paused, hoping for some morsel no doubt; unsuccessful, he prowled onwards, to richer pickings.

The kitchen was very basic, but perfectly adequate for the two of them. Opening the fridge John found the milk carton and put it onto the tiled worktop, next to the gas hob, by the sink. The kettle was filled and put onto the gas hob, once he had found the matches to light it. As the water was heating, John ferreted amongst the goodies in the welcome box left by the agent. Tea bags, a packet of biscuits, coffee and a few other basic commodities filled the box. John decided that a couple of mugs of tea, and some biscuits would be fine, until they were dressed and could visit the bakery for some of the lovely fresh bread.

He closed the door and window shutter, and walked back up to the bedroom with the mugs on a small tray he found next to the breadbin.

He sat down on the chair next to Anne and put the tray down. As he sat back he realised how relaxed he was beginning to feel. The tension was easing both from the travel and also from the past few weeks. What a nightmare they had left behind.

Anne picked up her cup, and took a sip.

"I'll get some bread soon. There is some jam and butter downstairs, we can have a late breakfast," John suggested.

Anne continued to look out to sea, and sip her tea.

They had initially had difficulty persuading Major Ross to let John join her in taking a break. John's project was so vital to the terrorism threat that was really ramping up at present. However, John had promised to keep in contact, and had set Mark up with the four new guys, and they seemed to be able to cope. Worst case scenario was that John would fly home for a while and then re-join Anne.

She was so badly affected mentally by the whole episode, not just the threat to her safety, but the whole unravelling of her team. The negative attitude that had caused Isobel's treachery towards her and the project had broken her spirit completely. John needed to be with her, and Major Ross hoped that she would come back, and not retire as she had talked about immediately afterwards. He would need her to train new researchers, now that the team had been decimated.

"I promise not to spend all our time talking about it, John, but I must get some of the things that have happened off my chest. Do you mind?"

"Of course not, my love. Do you want to chat about it now?"

"If you don't mind me ruining this perfect start to my recuperation." John turned to her and held her hands.

"Look, we are here, for you to recover from all the awful things that have happened. Ross has got them to pay for the whole vacation, as long as you are well again for the autumn. So you can talk about whatever you want. No problem."

"I just couldn't believe all that we've heard about Sarah, Paul and Isobel as we came away. How could we all have missed what was going on? I was stunned to know that Jonathon and Isobel were half brother and sister. Did you have any idea at all?"

"Not at all, but of course we wouldn't think of looking for it would we?"

"She sounded so bitter about him. Being left on her own to pick up all the debts, all the problems and not even having any children to show for it. You know that he put all the debt into her name, not his, don't you? She really was cut up about that."

"Unbelievable! She had it so tough, and kept all her problems to herself. Now what has she got to look forward to? Nothing, her whole life wasted, it could have been so different for her, and she is amazingly intelligent. In any other research establishment, she would have been top dog, wouldn't she?"

Anne nodded.

"Oh look, I think that is Giannis' boat coming in." Anne pointed towards the harbour wall.

"I think you're right. Come on, enough of this, let's get dressed."

The choice of the house had not been the best physically for Anne, but the location was perfect. A small local village, with hardly any tourists, on an island where tourists generally stayed on the other side of the island in Skopolos It was perfect for keeping out of the way, of not being asked questions, for relaxing. Hardly anyone spoke English, but yesterday everyone they passed had smiled and said hello or similar in Greek.

A little later on that day, they visited the bakery, and it was clear they had made the right decision. The baker's wife had come out from the back room, and watched them look at the small selection of breads, trying to decide what to try. She broke off small pieces of bread and stuffed them into their hands to try, smiling and welcoming all at the same time. After they had chosen and bought far too much, using a pen and paper to work out how much they had to pay, she hugged them both, and waved goodbye as they left the shop and walked over the lane back to their front doorstep. They were really going to enjoy this rest.

The sun was beautiful on their skin, as they lay in the meadow grasses eating the small cakes they had bought from the village shop. They had found the way onto the hill during their walk this morning. Between two local houses, off the path, they had seen a footpath. The woman had paused from sweeping up the fallen leaves and blossom from her shady patio tree, and nodded when they indicated if they could go up the path. It had been quite a climb, but the wild flowers were amazing, they just covered the hillside as far as the eye could see. The occasional tree dotted the meadow. The sun had enhanced the scent of the flowers, and the view was even better than from their veranda. Anne breathed in the fresh air, and relaxed. John just stared out to the horizon, deep in thought.

"Considering all the security, at both sites, it really is amazing," he eventually said. "Paul's chemical factory. Who would have thought it? Why? He was so well paid and had developed so much of the technology?"

"To be honest John, I really didn't listen to the details, I was so out of it."

"Well, he apparently had sold some of the research through Sarah to China, and then realised he could get a stunning amount more money by manufacturing chemical drugs. Of course, like us, that would be no problem from the point of view of the chemistry. China sent him the chemicals, which I didn't know are not illegal to own, did you?"

"Well no, but there again, I have never thought of taking drugs let alone making them."

"Then he was going to start up the production in that disused tunnel. He had bought all the equipment, but your escapade happened before he had made any. Some of those chemicals were incredible unstable, he was lucky he hadn't caused an explosion already."

"I did laugh about loads of the money being burnt." Anne chuckled, "serves him right."

"Well it won't do him any good in jail any way." John leaned back. Ten minutes later John turned to her.

"Do you know Anne, I have often lain in bed with you, and thought about us lying in the sunshine, with the warmth of the sun on our skin, up on the Malvern Hills. Instead here we are Anne." John leaned over and leant his head on his arm, and kissed her. "Here we are on a Greek island, with no-one around, just the two of us," and he kissed her again, "hidden by all these flowers, nearly at the top of a hill." Anne smiled, and knew what was coming.

They lay back afterwards, and both looked skywards. "Who would have thought it John, you and me, behaving like teenagers?" Anne giggled.

"Well you must have been some wild teenager. I never did anything like that when I was young!" John laughed.

"What about Sarah?" Anne asked as they walked further over the meadow-covered hillside. "Who would have thought she would fall for a Chinese man, and who would have thought a Chinese man would fall for Sarah, she is so wild and mad, you just wouldn't have thought they would gel. God knows what pressure was used by the Chinese state, to get Sarah to defect. They must have used pressure or money or both. Perhaps they were threatening Cheng. I don't think we will ever know. Pity her parents; doubt they will hear from her again. Isn't that terrible, unthinkable. Her father works for QinetiQ you know John."

"I know."

"Well at least we don't think her knowledge will jeopardise the roll out here, as everyone is of the opinion that the Chinese will use the information for more sinister uses, like the Russians. Enemies of the State will suddenly be disappearing. The production has started, so unless something really unexpected happens, then it's still full steam ahead. I wonder if China has the same problems with affording to care for their elderly?"

"What's going to happen to Paul?"

"To be honest I'm not going to concern myself with his downfall. He deserves any jail sentence they throw at him. Serves him right. We have now lost the technology to the Chinese, and although we are going to continue, we expect to find them using it from now on; probably going to track their citizens, especially when travelling abroad. That GPS tracking nanotechnology is brilliant, even if I say so myself; just think, you can locate anyone, anywhere in minutes. Amazing. Mark is still working on the skin absorption method, and is getting near the point where we can do initial trials. Now when I get back, we shall keep trying to solve the other problem, which will be truly ground breaking, and the technology could earn Britain the most unimaginable amounts of money."

"Will it work?"

"Well we are transferring a whole new team, some of the brightest very young talent, some of them brilliant hackers that have been spared jail so that they can work for us. We hope that it's possible to use thought processing, but it could take years from where we are now."

"John that will be amazing and although it sounds like science fiction, so did the Internet in our life time."

"Now come on that's enough talking for now. Let's go home and cool off in the swimming pool. It will help your ankle," John suggested.

"That's what I was thinking. It looked so inviting, so warm. Bet it isn't though." Anne laughed. John was so pleased to hear her relaxing.

Anne floated on her back in the tiny pool, which was perched on the ledge above two of the neighbour's vegetable and flower gardens. The local scrawny cats strolled past and around the pool. An older ginger cat, who was a little moth-eaten, sprawled underneath the table that John was sat at, reading a book. It wasn't that warm in the shade, due to the totally out of proportion palm tree, no doubt planted to shade the pool from the extremes of the summer sun, but casting unwelcome shade in the cooler May air. Anne was not going to be deterred and had decided a swim would help her ankle. She had swum up and down, which meant about five strokes maximum each way, for at least twenty minutes. Now floating, she was observing John's demeanour. He drank the coffee he had carried across the lane through the low wooden gate to the small patio surrounding the pool.

"John, what do you think has happened to Isobel?" Anne asked.

John paused from his book, took another sip of coffee, reached for a small piece of the bread, looked across the vista to the sea, way down the hill and across to the horizon.

"I don't know, Anne. I was not allowed to talk to her in hospital; the military police and security forces interviewed her once she came to. She apparently had the most awful hangover. She was removed by the forces and taken to a safe house somewhere. I really do not know what happens in these situations. She will be charged, and put on trial, presumably in secret, due to her knowledge of the research, and then placed somewhere secure. I cannot see her being released for at least five years, possibly ten. To be honest, she might not be released, due both to her age, and to her knowledge of the project."

"How awful John. I feel so sorry for her, despite her trying to sell us out. She had had a bad time with Jonathon and all that, and she was so very unhappy with the way the research was going to be rolled out. She was so lonely and dissatisfied with her personal life as well. You do know how jealous she was of you and me? I had not known how badly in debt she was either. Jonathon was obviously a pillock, but I did not know he had gambled all their money away. Fancy being married to someone who bet away all your money. Poor old Isobel.

I mean Jean was poor because she spent all her money on her parents' care, and she really did not spend money anyway. She wasn't bothered about belongings, her parents care was much more important to her, but Isobel seems to have wanted the better life, to buy things, to be loved and cared for, she craved it.

When you think about it, we scientists know so little about each other, we are so insular. Research fills our days, solving problems, working out new ideas, sharing them, but not talking about ourselves. I have you John, and I had Jean, but look at poor old Bill's funeral, apart from us, there were only Cilla's relatives. Isn't that so sad. Is our life really only research?"

Anne stood up in the water and walked to the pools' stepladder, gingerly raising herself up the steps. John brought her huge bath sheet over, and wrapped it around her. They both sat down at the table opposite each other.

John pondered what she had said.

"When you think about it, what do we know about Major Ross? Is he married? Does he have children? Do you know? Have you ever asked him? I bet he knows all about us though, especially if our homes are bugged," Anne said.

"Never asked him. I know about his service history, he has often spoken about it, especially when we were discussing my project, but nothing personal. Do you know I have never even thought if he lives on base, or in Hereford?" John mused.

"There you are. Our glory, we hope, will be our new use of the technology. I hope we put an end to suffering and pain, and save the NHS, that has been my absolute priority for all these years. Yours will be huge advancements in the security of British citizens, protecting our current way of life from insurgents and terrorists," Anne stated. "You could be another Robert Morris, with your developing of new radical methods of transmitting information."

"Robert Morris? Well it's going to take years I think, but let's see. Why Robert Morris?"

"Wasn't he the guy that gave the talk to students at the end of the nineties telling them not to use emails as it was not encrypted, and that the most secure way was to use the US mail?"

"You've got a good memory, Anne."

"Certainly have. Look at us, using that new bore to GCHQ, that's why."

John nodded in agreement, and finished his coffee, as the ginger cat stretched and rose haughtily then headed off purposefully to the wooden gate and disappeared underneath it before strolling down the lane.

"Coffee? Songbird," John enquired.

"Do you know I would love some," Anne beamed. It had been a while since they had relaxed enough for John to call her by her pet name.

August 2015

As they stood on the harbour wall waiting for the ferry to arrive from the other side of the island, Anne circled her ankle. It was so much stronger now; the swimming and walking the wild flower covered hills around the village had done the job. They were both as brown as berries. Fond farewells had been said all over the village yesterday. The Agnanti restaurant entertained them again last night, drinks being on the house.

The ferry came around the rocks, and the waiting passengers picked up their rucksacks, bags and suitcases, and formed a queue. Everyone trying to be polite but at the same time trying to jump the queue. Babies, pushchairs, young children rounded up and all ready to go home.

"Well Anne, back home to work," John mused.

"Yes, I shall miss the island, won't you?"

"We have had such a lovely time haven't we?"

"Fabulous. I feel healed, revitalised and ready for the trials' results."

"Come on Anne, let's fight our way onto the ferry."